Whitewashed Lies

An Alexis Parker novel

G.K. Parks

Copyright © 2018 G.K. Parks

A Modus Operandi imprint

All rights reserved.

ISBN: 1983208604
ISBN- 13: 9781983208607

For those whose lives are chaos

ONE

"You can open your eyes, Alex," James Martin said, his voice full of giddy happiness. It had been some time since I heard that tone. Obviously, our relationship was back on solid ground. He removed the pocket-square he had fashioned into a blindfold from around my eyes. "What do you think?"

"It's nice," I said tentatively, unsure why we were standing inside a completely empty loft apartment.

He let out a patient sigh. "The kitchen's a bit small, and I'm not sure about the marble flooring. The fireplace is a nice touch, and the balcony is breathtaking at this height. You should look around." He took my hand and pulled me toward the bedroom. Half the loft was the bedroom suite with attached bathroom. "The closet space isn't great, but I can make do."

"You're moving? What about your house? You love your house."

At one point in the not too distant past, I used to live in that house with him, but we were starting over. Taking it slow, like he insisted. I really fucked up, and after three months of hell, we realized things had to be different. I even agreed to couples counseling, and he agreed to be my sparring partner on occasion. Needless to say, we were still getting the hang of things which meant no sleepovers at his place. If it weren't for our weekly reservation at one of the finer hotels, I would have figured we weren't far enough along in our new relationship to share a bed.

"I'm not moving." Martin turned with a bewildered look, dropping the measuring tape he had been using to determine the depth of the walk-in closet. "Sure, this is a great apartment, but where would I put my home gym? The boxing ring would take up the entire living room, and there isn't space for either of my home offices."

A laugh escaped my lips, and I covered my mouth.

"What's so funny," he asked, smiling.

"Most people only have one home office."

"Hey, it came in handy when you needed a place to work." He gave me a sad smile. "It takes time to rebuild trust, Alexis, but I hope you realize the goal is for you to move back in eventually."

"Then who is this apartment for? The mistress you're keeping on the side?"

"No, it's for us."

I stared at him, not comprehending what he meant. "You just said we weren't ready to live together."

"Full-time," he clarified. "I thought this might be our weekend place. It's closer to the Martin Technologies building, and it's not that far from the federal building either. We could come here Friday nights, stay the weekend, and head back to the daily grind Monday morning. It'd be a little less scandalous than checking in at a hotel every weekend." He led me out of the bedroom and back to the kitchen. "Plus, it would be ours. It's neutral territory. No one could get kicked out. It'd be fifty-fifty. In the event things go south, we'd have to fight over splitting the property."

"I hate to break it to you, but the last two zeroes in my bank account are preceded by a decimal point. You know I can't afford this. I don't even think I could afford to pay the rent for a space in the adjacent garage. This would be your place. If we don't make it, there isn't a chance in hell I'd fight with you over any of it. I'm not with you for your money."

"I know. We'd be fighting over who would get stuck with the apartment instead." He pushed the purchase agreement toward me. "I had the papers drawn up a few days ago. I've already moved the money into escrow, but this deal will require your signature. We'd be co-owners." He put the pen on top of the paper. "Are you in this one hundred percent? Did you mean it when you said you wouldn't walk away or force me to leave again?"

"You know I won't."

He glanced down at the paper. "Prove it."

"What if I don't like the apartment? The closet sucks, and you're right, there isn't room for my treadmill or a proper workspace. The hotel suite might be larger than this place." I reached for the contract, hoping to find a price tag, but Martin took it from my hands.

"Do you really dislike it, or are you freaking out?"

I brushed a wayward strand of long brown hair behind my ear. "Both." I spun, surveying the amazing view and the balcony. "It's smaller than my place."

"Actually, it's bigger. The size of the bedroom is what makes it larger. But we can keep looking. We'll find something else. In the meantime, we can continue to order room service." He folded the papers and tucked them inside his jacket pocket.

"Hey," I put a hand on his arm, "is this what you want?"

"We're ready to take the next step, I think. I hoped this would be it, but it doesn't have to be this place. Any place will work. It's not like we're even going to be living here. It's just a getaway spot. Truthfully, the thought of sneaking away from work for a quickie was probably the biggest selling point. It's not like this apartment is that fantastic. So what if they have topnotch security features? We'll find something better."

That comment piqued my interest, and I decided to give the place a more thorough evaluation. Someone once told me I had to stop being afraid and go after what I wanted. Martin was what I wanted, but despite everything, the tiny voice remained in the back of my mind, warning me I would lose him just like so many other people I cared about.

"What else does the building have?" I picked up one of the real estate brochures that had been left on the counter.

Martin grinned, pleased I was willing to give this some serious consideration. "Let's take a tour." He palmed the keys and led the way back to the elevator. We had just reached the lobby when my phone rang. He narrowed his eyes. "Work?"

"Yep."

He checked his watch. "I should get back too. Can I drop you somewhere?"

"Not today." I gave him a peck. "Jablonsky's on his way."

He leaned down for another kiss. "Tell Jabber I said hello, and stay safe out there. I'll see you tomorrow."

I watched Martin get into the back of his town car and drive away. The doorman cleared his throat, politely waiting for me to turn around. When I did, he asked if I needed a cab. Declining the offer, I took a seat on a nearby bench and waited. Five minutes later, Mark pulled up.

"How'd you know where I was?" I asked.

Jablonsky snickered. "I am a federal agent. Plus, Marty showed me the apartment last week. What do you think?"

"I can't afford it."

"He can."

"That's not the point."

"The point is he needs you to make a grand gesture. He's worried when things get tough, your relationship will fall apart again. The apartment is supposed to force you to have something tangible to tie the two of you together. It'll keep you from walking away."

"But it won't. I have a place. He has a place. We could both walk away."

Letting out a frustrated growl, Mark flipped on the lights, wanting to get to the crime scene faster in order to cut the conversation short. "At some point, you'd have to come back together to unload the property. If nothing else, it'd be a pain in the ass, but it's supposed to be symbolic or some shit like that."

I cocked an eyebrow. "Did you learn that in couples

therapy?"

"No, from my divorce attorney." He glanced at me again. "Haven't you realized yet that Marty's testing you? He wants to make sure you won't run from commitment again. He needs to know you've changed or that you're at least trying." He pulled the car to an abrupt stop and double-checked the address, despite the three police cruisers stationed around the building. "It looks like we're late to the party."

Jablonsky took lead, marching into the evacuated office building and flashing his credentials at the police officer stationed at the door. The government plates and flashing lights probably tipped them off that we were federal agents. If not, the off-the-rack suit and sunglasses were a surefire bet. We probably didn't even need to show our IDs.

Detective Jacobs leaned against the doorframe, taking notes, while someone else photographed what remained in the room. At the sound of our approach, Jacobs turned, a curious look on his face.

"Parker," he greeted, "what are you doing here?"

Jablonsky stepped into the room before I could answer and crouched down. "Lt. Moretti gave me a heads-up when the police responded to the call. An explosion could mean several things, but he thought we might want to check it out. Parker's just along for the ride."

Jacobs glanced at me over my boss's head, and I shrugged. If Mark wanted to take lead, that was fine. After all, he was in charge.

"Was anyone hurt?" I asked.

Jacobs glanced down at his notepad. "No one was inside the building when the blast went off. It happened around six a.m. The offices open at eight. According to the bomb squad, the device had a timer. After the countdown, it went boom. We swept the rest of the building and garage, but we didn't find anything. Most of the rooms are locked up tight. We had someone come down here from Branded Telecom to open the doors, but the locks wouldn't disengage. We had to use infrared and thermals to check for other devices. The fire department came in and assessed the damage, but the structure's stable. The blast was contained to this area."

He pointed to several markers that went out into the hallway. "It was directional and similar in design to a claymore. Our techs are analyzing what's left in the hopes of identifying a signature."

"It blew out the glass," I mused, seeing the empty window panes across the hallway. "Any idea what the motive was?"

Jacobs shrugged. "Disgruntled employee is at the top of my list."

"Let's hope you're right, kid." Mark handed his card to Jacobs. "If you need some help on this, let me know. If not, we'll stay out of your way. Just keep us in the loop on where the investigation leads. It's possible this might connect to one of our cases."

"Which one?" Jacobs asked, but Mark snorted and headed toward the door. The detective focused on me. "Parker?"

I put a professional smile on my face, hoping to reassure him. "It's nothing you need to worry about. If the two are connected, I'll make sure you're read in. You have my word."

"If you say so."

Scrambling after Mark, I met him at the front door. He had stopped to speak to another police officer. From what I gathered, he was asking about building security. After copying a list of names and numbers from the officer's notepad, he went back to the car. Inside, he dialed a number and waited. He put it on speaker and let the automated message play. Disconnecting, he leaned against the seat and studied the surrounding buildings. Then he made a call to request access to nearby surveillance feeds. The police probably had done as much, but we weren't waiting to piggyback off their work. Despite his friendship with the major crimes lieutenant, Mark had the us versus them mentality, believing the federal government was superior to the local police department. I wasn't convinced, seeing as how I'd consulted for the police and had several friends in blue, but I wasn't stupid enough to say that to my boss.

Finally, he turned to me and asked, "Do you know what

they do inside this building?"

I glanced through the window at the high-rise. It was another nondescript building, but the interior offices had enhanced security features, like retinal scanners, biometric locks, and coded access. The explosion occurred on the fourth floor where there were offices, cubicles, and conference rooms. The building could have been used for anything. Based on the phone message, it was a telecommunication company, but I'd never heard of it.

I shook my head. "What do they do?"

"I have no idea." He started the engine and pulled away from the building. "I can tell you the company is a front for something, and it has a nice shiny cover story to go along with it." He switched lanes. "A place like this wouldn't be cleared out at any time of day or night. There would always be some kind of security detail on the premises, but no one was there. The blast came from within the building, so who reported it? I'm not buying it was some passerby who heard a boom."

"It could have been." Despite playing devil's advocate, I didn't believe it either. Letting out a sigh, I broached the worrisome tidbit we'd been ignoring. "You told Jacobs it might connect to one of our cases. Do you think it's the same type of incendiary device we saw in Turkey? Do you think this is terrorism?"

"Not yet." He glanced at me from the corner of his eye. "I think this was a dry run, just like what our counterparts have seen overseas. The first thing I want you to do is find out everything you can on the telecommunication company. I want to know what they really do. In the meantime, I'll start on the surveillance footage and the 9-1-1 call and see where that leads. Let's just hope I'm wrong about this."

"And to think, twenty minutes ago, my biggest problem was closet space."

TWO

Branded Telecom didn't have satellites, cell towers, or undersea lines. It didn't provide phone, internet, or cable to anyone. The company's website was vague. FBI forensic accountant Kate Hartley ran through their tax records and financial reports, but I didn't need her to tell me what I already knew. This was the only office building; although, they supposedly had satellite branches. Aside from general expenditures for the building and staff, the company had purchased a fleet of utility vans. Several had been parked near the building, but at least a dozen were unaccounted for. I didn't believe they were out on service calls. Narrowing my eyes, I ran the list of board members, pulling up information on the COO. After finding a phone number, I dialed and waited.

"Hello?"

"Is this Mr. Dutch of Branded Telecom?" I asked.

"It is."

"This is Special Agent Alexis Parker of the Office of International Operations. I need to speak to you regarding the bombing that occurred this morning." Normally, it was best to ask these questions in person, but I knew Det. Jacobs would be on top of things.

"Agent Parker, the police are here now. As I told them, the legal team of Branded Telecom will handle any questions. I was not in the building at the time and was only notified about the explosion a few hours ago. I can't help you." Without giving me a chance to ask anything else, he hung up.

"Asshole."

Putting the phone down, I picked another executive from the list and dialed. This time, I didn't bother to identify myself. Instead, I asked about their phone service and rate plans.

"Who are you? How did you get this number?" Ian Voight asked.

"You work for Branded Telecom, right? Your company has a bunch of utility vans, so I thought I'd let you put one of them to good use by setting me up with some phone service. If you have a great rate, maybe I can convince the entire building to switch over."

"Who are you?" Voight repeated.

"That's funny. I was about to ask you the same thing."

There was an uncomfortable pause on the other end, and I wondered why he hadn't hung up. I would have. Then he cleared his throat. "What does the FBI want with Branded Telecom?"

"We want those fancy caller IDs you just used to figure out where this call originated, and we also want to know everything about your company, including why an IED went off inside your empty office building this morning."

"You really ought to leave this alone." The line went dead.

Apparently, this would require actual legwork. The simple solution would be to phone Det. Jacobs, figure out who he had questioned, and tag along, but Jablonsky didn't want us following the police department too closely. He was afraid it would track back to matters of national security. So instead of phoning Jacobs, I took one of the government issued cars from the motor pool and drove to Ian Voight's home address. He threatened me, so it was best I pay him a visit in person. However, the address listed on his driver's license corresponded with an out of business diner.

I didn't like this. An explosion inside an office building was supposed to be straightforward, at least in terms of determining information about the targeted company. The difficult part was supposed to be identifying the bomber. Something wasn't right. I keyed in the address for Kevin Dutch. He said the police were with him. That meant his address should be legitimate.

I parked in front of the brownstone and looked around the neighborhood. Oddly enough, I spotted a Branded Telecom van idling half a block away. Stepping out of the car, I left my jacket unbuttoned to allow easier access to my weapon and moved down the sidewalk toward the van. Several people were on the street, so I did my best to blend in with the dogwalkers and foot traffic.

As I approached the van from the passenger's side, I noticed two men inside. They watched the surrounding area through the reflections in the side mirrors. If that wasn't suspicious, the dark jumpsuits and baseball caps they wore were.

I was fifteen feet from the rear fender when the driver gunned the engine. A horn blared from the white sedan he cut off, but the van kept going.

"Dammit." Eyeing the area, I couldn't help but feel like I was being watched. The crowded café across the street had a few outdoor tables, and it seemed like the men in suits were watching everything. I didn't spot the telltale curlicue wires running down the backs of their collars, but that didn't mean they weren't staking out the area. Continuing toward Dutch's home address, I phoned the OIO, making sure we didn't have any stings in place.

"It's not us," Agent Davis assured. "We didn't receive notification of an ongoing op from any other agency, but you know how that goes. Someone could be working in the area."

I glanced toward the café, but the men I'd seen had vanished. "Thanks for checking. I want to touch base with Branded Telecom's chief operating officer before heading back."

"Okay," Davis replied, confused why I was bothering to

disclose my intentions.

It wasn't like we were partners. At the moment, I was unattached, which was why Jablonsky had been venturing into the field with me. It was also why most of my time was spent conducting research and analysis from behind a desk. It was nice to get out and stretch my legs. However, my instincts said this wasn't the ideal scenario.

At the front door, a security camera was aimed at my face. Looking up, I rang the doorbell and waited. When there was no answer, I knocked, giving the occupant the benefit of the doubt that the bell was on the fritz. Noticing the lack of police cars, I wondered just how truthful Mr. Dutch had been when I phoned earlier. I could call Jacobs and check, but that would be premature.

I leaned over the railing, hoping to catch a glimpse of the interior of the home. The blinds were closed, and the drapes were drawn. This entire morning was turning into a bust, and the worst part was I had tipped off the men in charge of Branded Telecom that the federal government was on to their little cover-up. Jablonsky would not be pleased, but with any luck, the police would perform their due diligence. That way, I could say they screwed the pooch too.

I got back into the car, unable to shake the feeling of being watched. I kept my eyes on the mirrors, but I never spotted a follow car on my way back to the federal building. Once I parked in the garage, the tension melted away. The hairs at the back of my neck no longer stood at attention. Making my way to Mark's office, I knocked on the door. For once, I was going to admit my mistake from the get-go. It was about time I learned that lesson.

He slammed the phone down, grunting at the runaround he'd been given. I took a seat in front of his desk, waiting for him to acknowledge me. When he looked up, he shook his head.

"You didn't find anything," he said.

"No, and whoever these people are, they know we're looking into them. I'm guessing they'll scramble." I tapped my fingers against my thighs. "Why do you think Branded Telecom was targeted? And why aren't they willing to cooperate?"

Jablonsky swiveled the computer monitor to face me. "Do you see this?" He pointed to the six separate video feeds on the screen. "This is the security footage from nearby cams."

"None of them cover the building. How is that even possible? It's like the front door and parking lot are in surveillance blind spots."

"Not just those entry points. Every entry point. I gave Moretti a call to see what they had from the interior footage, but there isn't any." He turned the computer screen back around. "With all those security measures in place, the company decided they didn't need cameras, or so they say."

"Right."

"The 9-1-1 call isn't helpful either. It came in after the blast. Supposedly, someone in a neighboring building felt a tremor. They thought it was an earthquake and called to report it. The number links back to the adjacent office building, but it wasn't a personal line. It was the building's main line, so that doesn't help us identify the caller. The police are working on determining that also."

"When I spoke to Kevin Dutch, the COO of Branded Telecom, he said the police were with him, but when I drove by his house, no one was there. Should I check with Jacobs?"

"Might as well." He jerked his head toward the door, dismissing me. "Just be straight to the point, and don't share with your cop friends what we're doing."

"That won't be hard since I don't know what we're doing. When are you planning on filling me in?"

"You'll know what you need to know when you need to know it. After you check with Jacobs, see what kind of progress Hartley's made. Sometimes, the easiest play is following the money."

"Yes, sir."

I didn't like being kept in the dark, so after a short conversation with Jacobs who vouched for Dutch's story, saying their interview abruptly ended when the man insisted he had an appointment and left his house, I checked with our resident forensic accountant. Even the financial reports indicated this was a telecom company. They had all the necessary paperwork and reports filed. Too bad I didn't believe any of it would hold up in the real world. Deciding to follow the only thing that linked this morning's explosion to the OIO, I dug through our records on the recent overseas bombing. The OIO had several active agents and operations abroad, especially in contested regions of the Middle East. When I was first assigned to this post, I feared I would be sent to some war-torn country and forced to coordinate with military intelligence, our spy network, and the state department to monitor the area for potential international and domestic threats. Luckily, my lack of military training and inability to speak any Middle Eastern language kept the bulk of my duties stateside with the occasional European excursion. However, I had a feeling that was about to change.

Two weeks ago, one of our outposts had been attacked. It was a military installation, but several FBI and OIO agents were permanently posted there to work on deciphering potential domestic threats from our international enemies. A device had made its way onto the base and detonated inside a building. Amazingly, there were no casualties, but the blast caused several of the generators and power systems to go offline. For several hours, communication to and from the base ceased. The implications could have been catastrophic, which was why our agents abroad were determined to find out who was behind it and prevent it from happening again. Based on the reports and intel I'd seen concerning the matter, they were afraid that first attempt had been a practice run.

Very little intel had been provided on what remained of the IED, but from the photographs and reports, the situation sounded similar to what happened inside Branded Telecom this morning. Leaning back, I picked up the phone and dialed Hartley's extension. With any luck, the telecommunication company didn't have any ties to the Middle East or any military contracts. However, I had never been particularly lucky.

"They aren't military contractors," Kate said. "Based on what I'm seeing, they've never been government contractors either."

"That's great."

"Don't celebrate yet. I've seen shipments to several of our international bases." She clicked a few keys. "The shipping info lists communication equipment on the manifest. That's not particularly helpful."

"Why would they send anything if they aren't government contractors?"

"You'd need to ask them that, unless you have friends overseas. Ooh, maybe they were doing some kind of donation thing."

"Wouldn't there be a record of that?"

She searched through more of their information. "They didn't file it on their tax forms, so it probably wasn't a donation."

Typically, business transactions would require a warrant, but since the U.S. government was the receiving party, I didn't think it'd be necessary, especially if we found a record of the shipment on our end. "See what else you can dig up and give me a call when you know something."

"Alex, I don't think there's much to find."

"There has to be."

I stared at the computer screen. We were missing something. Clicking through photos of the explosion on the military base, I noted the similarities. The blast was directional. There were no casualties reported, and it blew out the glass from nearby windows.

Picking up the phone, I dialed Jacobs. "I have a million questions for you."

"Likewise. Tit for tat?"

Jablonsky wouldn't like this, but we didn't have much of a choice. "Deal. I'll go first. Did the explosion disrupt the electrical system?"

"I don't know. The responding officer said the lights were out, but by the time I arrived, power was back. I assumed the lights were off because the building was shut down for the night. It could have been an outage. But the locks on the doors were jammed, so make of that what you will. Why is that important?"

"I don't know."

"C'mon, Parker, tell me something."

"Ian Voight's home address is bogus."

"Voight's the VP of marketing," Jacobs said. "I spoke to him on the phone, but he was cagey. Now I know why. Anything else?"

"Yeah," I glanced back at Jablonsky's office, but my boss was occupied, "the IED was planted on the fourth floor. Who was the target?"

"Hell if I know. The names weren't on the doors, and there was no directory in the lobby. I asked Dutch about it, but he said no one works on the fourth floor."

"Convenient."

"And utter bullshit. For no one to work there, they sure have a lot of empty office space."

Another thought crossed my mind. "Did you get a list of employees?"

"Not yet. Dutch wanted to confer with counsel before providing that information."

"He's stonewalling. Shouldn't he want this solved?"

"I don't know. You tell me. What is going on?"

"I wish I knew."

THREE

"I think we have a problem." I leaned against the doorjamb to Jablonsky's office. "I spoke to Detective Jacobs, but he didn't have anything useful to say. Perhaps the bomb squad or fire department might have something we can use, but I doubt it."

Jablonsky snorted, not bothering to glance up from what he was reading. "They don't. No one physically cleared the offices inside the building. They used the dogs, the robots, and whatever other noninvasive methods of detection they have at their disposal. Doesn't anyone bang down doors anymore?"

"I'd be more than happy to."

That comment earned a quick glance and amused chuckle. "What's the problem, Parker?"

"Branded Telecom isn't a government contractor, but they've shipped dozens of crates to several of our installations around the world. Jacobs hasn't received an employee manifest, and from what we saw of the building, it's a very clean office space."

"I noticed that too." Mark scowled, deep in contemplation over the scene of the explosion. "No personal effects, nameplates, or a single scrap of paper or pen to be found anywhere. Sure, this is the digital age, but shouldn't someone have to write something down at some point?"

"One would think." I shifted my weight to the other leg and leaned my back against the doorframe. "I have a theory." I turned and looked at him. "Branded Telecom is a government cover. Something we haven't heard about because it isn't getting broadcast in our daily memos. I'm guessing DCS cooked it up."

Jablonsky bit his lip, somewhere between annoyed and awed. "Does this hunch of yours have any evidence to support it?"

"It's circumstantial. But I don't know how else to explain the odd occurrences, unless Branded Telecom is a crime syndicate, but that doesn't play well in regards to the shipments to our military bases."

"Did Branded Telecom send anything to our installation in Turkey?" Jablonsky asked, and I nodded. "When was the last shipment received?"

"Two months ago. Do you think they sent the bomb?"

He shook his head and tore through his desk for a folder. "I'll make some calls and see if that theory of yours holds water. In the meantime, keep it to yourself." He reached for the phone. "And stay away from the telecommunication execs until we know more." He jerked his chin up. "Shut the door on your way out."

Getting the message, I slipped away from the doorframe. It was getting late, but I didn't want to call it quits until I knew we were on the right track. Just hearing the words bomb, explosion, and IED made me sick to my stomach. Truthfully, we'd been lucky. Until we received notification from the police department, we had no reason to believe an attack of any kind was imminent. It was one thing if this was an isolated incident, but we didn't know enough to reach that conclusion. The overseas explosion on a base seemed to indicate this was just another practice for whatever was to come. I wanted to have a lead and a method of preventing an actual tragedy. Not everything was terrorism, so I refused to jump to that conclusion. But we needed to be prepared.

Grabbing my keys, I drove to the precinct. I hadn't

stepped foot inside the police station in several months. Surely, they missed me by now. Despite Jablonsky's initial insistence to keep the police in the dark, I had a feeling things might change. However, I wasn't going to spill the beans or provide any hints as to what hunches or theories I was exploring. I just wanted access to the building again, and since Jacobs was lead, he might want to personally escort me to the scene.

When I arrived, I flashed my credentials at the desk sergeant and asked to speak to the detective. Jacobs met me in the lobby, not surprised by the unannounced visit. He rolled his eyes, ushering me toward the staircase that led to the major crimes division. Once we crossed through the double doors, he folded his arms over his chest and gave me a hard stare.

"What are you doing here? We spoke three hours ago, and you didn't have a damn thing for me. So don't expect me to be in a sharing mood."

I gave him a sly smile. "I thought I'd stop by to ask if you wanted to revisit the telecom building. I was on my way and thought we could go together."

He narrowed his eyes. "Uh-huh."

"Hey," I held up my palms, "if you don't want to go, that's fine."

His grumble sounded more like a displeased growl. "You came here to invite me to visit *my* crime scene with you. Do you realize how fucked up that is?"

"Don't ask questions. Just go with her," Detective Nick O'Connell called from behind his desk. "If you ask too many questions, she'll eventually convince you the entire thing was your idea, and you'll end up driving. It's a no-win situation, buddy." I turned and gave O'Connell my death stare, but he just winked in return. "Are you keeping out of trouble, Alex?"

"Mostly. I might need a police escort to make sure I stick with the good behavior though."

Jacobs sighed. "Let me get my jacket."

While Jacobs went to grab his things, I sauntered over to O'Connell's desk. "Did you hear about the explosion this morning?"

Nick nodded. "Is that why you're here?"

"It sounded interesting, and you know how bored I've been lately. I thought I'd stop by and see how the real investigators were handling it."

"So you're just here to bust balls? Did you get tired of breaking Martin's?" My eyes went cold, and Nick held up his hands. "That was a joke. The last time I saw the two of you, you'd clearly made up. Are things still good?"

"For now."

He pointed a finger in my face. "That's the problem right there. There is no 'for now.' It's yes or no. No qualifiers or exceptions. Nothing's ever perfect."

"Careful, Detective, I don't want to have to tell your wife that you don't think she's perfect."

"Jen wouldn't believe you." He snickered. "Be careful and be nice. We don't get paid enough to put up with the job and your bullshit."

"I'll try." I spun on my heel and followed Jacobs out of the precinct. "Did you want to share a ride?" I asked when we hit the parking lot.

"You can drive," he said, recalling O'Connell's warning. Once we were on our way, he asked, "What are you hoping to find inside the building?"

"A motive. Evidence of who the target might be. Hell, at this rate, I'd settle for any signs an actual human works there." Realizing I was getting too close to my actual suspicions, I turned the tables and quizzed Jacobs on his impressions of the scene and his meeting with Kevin Dutch. While he had basically said all of it in our prior conversations, it was a nice way to distract him from asking more questions.

Pulling to a stop outside the building, I scanned the area, but it seemed just as lively as the rest of the neighborhood. It was just another early evening in the business district. Ducking beneath the police tape, Jacobs opened the front door, holding it so I could enter.

"Our techs should almost be finished processing the crime scene. By tomorrow, Branded Telecom will be back to work as usual," Jacobs said. "Mr. Dutch was adamant about getting back in the building as soon as possible."

"He doesn't want you snooping around."

"Probably not."

"That means we have to make the most of it now. Shall we go level by level?"

The detective let out an agitated exhale. "Lead the way. And for the record, I'd like to get home at a decent hour. Because of this shit, I'm working a double, and I'm not in the mood."

"No problem." I gave him a reassuring smile and set off to discover something that would support or disprove my suspicions.

After two hours, I was ready to throw in the towel. Most of the building was locked up tight. The areas that weren't were devoid of everything. It looked like the place had been professionally cleaned. The fourth floor was the only messy bit, but from what I gathered by observing the crime scene investigators, there weren't any fibers, fingerprints, or trace evidence to process, just the fragments of the explosive and the damage it had done. Jacobs spoke briefly to a few of the techs, and we returned to my car.

"I understand what you were saying." Jacobs sucked some air between his teeth. "I've seen a lot of office buildings. There's always a random photo, an inspirational quote, or someone's hand lotion or lip balm on a desk. I'd even settle for a chewed pen cap." He eyed me. "What is up with that place? Has the company even moved in yet?"

"Maybe not." That was a possibility I hadn't considered, but it would explain some things. As soon as I hit a red light, I sent a text to Kate to check if the telecom company had recently relocated.

"You know, texting while at a stoplight is illegal."

"Do you want to write me a ticket?"

"Next time." We didn't speak for the rest of the ride. When I stopped at the precinct, he opened the door and stepped out. "If there's a bomber out there, it'd be best if we knew about it sooner instead of later. You've always been straight with me, so I'm sure you'll let me know if there's a present danger."

"Of course."

He closed the door and tapped the side. As I drove

away, I couldn't help but wonder if this latest observation had any real impact on my hunch. Without having access to the locked rooms, there was no way of knowing the purpose of that building, but I was certain everything had been thoroughly sanitized. I just couldn't decide if that happened before or after the bombing, and if it was before, that meant someone at Branded Telecom knew the explosion was coming.

Noticing the time, I wondered if it was worth returning to the OIO building. Kate hadn't responded to my text. I had a feeling she had called it quits for the night. However, I knew there would be no point going home. The wheels in my head would spin all night, even if they were stuck in the mud. Returning to the office, I passed Mark's door. When I knocked, he made it clear I should go away, so I continued to my desk.

Hartley had left a post-it. Branded Telecom only existed at the one address. The satellite branches were bogus. Someone else was checking on the property records and company holdings. I doubted it would turn into anything worth pursuing. Without having a proper grasp of the target, it would be impossible to determine motive. As a last ditch effort, I read the latest intelligence reports on the off chance a terrorist group or organization claimed credit for the explosion, but there was nothing. As it was, news of the detonation inside a city office building hadn't hit the media. Jacobs and the police department were guarding that secret to prevent a panic and interference in their investigation, and the execs didn't strike me as the types to issue a press release concerning the matter either.

"Parker," Mark bellowed from down the hallway, aware the rest of the floor was empty except for a few agents inside the conference room, "go home."

Hitting the switch on the monitor, I pushed away from my desk and went to his office. "What if something else happens?"

"Sleeping at your desk won't stop it." He let his shoulders slump. "Since you expect me to lead by example, I'm going home too." He shrugged into his jacket. "I've sent out feelers to a few other agencies and called some of my old contacts. Keep your fingers crossed someone comes through. If we don't have a clue what's going on, there's no hope the police will ever figure this out on their own."

"They might." But I didn't believe it.

"Sure, and leprechauns are guarding a pot of gold." He led me to the elevator and stabbed at the button with his index finger. "Are you planning on chasing after rainbows?"

"Well, I could use a pot of gold." I snorted, remembering my morning with Martin at the apartment.

"If you find it, let me know. I could use a few coins." He smiled as the doors opened in the parking garage. "Try to get some sleep. This shit will be here in the morning."

I went home, ate dinner, and crashed in front of the television. While I channel surfed and stared at the moving picture box, my thoughts remained on the oddities surrounding the office building. I didn't care about the explosive so much as the building. It made a lousy target. Striking there didn't attract attention, inflict fear, or cause any real damage. The only harm it caused was forcing the building to shut down for a day while the investigators scoured the pristine crime scene for nonexistent clues. It was pointless. Or was it?

Rubbing my eyes, I sprawled out on the couch and stared at the ceiling. Despite the order in which things occurred, the building was cleared out. Could that have been the entire point of the explosion? And if so, the bomber should have realized the building wouldn't remain empty. The authorities would be crawling all over it. The only goal the bomber might have achieved was preventing the people of Branded Telecom from entering the building. Barring the possibility of an obvious theft, it seemed like a drastic way of shutting down a company for one day, but that would mean Branded Telecom was an actual company. I had my doubts, and I couldn't help but think whoever set the bomb recognized the telecom company for what it really was.

FOUR

"I am so over this." I shoved against the desk hard enough to roll my chair halfway across the room. "There's nothing to find. The only way we're going to get answers is by bringing in someone from the company, not that it's much of a company."

Kate gave me that frustratingly upbeat look of hers. "Or you could just listen to Jablonsky."

"He doesn't know everything." When I arrived at work this morning, he had called me into his office and insisted I drop the investigation. He didn't give a reason. He just wanted it dropped for the time being.

Hartley cleared her throat, jerking her chin to the side in the most obvious fashion. Cringing at the realization Mark was behind me, I scooted my chair back to its original position. Maybe he wasn't coming to see me.

"Is there something I should know?" He hovered next to my desk. His eyes went to the forensic accountant. "Did Alex ask you to do more research?"

"No, sir," Kate replied, practically saluting. "I was just giving her my report from yesterday. I should go."

"Chicken," I mouthed, but she was already halfway down the hall. "You need to teach me how to be that intimidating. Is it the scowl? Or maybe it's the stern non-wavering eye contact." I mimicked his gaze, squinting and blinking a few times. "That would make me cross-eyed or give me a headache. No wonder you're always in a bad mood."

"My mood is because of insubordinate agents who mouth off."

"You should have a word with Davis about that." I swallowed. "I just have one question. Is the investigation really DOA?"

"The police are handling it. They don't need us involved. Until I hear something solid from the people I've contacted, Director Kendall thinks it'd be best if we don't waste time or resources on this. If an attack is planned, we'll stumble upon it through the regular channels. We have a network in place and a number of substantial ops in the works. I need you to be a team player, Parker. Do you understand?"

"Yep." I slid the intel to the side of my desk. "You might as well take that with you so I won't be tempted."

He hefted the stack into his arms. "Bryant wants your input on the op he's running. He figured you might have some underground contacts who will prove useful."

"Yes, sir. Right away."

Ignoring the grumbling, I knocked on the conference room door and made myself as useful as possible for the rest of the day. Thoughts of the bomb and Branded Telecom played in the background of my mind, but I stayed away from it. If the PD hit a snag, Jacobs would phone, and if Kendall changed his mind, Mark would tell me. In the meantime, I had a dozen black market contacts spread across Europe who could help Bryant and his team track their arms dealer.

When they called it quits for the day, I ducked out of the office. It was Friday night. Martin and I had a date. After getting home and changing, I checked my messages. Not surprisingly, Martin called to say he was running late and would meet me there. At least some things never change, like gravity and Martin working late. Too bad the OIO wasn't as dependable.

* * *

"Did you enjoy that?" Martin asked.

"It was different."

"Is that the polite way of saying you don't like heights?" He took my gym bag and put it over his shoulder, balancing them both on one side as we made our way out of the indoor rock climbing facility.

"I don't, but that didn't bother me. We were tethered together." I met his eyes. "You wouldn't let me fall."

Putting an arm around me, he smirked. "Does that mean you trust me?"

I shrugged, deciding to bust his chops a little. "I guess, but there was a bungee cord hooked to the ceiling on the off chance you wanted me to tumble to my death."

He gave my shoulder a squeeze. "We weren't that high. You might have broken a leg, but that would have been about it."

"Aren't you chivalrous?"

He kissed my temple and pulled me closer. "You know I'm only teasing. What would you like to do now? It's early. We could catch a movie or grab a drink."

"I don't care. You decide."

He rubbed his hand up and down my arm. "Is everything okay? You seem preoccupied. I was almost certain you would have turned our climbing into a competition or a game. What's up?"

"Nothing." I licked my lips. "Work. Our latest investigation hit a dead end, so Jablonsky took us off it. It's just weird. I'm sorry. You deserve my full attention. It's the least I can do since you didn't let me plummet from those big scary cliffs."

"Now you're just mocking me."

"But you love it."

"I love you. There's a difference."

Waving that sentiment away with my free hand, I sighed against his chest. "I know it's probably too late now, but I want to see the apartment again and give it another chance. We need a place, unless you'd consider spending the night at my apartment."

"Would you be comfortable with that? I'm not talking about tonight or tomorrow. I'm talking about when things get complicated and hard and you're scared."

After a long pause, I said, "It'd be different this time."

"I hope it will be, but I'm not ready to test that theory yet. And I'm not convinced you are either." We continued our trek toward my parked car. His driver, Marcal, had dropped him off, but since we were spending the weekend together, he sent him home for the night.

"How do you know buying a place to share on the weekends will work any better?"

"I don't, but if we can make that work, eventually we'll be able to make the rest work. I need this, Alex."

"It's a lot of money. A lot of your money. It's ridiculous you can blow seven figures on an experiment you aren't even sure about."

"It's an investment, and while I might not be certain, I wouldn't be doing it if I didn't think there was a chance it'd pay off in the end."

"Promise me one thing," I said, waiting for him to nod, "when we're back on solid ground and we no longer need the weekend apartment, you'll take full ownership and profit from the sale. I don't want to feel like I'm being rewarded or paid for making this work. That's a slippery slope and a dirty business, and I won't have any of it. I don't want any part of the apartment to begin with, but I understand why you want us to own it equally."

"What if I use the profits to pay for some exotic vacation or a wedding?" He grinned. "Because at that point, we ought to be sharing all assets anyway."

"We'll deal with that later." I checked my watch. "Do you think it's too late to go sign the papers?"

"I guess we'll find out." He beamed and pulled me close for a swoon-worthy kiss. He cupped my face in his hands, leaning back to look into my eyes. "Are you sure about this?"

"I am."

He kissed me again and pulled out his phone, calling to see if he could get the building management and owners to agree to a meeting. While he worked on the plans, I let the feeling of serenity wash over me. This was for the best. I wasn't the same person I had been. Instead of focusing on the what ifs, I was determined to live in the present and appreciate the fact that we were together. Nothing would get in the way this time, not even me.

I sunk against his side, listening to the giddy tone of his voice and the excitement in his mannerisms. He was happy. We were happy. And then I noticed one of the Branded Telecom vans idling on the corner. A dark SUV was positioned across the street. Two men watched our reflections in a storefront window. A homeless guy was down the next alleyway. Either he was crazy, or he was speaking into the radio clipped to his sleeve.

"Martin, hang up the phone. I need my bag."

Confused, he promised to call right back and handed me my gym bag. "What's wrong?"

"Call Jablonsky." I removed my credentials and shoved them into my pocket. "Tell him we're being followed by Branded Telecom. He'll know what that means." Martin turned his head, and I nudged him with my elbow. "Don't let them know they've been made. Two guys at four o'clock. The van at twelve, and the SUV at ten." Slipping my nine millimeter under my jacket, I wasn't sure what to expect. After making a show of finding my car keys, I handed him back my bag while he held the phone to his ear, waiting for Mark to answer. "We should split up. Take my keys and head to the car. Circle the block. I'll meet you on one of the cross streets."

"Alex," he warned, but I gave him my no nonsense expression.

"It's okay," I insisted. "Go."

He took three steps toward the curb, phone pressed to his ear, when the SUV pulled up in front of him. The two men were right behind us, and I lost track of the third guy. Pretending to be oblivious, I took a left, hoping they'd stick with me and leave Martin out of it. Instead, the van shot across the street and stopped in front of me.

"Ms. Parker, we need to have a word," one of the men said from behind my back. The side door on the van opened, and something hard jabbed into my hip. I moved to turn, hoping to clear my weapon, but the guy put a firm hand on my right shoulder, preventing me from turning around. "You too, Mr. Martin."

"He has nothing to do with anything," I said.

"We'll determine that." The second guy took the phone from Martin's hand, disconnecting the call and turning off the device. Pocketing it, he gave Martin a shove in my direction.

Our eyes met. I didn't like the flash of anger that crossed Martin's face. It was impetuous and challenging. It was no secret he was in fighting shape and had recently completed a crash course in tactics and training. It made me wonder if he wasn't itching to try out his newly acquired skills in a real life situation. I gave a barely perceptible headshake and lifted my palms to hip level.

"Take it easy," I said, not entirely sure who I was addressing.

"We will," the man behind me said.

A black hood went over my head, and the world went dark. He grabbed me around the waist and heaved me into the van. I crashed down on my side. Before I could do anything, someone jumped on my back, holding me down and zip-tying my wrists.

"Don't you fucking touch her." Martin's voice was followed by the sound of flesh hitting flesh.

The swooshing metallic sound of the van door sliding closed reverberated around me, and I rolled toward it. Whoever bound my wrists grabbed my ankles. I furiously kicked in his direction, unwilling to cooperate for another moment. I was alone. I didn't know what they were going to do to Martin. I needed to get free. Instead, the staticky clicking of a taser followed by jarring, disruptive pain shot through my side and down my limbs, making them inert. The asshole bound my ankles, and the van went into motion.

I made an effort to pay attention to every turn and brake, keeping count in my head. After twenty minutes and a few final quick turns, the van came to a stop. The door opened, and someone slung me over his shoulder and carried me out of the van.

The next thing I knew, we were in an elevator, but I couldn't tell if we were going up or down. After several more sets of doors opened and closed, I was dropped into a chair. The hood was yanked off my head, and I was temporarily blinded by nothing but white light.

Blinking the disturbing, blinding haze away, I scanned the space in front of me. I had heard about these white rooms, but I thought they were nothing more than urban legends. The theory was they were used as tools for enhanced interrogation since they were basically sensory deprivation chambers. The void didn't provide any clear sign of a floor or ceiling. The room could be three by three or go on for hundreds of feet. After a more thorough scan, I located the outline of the doorframe a second before it opened.

A man ripe with the stink of government agent entered the room, dragging a stool behind him. He took a seat in front of me and offered an apologetic smile. "Sorry for the extreme precautions. We can't take any chances."

"Who are you?"

He didn't answer. Instead, he asked, "Why did you go to this address?" He removed a photo from his inner jacket pocket and held it up. It was the out of business diner. He reached into his pocket to retrieve a second photo, and I caught the slightest glimpse of a government ID clipped to the inside of his jacket. "And this address?" He held up a photo of Dutch's brownstone.

"I was working a case."

"That case is under police jurisdiction. They conducted their own interviews. You also returned to the Branded Telecom building later that evening with the lead detective. You searched the entire building. What were you hoping to find?"

"Who are you?" I repeated. He didn't speak, and I shook my head, giving him an evil smile. "Are you afraid your agency will disavow any knowledge of your existence if you tell me your name?" He frowned, not looking amused. "I bet they'd hate it that after the blindfold and the taser zap, I know exactly where we are. The Branded Telecom building, right?" I glared at him. "It's probably an even safer bet the FBI is not going to be pleased to find out one of their people was abducted by another agency in such a violent and unpleasant fashion."

"Agent Parker, we mean you no harm. This matter needs to be sorted and addressed. Once it is, you will be returned." Trying another tactic, he relaxed his posture as best he could. "You're right. We're both federal agents. We're on the same side. The problem is your investigation into our building has raised several flags. If certain parties take notice or the matter becomes publicized, it would threaten national security. Who have you told about your investigation? How many of the staff have you sought to question?"

"Ask my boss. Everything's in my report."

"You made no mention of your repeat visit in your report. Are you sure you haven't left anything else out?"

"There's one thing." I glared at him with utter hatred. "The CIA isn't authorized to operate domestically. That's the FBI's job. I believe this matter is out of your jurisdiction."

"This isn't a pissing contest." He stood, clasping his hands together and pacing in front of me. Whether he realized it or not, he just confirmed my suspicions that he was a spook. "Your office was instructed to back off."

"And we did."

"Then why did a dozen different requests for additional intel come in earlier this evening?"

"I don't know. I was reassigned to another case."

"We'll see." He left the room, leaving me to stare at the stool in stark contrast to the snow white backdrop. After several minutes, he returned. "It appears you're telling the truth." As if rewarding my cooperation, he stepped behind my chair and cut the zip ties free, dropping the small pocket knife into my lap so I could undo my ankles. "Do you know what this place is?"

"Its existence is highly classified and quite frankly illegal. Is this the reason it was targeted and attacked?"

The man nodded.

"How many prisoners do you keep here?"

"This isn't a black site prison. It's a fully equipped facility prepared to deal with any contingency. On occasion, we've used this room to question high-value targets. There are several similar sites worldwide. We might have dispersed some misinformation to prevent the enemy from discovering this place, but as you can see, our plan failed. We were forced to abandon it and regroup."

"That's why the building was empty and everything was wiped clean. That's why all questionable areas, like this, were locked up tight." I rubbed my wrists and stood, folding the knife. The man held out his hand. Reluctantly, I handed back the weapon.

"Yes."

"What am I doing here?" My anger and worry peaked, but I didn't want to tip my hand.

"It was necessary to determine if you posed a threat."

"I'm a fucking OIO agent. I swore an oath to neutralize threats."

"We are aware of that fact, Agent Parker. Now that you've been questioned and vetted, you may be asked to assist on a classified mission."

"Great." I glanced toward the door. "Would it have been too much trouble to call during business hours?"

"That would not have served our purposes."

"And kidnapping me did?"

"Rest assured we will not meet like this again. Any questions that need addressing will be handled through official channels. Like it or not, you're working for us now." He tossed the hood to me. "Put that on, and we'll take you back to where we found you."

"What about my companion?"

"You'll see for yourself." He nodded at the hood.

On the drive back, I tried to convince myself the good guys wouldn't hurt innocent bystanders, but I was having trouble believing these CIA assholes were the good guys. The measures they went to were too extreme for my tastes. I wasn't even sure how legitimate their credentials were.

FIVE

The van dropped me off where they found me. The operative in the back handed me my gun and identification. It was a miracle I didn't shoot him. If it had been the asshole who questioned me, I might have. Instead, I stepped out of the van. Before I could even turn around to ask where Martin was, they sped away.

"Alex?" I knew that nervous tone anywhere. Spinning, I caught the briefest glimpse of him before he hugged me. He held my face in his hands and did a quick scan. "Are you okay? Did they hurt you?"

"I'm fine." Gingerly, I reached up and touched his split eyebrow. "What the hell did they do to you?"

A gruff snort sounded behind him. "You should have seen what he did to one of them. The guy's in the hospital with a dislocated shoulder and a broken rib. Marty's lucky they didn't file assault charges."

"It was self-defense. Those sons of bitches took Alex." Martin stared into my eyes. "I can't lose you again."

"I'm right here. I'm not going anywhere. Promise."

Jablonsky made a gagging sound and stepped closer. "We need to take this off the street. There's already been enough commotion." He pointed to his car.

Martin opened the door for me. Once we were settled inside, Jablonsky headed for the federal building. After what just occurred, he'd want an explanation for what just happened. He deserved one.

"How'd you know to show up?" I asked, glancing at Mark.

"Marty called. When the line went dead, I decided to check things out. Luckily, one of you bothered to tell me where you'd be tonight." Mark gave me a pointed look. "By the time I got there, things had already gone south. One of the agents was picking his teeth up off the sidewalk. The other schmuck decided it'd be best to identify himself before opening fire. Obviously, you've rubbed off on my boy and not in a good way, but at least he was smart enough to surrender. When I arrived, they were having a chat in the back of a government vehicle."

"What did they want to know?" I turned to look at Martin.

He stared at his bloodied and swollen fists. "If I ever heard of Branded Telecom and if I had any government contracts." He met my eyes. "What's this about?"

"I don't know. I'm under the impression it's classified." Turning my attention back to Mark, I wanted blood or an explanation. At this point, option one was looking better and better. "It was also hinted that this is how these jackasses ask for help. Do you have anything to say on the matter?"

"I'm glad you're okay. Once we're back at the office, I'll get you squared away and tell you what I can." Mark gave me a brief look. "For what it's worth, I'm sorry. I didn't know it would go down like this, especially when you were on a date. I know you've been having enough problems lately. This was unfortunate."

"Unfortunate? Do you have any idea—"

Martin reached forward and put his hand on my shoulder. "He does." He gave me a grim smile, indicating he had already chewed out Jablonsky. I slipped my hand beneath his and intertwined our fingers, trying to avoid his sore knuckles. "All that matters is we're okay."

I nodded. "Yeah. We're okay."

The rest of the ride was in complete silence. After Jablonsky parked in the underground garage beneath the federal building, he led us to the elevator. Martin, in classic fashion, did his best to maintain a physical connection, but Jablonsky forced us apart, sending Martin to get checked out by one of the medics. As soon as we were alone, Jablonsky locked us in his office and went behind his desk.

"Are you all right? What went down?"

"No, I'm not all right." Crossing my arms over my chest, I stood in front of his desk, too wound up to sit. "Who do these assholes think they are? They could have politely identified themselves as federal agents, flashed a badge, and asked to have a few words in private. They could have said we needed to take a ride. Something. Anything. Instead, they box us in like we're criminals getting caught in a sting. They pull a gun and throw me into the back of a van."

"At least you cooperated."

"The taser burns on my back would disagree."

"Shit." Mark ran a hand down his face. "Marty said you played along."

"Until they separated us." I bit my lip and shook my head, fighting against the telltale tremble in my chin. "It's not fair. They could have been anyone. They could have done anything." I pointed emphatically at the closed door. "He's scared. He's fucking terrified what this means for us. How could they do this? Their building gets bombed, and I'm the damned casualty. Why did they go to these extreme measures? It's ludicrous and asinine and absolutely fucked up beyond all recognition."

"It is." Jablonsky let me vent. It was the safest move to make at this point. He knew it's what I needed before I completely lost it. He pulled a bottle of whiskey from his desk drawer and poured some into a mug, scooting it closer to the edge of the desk. "Their director will hear from me about this misuse of power."

"Good." I circled the office a few times before dropping onto the sofa in the corner.

"We need to talk about this case."

"I don't want it. I don't want to have anything to do with

it or those people."

He rocked back in his chair, watching me for a long moment. "Unfortunately, you don't have a choice."

"This is such bullshit."

Jablonsky unlocked his middle drawer and pulled out a file marked top-secret. That sent my eyes rolling. He opened the folder and skimmed the pages. Then he handed it to me to read. No matter how petulant I felt like being, there was no way out of this. I sold my body and soul to the United States government when I agreed to the reinstatement. Until I rectified that mistake with another resignation letter, I had no free will.

Too angry and stressed to concentrate, I slapped it closed and stared at my mentor. "Just tell me whatever I need to know. I promise not to shoot the messenger."

"DCS and the CIA have been tracking leads through their networks, hoping to determine the source of the explosive devices. So far, they have eliminated several potential leads from the list, but they don't have an identity yet. In the meantime, they want the FBI to be vigilant in determining the bomber's next target."

"How can we do that when we don't know who's behind this? If we don't know the bomber, we can't determine motive."

"They've speculated as to the motive. They believe the bombs aren't meant to inflict unnecessary physical harm. The device emits high-frequency waves. Those waves overload power grids and fry most electronics. We're talking everything from lights and wi-fi to weapons systems and satellite feeds."

"And they break glass," I added, thinking about the shattered conference room windows.

"That too." Jablonsky picked up the whiskey, deciding not to let it go to waste. After a sip, he put the glass down. "Since only their secret facilities have been targeted, they believe the bomber is using these distractions to infiltrate and gain intel."

"What kind of intel?" My mind went to the white void, and I snorted. "Don't tell me. Let me guess. It's classified."

"Yep. Basically, they want us to keep eyes on their

facilities and listen for any rumblings that indicate a strike is imminent. Surprisingly, they provided a group of addresses for us to monitor."

"So now we're security guards." The story didn't make sense. "How does the bomber get the device inside? These are suitcase-sized packages. These bastards must know more than what they're saying. They need to disclose before we put ourselves in harm's way."

Jablonsky finished the rest of the whiskey. "Director Kendall believes this situation would be better served if we work together. While DCS does its thing, we'll analyze the evidence and work this investigation like we would any other. That being said, the CIA doesn't want us drawing attention to this."

"Right, because abducting me and knocking Martin around was totally hush-hush." I got off the couch and paced. "We can't work this in the usual fashion. They want to keep us in the dark. As far as I'm concerned, they don't deserve our help."

"It isn't for them. It's for the innocent people who could be hurt. It's for the undercover agents, including our people, who will be put in jeopardy if this unknown party disrupts our system and gets whatever they're after. Let me make one thing clear. This isn't for those shitheads who ruined your night. You need to understand that. We do things we don't like all the time. It's called life."

"Fine." Blowing out a breath, I picked up the folder and leafed through it. The redacted intel was the cherry on top. "When do we start on this little project? As of eight hours ago, you told me I was off this case."

"Take the weekend. We'll get on top of it Monday morning. Honestly, there's not much we can do. I've assigned teams to monitor the potential targeted areas, but until we have something solid, it's a waste of time. And since the CIA is reluctant to give us anything to work with, we'll have to wait until Director Kendall gets us clearance for the full version."

"Agent Douche made it clear no one was supposed to know about this without being vetted. How could you assign teams?"

"They believe it's an exercise. Hopefully, they won't be abducted and questioned."

"Yeah, hopefully not." I glanced at the closed door. "What do I tell Martin? I've been given strict instructions not to speak to anyone about this. I'm probably not supposed to talk to you either."

"Tell him it's office politics and an interagency pissing contest. We screwed with them by accident, so they decided to be assholes and drag you in for questioning. It isn't entirely a lie." He gave me a grim look. "And I wouldn't put it past them to have bugged your phones or apartment, so be careful what you say and do."

"Need I point out what they're doing is illegal? They don't have jurisdiction to operate domestically. What the hell is going on?"

"I wish I knew. I guess that's what we're going to find out." He put a hand on my shoulder. "Don't let this crap get stuck inside that thick skull of yours. Marty's a big boy. He's okay. You're okay. Don't do what you always do."

I laughed because if I didn't, I'd cry. "We were going to sign the papers on the apartment. Normally, I'd take this as a cosmic sign of why we shouldn't be moving forward, but I'm not getting into that headspace again. I just don't know what he's thinking."

"Go find him so you can get back to your date. You deserve some happiness in your life."

Martin was in the lobby, typing out a message on his phone. I dropped into the chair beside him, putting my cheek on his shoulder and rubbing a finger over the icepack that covered his knuckles. He put his phone down and turned to look at me.

"I figured you'd be working the rest of the night, so I texted Marcal for a ride home. Maybe we'll try this again when men in shitty suits aren't dragging you into the back of utility vans." The bitterness and anger strained his vocal cords. He coughed and looked away. "I wanted to kill them."

"Mark made it sound like you almost did."

He smirked, but he wouldn't make eye contact. "Not really. I couldn't figure out why you went with them willingly, but you must have recognized them for what they were."

"Sort of."

He laughed bitterly. "Dammit, Alex. You cooperated in the hopes of protecting me."

"I will not apologize for that. You ought to bet your ass that if I'm in a position to actively stop bad shit from happening to you that I'm going to do it. Every fucking time. And you're the same damn way. You have the bruises to prove it, so don't get on that high horse. This situation was different from last time, and you know it. They weren't hitmen. They were government agents."

Finally, he made eye contact. "You figured if you went along with them, they'd leave me alone. But they didn't."

"I know. I ended up getting into it with the asshole in the back of the van, but that didn't turn out so well."

"Did he hurt you?" His green eyes found mine, the anger blazing in their depths.

"He could have, but he used nonlethal techniques to subdue me." Instead of waiting for Martin to ask why this happened, I volunteered the answer. "One of my cases overlapped with their operation, so they wanted to exact some revenge. We're supposed to be on the same side, but instead of working together, they do stupid shit like this. I'm really sorry they ruined our night."

"Me too." He looked at his watch. "Do you want a ride home or back to your car?"

"What about our weekend?"

He shrugged.

Blinking, I shoved my feelings aside. He had been through a lot tonight. Perhaps he needed some time to process. "Okay. Whatever you want."

He brushed his thumb against my cheek. "What do you want?"

"To wake up next to you in the morning."

SIX

I didn't sleep well. Thankfully, my nightmares weren't the problem. I was just worried Martin finally realized I wasn't worth the trouble. I'd been warning him about this since before we started dating, and after being apart the last few months, I knew if we split again, we'd never get back together. We'd be too damaged and broken to salvage anything. As it was, we were still on the mend. Resolutely, I decided that despite everything else, he had to be my priority. The job in general and this case specifically were too much of a strain on our precarious relationship. Even after this case, there'd be another and another. It was up to me to keep my focus on us.

Martin jerked, grunting in his sleep. After saying his name several times, I gently ran my palm against the uninjured side of his face, and he calmed. In the dark, I couldn't tell if he fully woke up, but he wrapped his arm around me and settled back to sleep. And nightmares used to be my schtick.

"Don't leave me," I whispered. Eventually, I drifted off in the warm cocoon of his embrace.

When I opened my eyes again, it was morning. I stretched my arm across the bed, searching for him but coming up empty. At least the bed was warm, so he couldn't have left that long ago. I heard voices, and the door to the suite closed. Footsteps approached the bedroom. I held my breath, not wanting to face the uncertainties of another day.

Martin slipped back into bed, snaking an arm around my waist and kissing my shoulder. "Morning, beautiful," he murmured.

"I was afraid you left." I hated the way I grasped his arm, like it was a life preserver and I was drowning.

He snickered. "I don't think I could get too far like this. The townsfolk would force me back inside with torches and pitchforks." He slowly extricated his arm from my death grip. "How are you feeling?"

Needy and insecure. "I'm okay." I turned to look at him, but he was facing away, reaching for something on the nightstand.

"Just in case, I had the concierge track down some aloe. Between the burn on your back and my rendition of Frankenstein, I thought we could use it." He squeezed the tube and gently rubbed the cold, wet gel against my side.

As soon as his fingers left my skin, I rolled over to face him. The left side of his face was bruised and swollen. He didn't have a black eye, but his cheek was red and twice its normal size, practically running into the swollen cut on his brow.

"You need ice." My gut filled with a familiar pang of guilt. "It's a good thing we didn't drink the champagne last night. Stay here. I'll be right back." After grabbing a washcloth from the bathroom, I dipped it in the melted ice bucket and pressed it gently against his cheek. "It'll bruise like a bitch, but if we get the swelling under control, you can cover it with makeup."

He smiled. "So some other guy can kick my ass?"

"No," I grinned, "but I like my men pretty. And even if you have the body of a middleweight MMA fighter, you shouldn't look like you just stepped out of the ring after a particularly brutal bout."

"Who are you calling a middleweight?" He tickled my sides and pulled me on top of him. He winced and groaned but refused to let go.

"Are you okay?"

"Just a little sore. I'm not sure if it's from rock climbing or the fight. Probably both."

"It's the rock climbing," I affirmed, choosing to believe that's why my back and shoulders were stiff and not from the stress I was carrying.

"I would order massages from the spa, but I know how you feel about strangers touching you." He rubbed his palms up and down my back. "Maybe I should treat myself, and when I get back, I'll take care of you."

"I've decided I don't like the idea of strangers touching you either." Wiggling out of his grasp, I sat up, placing my palms on his shoulders. "How about I give you a rubdown instead?"

He grinned devilishly. "You aren't a professional, so does that mean I can ask for a happy ending?"

"If that's all you want, fine. But I think I can come up with something a little better than that."

"Oh yeah?"

I crinkled my nose playfully. "Yeah."

*   *   *

"How was the rest of your weekend?" Jablonsky asked when I entered his office on Monday morning. "Did you get Marty squared away?"

"Sure." I took a seat in front of Mark's desk. "Once we found concealer to match his skin tone, he was good to go."

He stared at me for a moment. "The two of you haven't spoken a word about what happened since that night, have you?"

Letting out a sigh, I picked up my coffee cup and took a sip. "Can't we cut the small talk and get down to business? Detective Jacobs left a few messages on my work voicemail, so we'll need to address that. Has Director Kendall made any headway in getting us cleared with Clandestine Service or whoever's in charge of this shitfest?"

Nodding, Jablonsky slid a dossier to me. "That's the full version or what our counterparts are claiming is the entire situation. I have my doubts, but be that as it may, it's a better starting point than what we were given last week. I spoke to Lieutenant Moretti on Saturday. Dom's agreed to put the investigation on the backburner if I personally guarantee there are no other targets in this city." He sighed. "I can't exactly do that, which explains why the detective's been hounding you. Do you want me to take care of it?"

Jacobs and I had a history. It'd be best if I handled it. "I need to know what it is we're doing before I say or do anything that may contradict that. It's not like I can tell him the truth." I stared out the open blinds at the view of the bullpen. "Do you think the police department has any idea what's going on?"

"I'm not sure it matters. No one was hurt. There were no witnesses, no security footage, and no leads. Even if they bang down the doors to the office building or place officers in the lobby, it won't lead to anything."

"How can you be sure?"

"Because we ran down everything we could and never found anything. They won't either. The Defense Clandestine Service is great at cover identities. They know how to sell their people and companies as something they aren't in order to infiltrate terrorist cells and feel out American opposition. They won't drop the ball because the boys in blue come knocking."

"Fine."

Jablonsky knew I was far from pleased to be helping on this assignment. "Our priority is figuring out the bomber's motive. I don't think we'll be able to determine who's behind it, not with the intel we've been given, but I'm confident we'll find a pattern and figure out what these two targets have in common. I'll work the bomb angle. We have the schematics concerning the overseas explosion, so I'll need you to get Jacobs to give us a copy of every report and photo that was taken from the telecom building. Double-check with the fire department and bomb squad to make sure they don't have anything hanging around that they forgot to include or forward."

"Yes, sir." I scooted the dossier to the center of his desk.

"Anything else while I'm running errands?"

"Not that I can think of, but if it takes all morning to get the files, you might as well pick up lunch on your way back. I'll have a turkey club on rye."

Not bothering to hide my annoyance, I glared at him and left the office. Maybe I should pick up a whistle before leaving. If it was supposed to deter rapists from attacking, it might prevent overzealous CIA operatives from kidnapping me. Then again, that's probably why the FBI issued firearms.

The drive to the precinct seemed shorter than usual. Unsure what I was going to tell Jacobs, I hoped he might be out on a call so I would have some extra time to come up with a feasible lie. However, when I entered the major crimes unit, he was staring at the case file.

"Detective," I greeted, resting my hips against the desk, "I got your messages."

He nodded, but his focus remained on the aftermath of the explosion. The images the crime techs had taken showed the extent of the damage. Someone had superimposed lines with markers to show the blast range. He leafed through a list of alleged employees. Finally, he slapped that down, scribbled a few notes, and leaned back to look at me.

"The fourth floor was empty. In fact, I'm pretty sure it was intentional. My guess is the explosion was an inside job. Nothing tracks beyond paper when it comes to Branded Telecom, so maybe it's an insurance scam. Start a company, make things look legit, set a fire or stage an accident, collect the money, and do it again elsewhere." Jacobs fidgeted as if something about that theory didn't quite fit with the facts. "What do you have for me?"

"Nothing. I'm just here to collect some files. Jablonsky's bored. He wants to see if we've seen this type of incendiary device used in the past."

"What did the LT say about this?"

"I'm not sure. My boss said he spoke to yours on Saturday. All I know is he sent me to get the files. I'm guessing that means Lt. Moretti agreed."

"Let's find out." Jacobs ushered me toward the office

and knocked. When a gruff response followed, Jacobs pushed me ahead of him. "Sir, Agent Parker's here to collect some files."

Moretti looked up, letting out an amused snort. "Jabber knows I've got a soft spot for you. If he'd shown his ugly mug around here, I'd have turned him down flat." His eyes went to Jacobs for a second. "Have you made any progress?"

"No, sir."

"And you want everything we have on the bomb schematics," Moretti said, knowing precisely why I was here.

I gave him a contrite smile. "Yes, sir."

"Fill out a chain of custody form, and we'll give you what you want." He pointed an accusatory finger at me. "Tell Jablonsky I expect to be kept in the loop and he owes me."

"Will do," I replied, following Jacobs out of the office.

Once we were back at his desk, he removed a clipboard from one of the drawers and handed it to me. "Fill that out." From his tone, he wasn't happy with the current situation. "I'll check with forensics and make sure they've completed their initial reports and everything is included."

He walked away, and I concentrated on the paperwork. By the time I was finished, he was hovering over me. Taking the clipboard, he flipped through the pages, checked the information, and signed the bottom. He handed me a copy and placed a rubber band bound manila folder on the desk.

"Is this everything?"

He nodded.

"Great." I moved to get up, but he put a hand on my shoulder, holding me in the chair.

"Not great." His eyes conveyed hurt from being betrayed. "I thought you were going to be straight with me. What is this about?"

"I can't say."

"Can't or won't?"

Pressing my lips together, I picked at the rubber band. "I don't know what this is about. I'm not sure what's going on or why it's happening. All I know is I'm stuck working on this shit, and I would rather be doing anything else. I'd much prefer that you deal with this. I don't want it, but we don't get to pick and choose our assignments."

He removed his hand from my shoulder and dropped into his desk chair. "Why is the OIO suddenly so interested in bomb schematics? You must know of another similar detonation."

My mind flashed to what I had initially said when Jablonsky and I first appeared at the crime scene. "That's what we're hoping to determine."

"Dammit," he slapped his palm against the metal desk, "did you forget how to answer a question with yes or no?"

"Maybe."

He closed his eyes, frowning deeply and inhaling to keep his cool. "This isn't a game. Do you understand that?"

"I do." I stared at him for a long moment. "You have my word that I'll do everything I can to make sure no one gets hurt. We don't know enough to determine if that's a possibility at this point. You might be right about this being an insurance scam, but we won't know until we have time to conduct an analysis." I hefted the file and stood. "Thanks for cooperating."

He shook his head, turning toward his computer screen. "Thanks for lying to my face."

SEVEN

Jablonsky gave the leg of my chair a kick, causing the wheels to roll to the side. After most of the office emptied for the night, we moved our investigation to one of the conference rooms. The lighting was better, and it gave us space to spread the intel out.

Staring at him with contempt, I let out a resounding sigh. "What?"

"Talk to me. You've barely said a word since you came back from the precinct." He reached for a cold egg roll.

Crinkling my nose, I turned back to the police reports. "You shouldn't eat that crap."

He took a bite and let out a satisfied hum just to annoy me. After he finished chewing, he pushed away from the table. "Parker, what's going on? You used to love Chinese takeout. Is this what happens when I lend you out to another agency for a few months?"

"It's not about the food."

"No shit." He pushed my chair away from the table, standing between me and the file. "I'm not playing guessing games with you. We have too much work to do, so what is your problem now? I'm getting really sick and tired of your attitude."

"Jacobs was right." I climbed out of the chair and walked the length of the conference room. "The blast was directional. The device wasn't placed there by accident. It wasn't couriered over, and it didn't get delivered. The fourth floor was intentionally cleared. Plus, the IED went off in the early morning hours. Someone must have set it to go off at that time. And what about the guy who made the 9-1-1 call? Did we ever determine who that was? I'm betting it was probably one of those CIA dickheads who decided it'd be fun to abduct an OIO agent and knock the living daylights out of an innocent bystander."

"Marty held his own."

"For once, Mark, this isn't about him, so don't go there."

"You think DCS is jerking us around?"

I held up my hands in a 'who knows' gesture. "What do you think? You said we have to work on this, and we have to play nice. But what does this look like to you?" I crossed to the table and yanked the photo from the file. "Whoever set this bomb was inside the building prior to the explosion, but conveniently, there are no cameras, no footage, and no proof any of that ever happened. If the bomber already gained access to the inside of the building, why didn't he steal whatever sensitive intel he wanted? Isn't that what this is about?"

"Maybe he took the intel and used the bomb as a diversion tactic," Jablonsky suggested.

"Fine. But how did he get inside a secure black site in the first place? I don't think you can walk through the front door without someone noticing." I set my jaw, hating the thoughts running rampant through my mind. "I don't care what we've been told. This reads like an inside job."

"Why would the CIA detonate an explosive inside their own building? Do you think they were testing a weapon?"

"Based on what I remember while being hooded and tased in the back of a van, I can't be certain they took me to the Branded Telecom building, but I assumed they did and no one bothered to correct me." I considered the white room and what I had learned from various walkthroughs of the crime scene. "It's not a prison, but they have areas reserved for enhanced interrogations. Who knows what else goes on inside that building? It's in a virtual dead zone. No exterior monitoring. No internal cameras. They don't want a record of whatever goes down. That doesn't seem particularly legal. Maybe someone grew a conscience and wanted to draw attention to some unsanctioned activity."

He narrowed his eyes, thinking about what I said. "If this was any other building, I'd say it was a disgruntled employee who knew the interior specs and wanted to lash out, but this isn't your typical telecom company." Reaching for the folder concerning the similar bombing at the military installation, Jablonsky took out the crime scene photo and placed it on the board next to the one from the telecom building. "What you're suggesting is indicative of a rogue operative or a double agent. That doesn't make sense since these two events happened worlds apart. If it were an individual acting alone or as a puppet for another entity, it'd be easy enough to track, especially for DCS. Thus, the same person can't be responsible for both explosions. I'd stake my pension on it."

"That doesn't mean the parties responsible aren't part of some rogue faction."

"Dear lord," Jablonsky snickered, "how many cheesy spy novels have you read in your lifetime?"

"Then explain to me how someone snuck inside a CIA building that has tighter security than Fort Knox, set off an explosive, and escaped undetected."

Jablonsky picked up the half-eaten egg roll. Taking another bite, he finished chewing and wiped his mouth. "The CIA let it happen. They wanted it to happen, and that's why they're so damn pissed we're looking into it. They're afraid we'll arrest the culprit before they can use him for whatever scheme they're planning. That would explain why they grabbed you off the street and have given us guidelines on how to assist. DCS must be in the midst of executing a play, and they don't want to risk us screwing it up. That's the only thing that makes sense."

"What about the police?"

He ground his teeth, giving me a mirthless smile. "We

put a stop to their investigation when we procured the files. Without these, they're dead in the water, and they're too strapped with other cases to waste time on a victimless crime."

"Does that mean we should also call it quits?"

"It means something serious is going down, and the CIA is too stupid to ask for our help. We're supposed to handle domestic threats, so they must have gotten their teeth into this case somewhere overseas. And when it came to our shores, they didn't bother to disclose. They think they can handle it, but from what I've seen so far, I doubt it. They probably asked for our help to keep tabs on us and leash our investigation."

"Agreed."

Taking the photos off the board, he put them back in their respective files. "Let's call it a night. First thing in the morning, I have several calls to make to Washington. Someone is bound to know something, and they're going to tell me what that something is. Make sure you keep these suspicions between us. We don't want to cause a panic or else those CIA assholes might really make you disappear."

"And with that lovely thought, I'm out." I held up my hands and stepped away from the table.

"One second, Parker." He watched me anxiously bounce on the balls of my feet, inches from the conference room door. "You never told me what's bothering you. It's not just the case. So what is it?"

"I had to lie to Jacobs. He knows, and he's pissed."

"He'll get over it."

"I know. I'm just tired of the lies and the half-truths and being jerked around and forced to follow these stupid orders for no damn good reason. Perhaps some of that has something to do with Martin."

He nodded. "Get some sleep. You'll feel better in the morning."

On my way home, I phoned Martin. "Hey, how was your day? Did the other boys on the playground tease you?"

"It was fine. I'm not sure anyone noticed, although Charlie said I looked rested."

"Perhaps you need to cover those dark circles more

often."

"Perhaps. So how was your day?"

"I don't want to talk about it."

He paused. "Oh-kay."

"Can I ask you something?"

"Anything."

"Do you still want to sign the papers on the apartment? I understand if you don't. It's not like you've mentioned it since the incident."

"Sweetheart, nothing has changed, but after our plans were derailed Friday night, I was afraid I might be pushing you into it. I didn't want to pressure you. It is a big decision. If we're not ready or you're not sure, then we should wait."

"I am sure. Are you?"

"Absolutely. When do you want to do this? I don't know how much longer they'll continue to wait on our decision."

"In that case, the sooner, the better."

"Yeah?" The sound of his happiness lightened my mood.

"Yes."

"I'll arrange it and let you know what day and time." He let out a contented sigh. "I love you. I wish it wasn't Monday. The weekends are always too short."

"You could come over."

"Don't tempt me. One of these days, the answer will be yes but not yet." I heard voices in the background. "I should go. Luc and I are preparing for a conference call. I'll talk to you in the morning. Sweet dreams."

Disconnecting, I knew why he was hesitant, but his words held the slight sting of rejection. With any luck, things would be different once we had the apartment. From a logical standpoint, a place to sleep was a place to sleep, but it would make a difference to him. Our place. The words signified a special meaning. A commitment. The thing that I typically ran from.

Forcing my mind away from those thoughts, I let myself into my apartment, changed, and ran for an hour on the treadmill with the music blasting. It was freeing.

After a shower and a quick snack, I settled into bed with a book. Work should stay at the office. I was tired of bringing it home and letting it rule my life. However, fate often had different plans.

The next morning, I went back to the grind. After skimming the morning memos, I knocked on Jablonsky's open office door. He looked up, groaning at my presence. The phone was pressed to his ear, and he put his hand over the mouthpiece.

"Our bomb experts updated their reports on the first detonation," Jablonsky said, holding up a file. "Get started on the comparison, and run everything through the database to see if this asshole ever detonated anything prior to a month ago."

"Yes, sir."

Returning to my desk, I read the updated report. The experts reconstructed part of the fuse and identified two additional compounds used in the construction. From the included schematics, they were close to reconstructing the device used overseas. I was no expert, but the configuration looked incredibly similar to the one used in the telecom building. After a careful comparison of the components, I made a list of the commonalities. The differences seemed inconsequential, but only a bomb tech would know for sure.

Using the common features as the means for my keyword search, I sifted through the vast computerized database, hopeful the two detonations were related. Several pages of entries popped up. I clicked on the first digitized case file, checking to see if it was related. After ruling it out, I proceeded to follow the same pattern with the rest of the entries.

My cell phone rang, and I grabbed it. "Parker," I responded, distracted by work.

"I take it you're busy," Martin said.

"Sorry, I'm just looking for something. What's up?"

"Can you get away around noon?"

I chuckled. "You don't have to be so literal about a nooner."

"I wasn't, but that's not a bad idea." He paused, as if giving the thought some careful consideration. "The papers will be ready to sign this afternoon, and the apartment is ours. We could christen it afterward, but that means I'll need to move some meetings around. I've already rescheduled two for today in order to make time to sign the bill of sale. Maybe tomorrow?"

Giggling at the ridiculousness, I shook my head. "So we're doing this?"

"Only if Jabber can function without you for an hour," Martin said, providing me with a final way out if I wanted to take it.

"I'll make it work." The thought of Martin making such a vast investment in our relationship and potentially our future was reassuring, but it sent a kaleidoscope of butterflies through my stomach. We'd already failed twice. It was conceivable we'd crash and burn again.

"Great. Shall I pick you up?"

"I'll meet you at the Martin Technologies building at 11:30," I declared, unsure what I'd have to do between now and then. "No matter what happens, I will be there."

We disconnected, and I went back to my assessment. Four pages into the search results, I found a potential match. Copying down the case number, I opened another window and pulled up the full file. A similar IED was used four months ago at an American outpost in southeastern Europe. Two servicemen suffered second degree burns, but no fatalities were reported. The explosion originated in a file room. The security equipment was compromised, and the bomber was never identified. From the investigation the MPs ran, they believed one of the hired civilian personnel was working on behalf of a terrorist cell. The man in question, known as Guillermo Vega, disappeared the same day. His identity was a fake that passed the initial security check. They believed he staged the explosion to gain access to classified intel.

Printing a copy of Vega's photo ID, I stared at the image. Too bad we didn't have surveillance footage from the latest bombing to use as a comparison. Struck with an idea, I went upstairs to speak to Agent Lawson. The nearby CCTV feeds didn't cover the telecom building, but it was possible the bomber walked past one of the cameras at some point. If we pulled enough footage, we might find Mr. Vega.

Agent Lawson practically laughed in my face at the notion. The area in question was too large. With nearly two hundred and seventy degrees of possible approach vectors, there would be no way of knowing which CCTVs to examine. It'd be the proverbial needle in a haystack, and we didn't possess the processing power or speed needed to make this work. If we had a supercomputer or the resources of the NSA, we might be able to make it happen, but even that was iffy.

Dejected, I returned to my desk to find Jablonsky leafing through my notes. He looked up and offered a grim smile. "Is your go-bag in the car?"

"Why?"

"We're wheels up in thirty. You know the only way to get anything done right is to do it yourself."

"Fuck. I can't." Checking the time, I needed at least two and a half hours. "Mark, I seriously can't leave right now."

"I can give you an hour if you need to pack."

"I need three. Martin and I are signing the papers on the apartment at noon. I promised I'd be there. I won't miss it. I can't."

Biting the inside of his cheek, he thought for a few moments. "Fine. You have three hours and not a second more. I'll pick you up once the papers are signed, and we'll leave from there. Consider it an engagement gift."

"But we called off the engagement."

"You're buying an apartment together. What do you think happens next?" He rolled his eyes, muttering under his breath and heading back to his office.

"Where are we going?" I called.

He stopped and turned around. "Turkey."

EIGHT

"Is that all you need?" I rubbed my palms against my bouncing thighs.

The realtor looked up from the paperwork. "That's all we need from you, Ms. Parker." His eyes shifted to Martin. "It appears you're on the hook for the painful part of this transaction."

Martin smiled good-naturedly. "That's not a problem." He put his hand over mine, wondering why I was so wound up. "Are you okay?"

"I'm fine." I made a point of looking at my watch. "I really need to get out of here. Do you mind?"

"Just a little, but I'll get over it." He leaned over for a kiss but caught my eye and chuckled to himself. "I'll walk you out." He turned to the realtor. "Don't add any more zeroes in the next five minutes."

We lingered outside the doorway to the office. "Thank you." I grasped his face and kissed him hard. "I should be back by this weekend. Do not buy any furniture without me. You agreed we'd pick it out together."

"I'm buying a bed, and whatever the kitchen needs. The rest is up to you."

"Good." I kissed him again, and he realized I was nervous about my impending trip. "Mark's going to kill me if I don't walk out that door in the next two seconds."

"You better get going. I love you."

I smiled. "I sure as hell hope so." I jerked my chin at the office door. "And for the record, I intend to pay for the furniture. You better accept it because I have to feel like I'm contributing." I gave him a wink. "I'll see you around, handsome."

Turning, I marched out of the building and to the waiting SUV. Jablonsky had turned on the flashing lights but somehow resisted the temptation to flip the siren. Climbing into the vehicle, I settled into the seat. The last place I wanted to go was the Middle East. Perhaps I was a total chicken shit, but going to one of our forward operating bases to investigate a crime scene firsthand seemed like asking for trouble.

"It'll be fine," Mark said, reading my mind. "That region hasn't seen action in a while. There are hundreds of troops stationed there. We're going to meet with a few of our overseas agents, get the lay of the land, hear what the rumor mill has turned out concerning the detonation, and get our asses home."

"Yep." My phone buzzed, and I glanced at it. Laughing at the message, I shot back a quick reply to Martin's desire to get the last word concerning my contribution to the new apartment and tucked my phone away.

"What'd Marty say?"

"How'd you know it was him?"

"He's the only one who can make you smile like that." He glanced at me for a moment. "You seem so different now when it comes to him. That's a good thing." He nodded to himself. "But you need to focus on the job, Agent Parker. I don't want those squids, flyboys, and jarheads to get the wrong impression."

"They won't." I took a deep breath, feeling the anxiousness start to bubble again, and grabbed the case file. Flipping through it for what felt like the fiftieth time, I asked, "What was the impetus for this sudden trip? Last night, you were going to make some calls. What did you find out?"

His grip on the wheel tightened, and he continued to stare at the road. "There are several discrepancies in the reports we received. We need to ask some questions and iron out the wrinkles. It looks like there's a lot more to the story than a sole infiltrator looking for intel. I just don't know what we're going to find. It might be nothing."

"How many spooks are on base?"

"It's tough to say. As a general rule of thumb, one or more is placed with our elite units, and several elite units operate out of that base. That doesn't include those working as oversight or intelligence gathering."

"You think they whitewashed the reports?"

"Only if they have something to hide."

For the remainder of the drive, I mulled over that possibility. That would mean the reports we read could be fabricated. The two OIO agents stationed at that base might not have gotten much of a chance to investigate. Given the size and location of the FOB, it was likely there would be other policing and intelligence agencies represented, but any communication in and out of the base would be scrutinized for possible security breaches. Information could have been redacted, and key facts could have been erased. It was no wonder Jablonsky thought an overseas trip was in order.

After boarding the Gulfstream, I dug through the police reports on the Branded Telecom explosion. At least I knew the facts of that case hadn't been compromised. The more familiar I was with that case and the IED used, the easier it would be to draw comparisons and note similarities. For the next eight hours, Mark and I spit-balled ideas, made notes, tossed around theories, and otherwise came to the same conclusions we had the previous night. We didn't know a damn thing, and the reason for that was beyond our control.

I mentioned the explosion from the southeastern European base and produced a blown-up copy of Vega's identification. "That's not his real name, but it's all we have right now."

"So this might have begun four months ago." He chewed on his bottom lip, making a mental note for later. "That might mean something. I'm just not sure what."

We landed tired, hungry, and aggravated. With the time

difference and the lengthy flight, I felt as though I'd lost an entire day. According to my current time zone, it was sixteen hours from the time we left, making it just after four a.m.

"We should have left three hours later than we did," I mused, hoping my eyes would grow accustomed to the darkness surrounding us. It was odd to be out of the city and in the middle of a desert. Luckily, parts of the base were lit up. "At least there'd be people to greet us, and the coffee would be made."

Jablonsky handed me my bag and threw his over his shoulder. "Most of the base will be awake in the next hour. You'll see platoons of men jogging around the perimeter. They like to rise and shine."

"I'd just like to get something to eat and maybe stretch my legs. Sleep might be nice at some point."

"Unfortunately, that will have to wait."

We walked several feet from the Gulfstream and were greeted by two men in fatigues. Corporals Yula and Stein were sent to give us instructions and get us squared away. They showed us to officer's quarters where we stowed our belongings. Then they gave us a brief tour of the base, along with the list of places that were off-limits and numerous behaviors that were not encouraged. After our crash course in surviving on a military base without getting shot by enemy or friendly fire, we were dropped off at the mess hall.

"Apparently, you're getting your wish to eat." Jablonsky grabbed a cup of coffee but gave the chow a wary look. "I might wait until we get back home before I eat again."

"Says the man who scarfed down cold egg rolls last night."

"Suit yourself, but I'm having flashbacks from my days in the navy. Those weren't good days."

"You were stationed stateside. How bad could it have been?"

He glared as if I just outed him. "The food was *that* bad."

My growling stomach didn't seem to care. I grabbed a tray from the line. While I picked at the scrambled eggs and sausage on my plate, a man in a khaki shirt and camouflage pants approached our table. He yawned, scratching at the scruff on his neck and rubbing his eyes. Compared to the rest of the five a.m. crowd, I doubted this guy was military. He sat down.

"Agent Jablonsky? Agent Parker?" he asked, and we nodded. "I figured. No one else hangs around in suits. You two stick out like sore thumbs. Did you just land?"

"Forty minutes ago," Mark said.

"Talk about a red-eye." The man blinked a few times. "Sorry, I'm Dean Harrison. Agent Dean Harrison. There isn't a chance that one of you is here to replace me, is there?"

Jablonsky chuckled. "I've served my time with shitty OIO assignments." He jerked his chin toward me. "Perhaps you could convince Parker to take your place."

"Don't waste your breath." I graced him with a friendly smile. "I just signed papers on an apartment nine hours ago."

"Damn, if only you'd gotten here yesterday." Harrison yawned again, covering his mouth. "Sorry, I'm not an early bird. When would you like to get started?"

"Right away." Jablonsky stood, picking up his coffee cup and draining it. "We'd like to see the explosion site first, and we'll need to review your reports and interview anyone involved or who might have seen something."

"Okay. I'll take you over there, and while you're looking around, I'll pull those reports and have my partner set up interviews. Is there anything else you need?"

"More coffee," I said, taking a final bite and dumping the rest of my tray in the trash.

"We have a pot in our office."

"Great. Lead the way, kid." Mark gestured toward the door.

Harrison didn't feel the need to make small talk as he guided us across the base. We came to an abrupt halt outside a building, and he handed the guard stationed out front his identification. The guard ran it through the computer and eyed Jablonsky and me.

"Who are your friends, Harry? I'm gonna need their

IDs."

"OIO Agents Jablonsky and Parker," Harrison replied while Mark and I handed over our credentials. "The paperwork went through last night." He glanced at Mark. "About ten hours ago?"

"Probably," Jablonsky replied.

The guard didn't appear to care. He scanned our IDs, clicked a few keys on the computer, and picked up a phone. After a short Q&A session, he hung up. "You've been cleared to enter this building. Keep your IDs visible at all times." He hit a button, and the electronic sound of a lock releasing emanated from the door behind him.

Harrison led the way inside. Upon entering, I couldn't tell any type of explosive had gone off. Several military personnel were at their stations, working behind desks or computer screens. There was no obvious damage, but that soon changed.

"Watch your step," Harrison said, taking a left. The floor was cracked, pockmarked with dips from what I imagined had been shrapnel. "Normally, they'd have everything cleaned up by now. I'm not sure what the delay is, but it worked out to your advantage."

"I guess so." My eyes darted toward the shiny new door hanging above an even more damaged floor. "How far did it spread?"

Harrison turned and pointed to the path we just took. "That's the end of the blast zone. The epicenter is right through here." He opened the door and reached for the light switch. "We replaced the lights and rewired the whole damn room. Other than that, nothing has really been touched, aside from the door. The files that weren't damaged were moved to another part of the facility, but the cabinets and furniture that were in the room at the time of the explosion are still here." He scanned the debris. "I don't know what you're hoping to find. It's pretty much just rubble."

Jablonsky narrowed his eyes at the destruction laid out in front of us. "What about the device?"

"What remained of the IED was taken to our bomb experts and dismantled."

"We'll need to talk to them too," Mark said, dismissing Harrison with a wave of his hand as he turned toward the far corner of the room.

The resident OIO agent gave me a look. "I'll get started on your requests. If you need anything, talk to the MP stationed at the front of the building. I'll be back in an hour."

"Take your time," I said, certain Jablonsky was on to something.

As soon as we were alone, I gave the room a quick check for signs of surveillance equipment. Coming to stand beside my boss, I noticed the scratch marks on the floor that had caught Mark's attention. He pointed to a few pristinely shaped holes but remained silent, flipping open his notepad and reaching for a pen. I did the same.

Breaking the room into a grid, we conducted a thorough search, marking down signs of damage as we went. The blast didn't originate in the center of the room but closer to the back wall, facing the doorway. It shattered the interior glass windows, but it didn't yield any scorch marks or burn patterns.

Narrowing my eyes at one of the drilled holes in the floor, I crouched down to see how deep the hole went. Pulling out my key ring, I used the tiny flashlight to shine a beam through the hole, but the light didn't reflect back. Flattening on my stomach, I pressed my eye against it but couldn't see anything below me.

"Do me a favor and shine this light through that hole." I tossed Jablonsky my flashlight and kept my face to the ground. "Shit." I sat up, brushing dust and debris from my clothes.

"What's down there?"

"Hell if I know, but there's definitely something below us."

NINE

"The IED must have been placed here." Jablonsky indicated a spot on the floor. It was equidistant from the four sets of drilled holes in the tile. "I'm guessing it was shoved underneath a table that was bolted to the ground."

"Why would they bolt the table to the ground? We're not on a ship." Before he could answer my question, the realization dawned on me. "This was an interrogation room at some point."

He shrugged. "This building might have been used for more than just housing files and storage."

Surveying the room again, I noted the small window in the corner. Interrogation rooms rarely had windows. They posed too many security risks, and we were on ground level, making a sub-level even more suspicious. "I want to go downstairs and check it out."

"Good luck."

"We'll see."

Leaving the room, I scanned the hallway for any indication of an elevator or staircase. Since I didn't remember seeing one on our way inside, I headed in a different direction. Unfortunately, the building was a giant square that spit me out at the front. Two men in uniform brushed past, glancing curiously at me.

"Ma'am?" the MP asked from his post. "Do you need something?"

"Two things." I gave him a sexy smile, figuring a little flirtation might help my cause. "First, is there a ladies room?" I didn't need the bathroom, but it was always best to use that as an excuse for wandering the hallways.

"You'll find the facilities down the corridor. It'll be the third door on the right."

"Thanks." I flipped my hair, turning up the charm. "I must have walked right past it and never even noticed. This place is just one big loop, isn't it?"

His shoulders moved upward half an inch before dropping back. Obviously, this soldier was married or gay. Or maybe he didn't know how to chitchat. Holding the smile, I figured the effects of my flirtation might be delayed because I was still on east coast time.

"Did you need something else, ma'am?"

"Yes." I needed him to stop calling me ma'am. "What's beneath this building?"

His eyes darted to the door, probably out of habit. "A bunker."

"How do I access this bunker?"

"You don't." His eyes went hard. "Authorized personnel only."

"What's in the bunker?"

He held eye contact. "It's used for storing munitions and can be utilized as a defensive position in the event of an attack."

"Like to stop bombs?"

"I believe Mr. Harrison was assigned to assist you on that particular matter."

I took a small step backward. "Right. Thanks." I pointed down the corridor. "Third door?"

"Yes, ma'am."

"Great." I walked away and ducked into the bathroom. After a few minutes, I exited and returned to the epicenter. Jablonsky was crouched down, examining the corners of the room where the floor met the walls. "It's a bunker."

"That sounds like bullshit. There'd be at least a foot of

concrete between this room and the area beneath us. There's no way the bolts would have penetrated deep enough to see inside, unless they were drilled through and that would compromise the integrity of the bunker. Who's the moron who told you that?"

"The MP out front."

"I wonder if he's actually stupid enough to believe it." Shaking his head, Mark scooted over. "Take a gander at this."

I leaned over, glancing down at the seam where the wall met the floor. At some point, the floor had been redone quickly and sloppily. Taking out a pocket knife, Jablonsky pried the corner of the tile up to reveal a painted cement floor underneath the pockmarked tile.

"Maybe the bunker idea wasn't that farfetched," he admitted.

Glancing out the blinds, I snorted. "How many interrogation rooms have you seen with windows?"

"None."

"Maybe the holes were to hold something else down besides a table."

Before we could ponder that question any further, Agent Harrison returned. "Are you about finished?"

"After you answer a few questions." Jablonsky turned on our fellow agent as if he were nothing more than a confidential informant. "What's the purpose of this building?" He pointed to the holes in the floor. "What was here?"

"As far as I know, this is where they house files. Maybe they had some cabinets or permanent shelving installed at some point in the past." He knelt down and inspected the holes with the tip of his pen. "That's odd." He pulled a handkerchief from his pocket and twisted the corner into the hole. "There's no residue from the bomb." Everything else in the room had a layer of ash and dust.

"Were you ever inside this room prior to the explosion?" I asked.

Harrison scrunched his eyebrows. "Not that I recall."

"We need access to the area beneath this room," Jablonsky said. "See if you can make that happen."

"I'll try. In the meantime, I've lined up those interviews. You should get started on them," Harrison insisted.

Jablonsky and I exchanged a look. We didn't want any more evidence or facts to disappear, but we were out of our depth. This wasn't our crime scene, and we were so far out of FBI jurisdiction I doubted any of Mark's contacts would be able to help. Our best bet was getting one of our interviewees to shed some light on the matter, assuming they hadn't been ordered to perpetuate the CIA's misinformation, or this entire trip would be an utter waste of time.

After being led to another similar building, Harrison opened the office door. "Hey, Kylie. These are agents Jablonsky and Parker."

Mark and I nodded at the woman with the severe bun. Aside from a heavy layer of eyeliner, she wore no other makeup and looked like she was barely over eighteen. The gold plate on her desk read Special Agent Kylie Arbuckle. She gave us a professional smile, sizing us up the moment we walked into the room.

"Jablonsky?" she asked, and Mark jerked his chin upward. "There was a call for you." She handed him the note.

Mark read it and looked at me. "Get started on the interviews while I make a phone call."

"No problem," I replied as he walked out of the room without a moment's hesitation.

Harrison cleared his throat. Brushing past me, he moved to a messy desk and put a stack of files on the floor. After wiping crumbs off his chair, he spun the empty seat toward me. "Make yourself comfortable. I'll speak to base command about getting you that authorization."

Once he was gone, I moved toward the desk. Without being too finicky, I swiped my hand against the chair and sat down. Under normal circumstances, I would have read the notes and files on his desk for possible connections to my case, but Kylie was watching me. Resisting the urge to snoop, I leaned back and closed my eyes for a moment.

"Long trip?" she asked.

"Yep." Opening my eyes, I looked up at the ticking wall

clock. "But we power through. We don't need to sleep or eat. We're supposed to be robots." I gave her a friendly smile. We were chums. She could confide in me. "How long have you been stationed here?"

"About two years. It's my first assignment since I became an agent."

"That sucks."

"It could be worse."

"Did you investigate the bombing?" I didn't recall seeing her name on the reports, but then again, I didn't see Harrison's name either.

"The military did. They have highly specialized bomb techs, so they were first on the scene. After that, CID gave it a look. Once everything was cleared away, we gained access." She let out a heavy sigh. "There wasn't much left to see. The blast destroyed the room, shattered the glass, and took out part of the hallway."

"Any idea how the perpetrator gained access or brought a bomb onto the base?"

She shook her head. "I'm sure you've read the reports."

"I have." Deciding to wait her out in the hopes she'd share, I picked up a blank notepad from the corner of the desk and a pen. "Have you questioned the potential witnesses?"

"No one saw anything. You said you read the reports. That's everything we know."

"What were you working on prior to the explosion?"

She glanced at the doorway. "An investigation into possible cyber attacks originating in Syria. Allied intelligence agents picked up chatter while conducting a raid of a suspected terrorist stronghold. They passed the intel off to us to assess. We were in the midst of the analysis when the IED went off."

"Did these cyber attacks pose a domestic danger?"

Her gaze shifted to her desk. "We don't know."

"You haven't finished the analysis yet?"

She shook her head. "We lost the intel when the base systems blacked out. That explosion knocked everything out. It took down our internet and fried several systems. We're lucky to have recovered any data from our hard drives."

"I thought the damage from the blast was contained."

"Physically, it was, but electronically, it struck the entire base."

Before she could say anything else, a man in uniform knocked politely on the door. After introducing himself as one of the interviews we requested, I ran through the questions while Agent Arbuckle left to conduct other business. After I completed two interviews and half of a third, Mark returned from his phone call. He took a seat at Kylie's empty desk and took over the questioning.

While he asked for the same details and received the same answers I had, my mind wandered. The detonation was contained, so how could it knock out the entire base? From what I'd seen, this place was huge. I was losing sight of the forest from the trees. We had known about the power outage and communication blackout prior to our arrival, but after seeing the room, I'd gotten distracted with other things. And the damn jetlag wasn't helping.

Flipping to a new sheet of paper, I wrote down the facts we knew while Jablonsky's questions droned in the background. After filling up an entire sheet with my impressions, questions, and facts we'd learned since arriving on base, I flipped to another page and scribbled down random theories.

"Parker," Mark said my name, and I dragged my eyes from the paper, "what are you doing?"

"Trying to find the forest."

He gave me a concerned look. "Yeah, okay." He scooted closer, and I realized we were alone in the office. "The holes were drilled to allow wiring to penetrate through the concrete. Beneath the room is a bunker, but they compromised it when they decided to use it to house the generators and computer systems. The entire nerve center of the base is below that building. That's why it was targeted. Whoever planted the IED knew where to place it in order to inflict maximum damage. Apparently, the wiring was supposed to be reinforced and incased in glass and steel, but the bomb blew right through it. Whatever electromagnetic pulse it released was strong enough to damage the underground systems. Even after the wiring was replaced, some of the data drives wouldn't power on."

"Did our agents tell you that?"

He let out a derisive scoff. "I doubt either of them has ever investigated an actual crime scene, so there's no way in hell they'd know about any of this."

"Then how'd you find out?"

"I asked the right people the right questions." He flipped through the personnel records of our interviewees. "No one's been able to shed any additional light on the situation, and I'm sure they won't. From what I gather, they've been ordered to stick with the cover story, and a good soldier always follows orders."

"No wonder I never enlisted. So how'd you get these good soldiers to give up this much information?"

Mark smiled. "I happen to have a few buddies in the state department who lunch with various generals. When a five star calls and asks the base commander to provide a complete rundown, you get a complete rundown."

I gave him a skeptical look.

"Or at least a more complete account that doesn't interfere with whatever cover story is currently in play."

"Is that why I'm feeling the urge to do a Jack Nicholson impression right now?" I asked.

"Don't do it, Parker."

I grinned. "Why? You can't handle the truth?"

TEN

We spent the rest of the day conducting additional interviews and reviewing the intel base command provided regarding the detonation. Not surprisingly, we'd been denied access to the bunker. Around dinnertime, Jablonsky and I went back to our shared quarters. I lost track of how long we'd been awake, but we were past the twenty-four hour mark.

"Dammit," I dropped onto the twin bed at the far end of the room. "I feel like we didn't accomplish anything by being here."

"We know the motive behind the bombing. It was to disable the base's data systems. I don't know how much intel was lost, but I'm guessing quite a bit." He blinked a few times. "That's probably the same reason the telecom building at home was attacked. We know it's a black site. Somewhere in that building must have been several servers and databases. The blast probably corrupted the data. The bomber doesn't want to steal the intel. He wants to make sure we don't possess it." He took off his shoes, shed his belt and tie, and lay down on the bunk. "I'm assuming the locations the FBI was asked to monitor house additional servers. The CIA probably wants to safeguard against losing any more data by having us guard it."

"Why didn't they tell us that in the first place?"

"I don't know. There's probably more to it than that."

I kicked off my shoes and pulled my knees to my chest. "Did you ask anyone if they recognized Guillermo Vega? I saw you take the photo out when you were talking to the CID investigators."

"They didn't recognize the name or the man, but someone slipped this to me." Jablonsky dug into his pocket and pulled out a USB. "It's base security footage from an hour prior to the detonation. The suspected bomber is caught on the feed. He had an access card and ID."

"So we know the bomber. Why didn't you say so?" I jolted upright.

"We don't know the bomber. The ID was faked. The system was hacked to allow entry for the unsub. From what I've seen of the footage, it isn't the best quality. Once we get home, I'll have our techs run it through facial rec. We can conduct a comparison to see if the man in the footage is Vega."

"It is his M.O.," I mused. "Were you going to tell me any of this if I hadn't asked?"

Mark chuckled. "I was going to tell you on the plane ride home. I was afraid if you knew anything now, you'd want to poke around." He reached for the light switch. "Now go to sleep. We have an early flight."

*   *   *

I bolted upright and scanned the unfamiliar room. "What the hell is that?"

Jablonsky grumbled from the bunk across from mine, not bothering to turn over. "Incoming wounded," he mumbled. "Go back to sleep."

"Wounded?" I blinked a few more times, throwing my legs over the edge of the bed. My nine millimeter was in hand, and I wasn't comfortable enough to put it down yet. "Are we under attack?"

"Alex, go to sleep. Our flight leaves in eight hours. Shut up until then."

I listened to the warning bells outside. The base had

been alerted about something. According to Mark, that was incoming casualties, but that was far from comforting. I wasn't used to being in a war zone. The things I had dealt with were rough, but I couldn't imagine being on the front lines or in the trenches where anything could happen at any time. The men and women who served were owed a debt of gratitude.

The sound of helicopters grew louder. After a while, the warning sirens stopped, and the base was quiet again. Taking a deep breath, I settled back onto the bunk, placing my nine millimeter beneath my pillow. My head ached. I was tired and hungry, but my senses were on overdrive as a result of my overactive mind and imagination. Just as my thoughts started to quiet, a thundering snore sounded from the other side of the room.

Getting out of bed, I put on my shoes and grabbed my credentials. Running my fingers through my hair, I left the room and headed for the enlisted club. It was basically just a bar, but the base commander had granted us access to most of the on-site amenities, as if this were a resort. Plus, it'd probably be easier to get inside the e-club than the o-club without an escort. Actually, I didn't even know if they were segregated like that anymore. Perhaps I'd gotten the idea from watching too many old movies.

After flashing my credentials and temporary base ID, I entered the bar. It was dark out, but for those accustomed to this particular time zone, it was early in the evening. For me, it felt like morning after pulling a few consecutive all-nighters. Taking a seat at the emptier end of the bar, I glanced around at the two dozen people in fatigues, khakis, and basic black. I stuck out like a sore thumb.

"What'll it be, Agent?" the bartender asked. His eyes flicked upward from the ID hanging around my neck.

"Something to kill a headache." I gave him a smile. "And I'll take anything edible to go with it."

He chuckled. "Is this your first military base?"

"Am I that obvious?"

"Yeah." He laughed. "We have a full menu at decent prices. Pick your poison." He handed me the laminated sheet, and I flipped it over.

After deciding on some boneless wings, fries, and a beer, I propped my head on my elbow and surveyed the room. A few of the guys eyed me like I was fresh meat. Another group was leery and cautious, as if I might be an unexploded landmine. Truthfully, both groups were probably right.

"Parker?"

I turned at the sound of my name. "Hey, Kylie." She took a seat on the barstool next to mine, and the first group of guys lost interest. "What's up?"

"Not much. I figured you would be asleep by now. Is the time difference messing with you?"

"The time difference, the sirens, Mark's snoring." I rolled my neck from side to side and picked up the beer. After taking a sip, I held the cool bottle against my temple. "This trip was a complete waste of time."

"I'm sorry about that. What can I do to make it up to you?"

"You could tell me how an alleged enemy insurgent passed the security checks and moved freely around the base."

"I don't know."

"Yeah, no one does." I rolled my eyes, too aggravated to bother being diplomatic. "Any idea how he got the IED inside the building or had enough time to set it up in what I imagine was a sensitive location?"

"It isn't a sensitive location. It's just a file room."

"Right." The bartender dropped the platter of food on the bar, and I skewered one of the wings with my fork. After chewing thoroughly, I took another sip. "Except it is a sensitive location. So either you're full of shit, or whoever read you in on these matters is full of shit." I was tired, aggravated, and didn't feel like pulling any punches. Focusing on my food, I shrugged my shoulders. "It doesn't matter. I'm going home tomorrow to work the investigation just like any other."

"Where'd you get your intel?"

"A little bird." I snorted. "How many spooks are on base?"

She smiled. "You mean how many are on base that I can

identify. At least eight. Several are assigned to missions with the elite units, but I'm sure there are others who remain on base at all times." She glanced around to see if anyone was paying any attention to us. "Why? Does this have something to do with them?"

I didn't say anything. Instead, I worked my way through the wings and fries. After washing everything down with the remainder of the beer, I pushed the plate away and reached into my pocket for some cash. Placing a few bills on the bar, I gave the bartender a smile and got up.

"It was nice meeting you, Agent Arbuckle. I hope your next assignment is better than this one."

"Wait." She tossed some money on the counter to cover her drink and jogged after me. "Talk to me, Parker." We were outside now, and I continued on a path toward my temporary quarters. She nodded to a few men as they went past, but once we were alone, she grabbed my arm. "What's going on?"

"Below that file room is a secure bunker that contains the nerve center for the base. That's why the power went out. That's why your databases were corrupted. That's why you lost intel on your current investigations. Apparently, backing things up to the cloud isn't a great idea after all."

"What do you want me to do about that?"

"Nothing. I wanted access to the bunker to take a look around, but base command won't allow it. That's it. There's nothing more to say. Now if you'll excuse me, I'm going to get some sleep before my flight."

I was fifteen feet away when she called out, "I know a way into the server room. If you want to take a look, I'll get you inside."

Stopping in my tracks, I turned around and scrutinized her. "I thought you didn't have access. What changed?"

"You're leaving tomorrow. What harm can it do? Plus," she blushed, "I think you're hot. Maybe we could sneak back to my quarters afterward."

"Oh." I blinked a few times, confused by the sudden shift in the conversation. I didn't even notice if she had been flirting. Frankly, I had no idea she was into chicks. Damn, sleep deprivation was taking its toll. "I'm flattered, but my boyfriend and I have an agreement. Neither of us is allowed to sleep with other women."

Her face turned a deep crimson. "You're not gay?"

"Nope."

"I'm sorry." She shook her head. "Harrison said you were interested. He just wanted to humiliate me. He's such an asshole."

"You should report him."

"What's the point?"

Deciding not to open that can of worms, I let out a sigh. "Can you get me inside the bunker?"

"Yeah. Come on."

She led us down an unfamiliar path toward a hangar. Taking a quick right, we went around the side of the building and turned left toward the site of the explosion. Instead of entering the building through the front door like we had done this morning, she took me around to the rear. There was another doorway, but this one didn't have a posted guard. It also didn't have any visible means of entry. Kylie slid her fingers against the doorframe, working her way lower and to the side.

"I don't think the building wants to be felt up," I remarked.

She continued moving sideways, practically in the surrounding brush, when her fingers latched on to something. I heard a faint click, and she turned with a twinkle in her eye. "You're wrong. It was just waiting for me to find the right spot." She eased deeper into the surrounding bushes, remaining at a crouch. "In case you're curious, I always find the right spot."

"I bet you do." Ignoring the obvious innuendo, I glanced around, but I didn't notice anyone nearby. I did, however, spot at least two surveillance cameras that had a decent shot of the area. Sidling up beside her, I looked at the hatch. "That leads to the server room?"

"Yep."

"Have you been down there before?"

"Plenty." She gave me a sly smile. "Oh, you meant inside the bunker."

Ignoring her, I peered into the dark hole, seeing a ladder

that led straight down. "I was told it's authorized personnel only."

She nodded. "I haven't been inside. I just happened upon the schematics when we were going over the building layout and fallout from the IED. We were told CID would investigate inside, and we were forwarded their findings. It was beyond the scope of our position since base destruction has nothing to do with determining potential threats to us or our allies here or at home."

"Now you're just quoting the OIO's mission statement." I jerked my chin toward the cameras. "I suggest you get the hell out of here. You were told this was off-limits. Being here is a clear violation."

"We're civilians. We don't fall under military regs."

"It doesn't matter. They'll have your ass either way." I gave her another look. "Get out of here. You don't want to get mixed up in this shit."

"It's too late for that." She stepped away from the opened hatch, allowing me total access. "I'll be your lookout," she met my eyes, "unless you've changed your mind. Like I said, we could always walk away and pretend this never happened. You'll fly back home and work the case like you would any other."

Her words were really pushing my buttons and not in a good way. Taking a breath, I threw one leg over the edge, finding the ladder rung with my foot. "Leave the door open. The last thing I want is to get stuck inside and miss my flight home."

"Yes, ma'am."

Biting my tongue, I slowly made my way down the ladder to the bunker below. My last case had involved underground tunnels, and I was starting to have flashbacks. Thankfully, the bunker was nothing like those tunnels. The walls were made of thick concrete, and the room was lit with various colored blinking lights from servers and computer equipment.

Taking out the flashlight on my key ring, I shined the light at the ceiling, searching for signs that I was beneath the site of the detonation. The bunker appeared vast, separated into various sections and rooms by additional concrete walls. Finally, I spotted some ceiling cracks. They weren't very severe, spiderwebbing out from tiny pinpricks. Those must have been the holes in the floor.

Sweeping the beam of light to the floor, I knelt down and ran my finger against a faint layer of dust and ash. That definitely came from upstairs. Taking a moment, I looked around the area. Several servers donned the side of the partitioned off space, but it was the other side of the room that caught my attention.

The light bounced off the ground and reflected against a set of metal bars. Moving closer, I assessed the small prison cell. It contained a cot, a table, and a chair. Why would they have a cell inside what was supposed to be a secure area? It made no sense. I pondered the reasoning, coming up with nothing short of a plot for a few post-apocalyptic sci-fi flicks.

The door to the cell wasn't locked, so I opened it wide, making sure it wouldn't close on me. Cautiously, I entered. It was empty, just like the rest of the converted bunker turned server room. Aside from a few wayward cables and plugs, there was nothing inside to indicate who might have been held here or if anyone had ever been kept inside.

Shifting my focus to the damage caused by the IED, I gave the computer array a quick glance. I had no idea what any of the equipment did. I wasn't a techie. The numerous towers seemed to be functioning. The room was fairly warm from all the electricity, but given the small amount of physical damage that had been done by the bomb, the attempt appeared to be an utter waste of time.

Heavy footfalls thundered into the room, and I barely had time to get my hands in the air before being surrounded by several M16s. What the hell happened to my lookout?

"Who are you?" one of the MPs barked.

"FBI Agent Alexis Parker. I'm with the OIO. My colleague and I landed early this morning to investigate the scene of the explosion." Slowly, I held my identification outward from where it hung around my neck.

"You are not authorized to be in here," the soldier said. "We've been granted permission to shoot on sight."

"Even if I go quietly?" I hoped he had a sense of humor.

He yanked the ID that was around my neck, holding the beam of his flashlight toward it to make sure I wasn't full of shit. Then he blinded me with the light. "What are you doing down here? How'd you get in?"

"The trap door at the rear of the building." I knew they must have seen the security footage.

"You triggered an alarm. You're lucky we didn't kill you."

"I'm sorry, fellas. Really. I won't let it happen again." I held up my hands a little higher.

Cautiously, the four men maneuvered around until I was surrounded. One of them removed my nine millimeter while the others stood watch. "Until we verify your identity with base command, you will listen to our instructions. If you try anything, you will be shot. Is that understood?"

"Yes, sir." Hopefully, this was posturing. Maybe it was a game to scare the outsider. Maybe it was some scheme those CIA twats had hatched up for shits and giggles. Either way, I let the men take me through the bunker, up another staircase, and out the front door, all while being held at gunpoint. Apparently, it was up to base command to decide what was to become of me. With any luck, I'd get banned and sent home. At least, that was the punishment I hoped to receive.

ELEVEN

"I cannot apologize enough," Jablonsky said. "Had I any idea that one of my agents would act so idiotically, I never would have brought her along. I'm sorry for the trouble she's caused."

The base commander rubbed his eyes. "How did you gain access to the bunker, Agent Parker?"

"The layout was part of the investigation file that was passed along to the OIO agents stationed here." I replied, doing my best not to throw anyone else under the bus. "The rear hatch is easily accessible to those who know where to look for it."

"The hatch requires valid ID. You do not possess the security clearance. Who opened the door?" the commander asked.

I remained silent, feeling as though the entire evening was a setup. The situation didn't sit well. The nagging buzzing in the back of my mind made me twitch. Something else was going on here.

"Answer him." Mark's words came out as a low, rumbling growl.

"Agent Arbuckle offered to get me inside the bunker."

The base commander didn't speak. Instead, he picked

up a stack of papers on his desk, tapped the edges against the tabletop, and placed them in a neat pile. "You will return to quarters and remain there until your flight. MPs will be stationed outside your room should you try to leave again." He stared at me for a moment. "I understand you were sent to investigate, and upon your arrival, you were given strict guidelines by which you were to conduct yourself. But you failed to comply. I'll be forced to file a report of the incident and a complaint with your office. The men and women on this base are under my command. Their protection and security is my top priority. Your actions were entirely unacceptable. I don't want to ever see you on my base again. Is that understood?"

"Yes, sir."

Jablonsky grabbed my upper arm before I could say what was really on my mind. "Let's go, Parker." He turned back to the commander. "She will be reprimanded, as will the other agent involved. I apologize again."

We were escorted back to our temporary quarters. Mark took a seat on his bunk and blew out a breath. I opened my mouth to say something, but he put a finger to his lips and shook his head.

"Mark?" I ignored the gesture, but he shushed me.

"Now is not the time, Agent Parker." He stared at me for a long moment, communicating with his eyes that he didn't believe the room was secure for us to talk. "Get some sleep. We have a long flight ahead of us, and I have to figure out what to do with you."

"Yes, sir."

He dropped back to his bunk. I did the same, not bothering to take off my shoes. There wasn't a chance in hell I'd be able to sleep. There was too much to think about. I wanted to write everything down, but in case we were under surveillance, I couldn't risk it. Instead, I stared at the ceiling and fidgeted until the MPs knocked on the door to take us to the mess hall for breakfast.

"Weren't you starving?" Mark nodded at my tray.

"I ate last night, and I'm afraid they might poison me."

"Probably." He glanced around, noting our guards. "Stay here and stay out of trouble." Before I could respond, he disappeared into the crowd of hungry soldiers. The MPs stood beside my table, making it obvious I was the only one in trouble.

"You can sit down, if you'd like," I offered.

"No, ma'am."

"Suit yourselves."

Since my escorts weren't winning conversationalists, I sat quietly and observed my surroundings. I didn't spot Arbuckle or Harrison and wondered what fate they might be facing. I wasn't convinced Arbuckle hadn't been recruited by the CIA or tasked to assist on whatever game they were playing. I had been slow on the uptake. Until the base commander said the hatch required authorization, I hadn't really considered how Kylie opened the door. I should have thought of that sooner. Then maybe I wouldn't be in this mess. Yet, I couldn't help but think I was meant to see inside that bunker, even though I lacked the authorization. Why wasn't the OIO given authorization anyway? It was a bomb on a base. We had agents stationed here, and we were on the same side. None of this made any sense. The more I thought about it, the more convoluted it became.

By the time Mark returned, I was agitated. He and Agent Harrison joined me at the table. Harrison offered a polite smile and leaned closer.

"I'm sorry. Kylie should have known better than to get you into this mess. She will be punished." Harrison looked up to see if the MPs were paying attention, but they pretended they weren't. "I understand you and Agent Jablonsky were tasked with investigating the crime scene. I'm sorry the parameters for that investigation were limited. Base security is a serious matter, particularly after the incident. I'm sure you must understand that."

"Uh-huh." I eyed him with contempt.

"I hope you had enough time to investigate the scene of the explosion and had the chance to speak with each potential witness," Harrison said, turning his attention to Mark.

"We did." Jablonsky took a sip from his mug. "Should anything else turn up, you will forward the intel to our office."

"Absolutely."

"Okay." Jablonsky made a show of looking at his watch. "Take care of yourself, kid." He stood. "Parker and I have a flight to catch."

In utter silence, the MPs led us to the airstrip. At the plane, one of the MPs returned my nine millimeter. They must have thought I looked insane enough to do something stupid with a handgun on a base full of heavily armed soldiers. Shaking my head at the sheer ridiculousness, I checked my weapon to find it unloaded. Stowing it in my bag, I climbed aboard the Gulfstream and waited for Mark to join me. He didn't speak another word until we were in the air.

"How many more assholes are you going to let manipulate you?" he asked.

I shrugged, choosing to stare out the window at the clouds beneath us. "Y'know, I screw up a lot, but someone orchestrated this." I snickered. "Did you know Kylie tried to pick me up at the bar? I was minding my own business, and she appears out of nowhere, starts making small talk, and then when I'm ready to leave, she says she can get me inside the bunker."

"Were you drunk?"

"No."

"But you were tired. You might not have been thinking straight."

"I wasn't." I let out a sigh. "Just straight enough to turn down her advances." I turned in my seat to face him directly. "When I asked her how or why she could get me inside the off-limits bunker, she said it was because she thought I was hot."

He laughed. "Damn, that's the oldest trick in the book. Is there something you want to tell me? Or maybe Marty needs to know something."

I glared at him. "I wasn't interested, and I turned her down."

"But you wanted access to the bunker, and to make the situation less awkward, she said she'd get you inside. I don't care how you ended up down there. I just want to know what they're hiding beneath that building."

"A holding cell. It was empty. I have no idea if someone was inside when the bomb detonated, but from what I could see, the damage was minimal. The only obvious sign that there had been any type of explosion was some dust and ash that floated down from the holes they drilled in the concrete ceiling."

He rubbed his mustache and picked up a pen. After tapping it against the tray table for a few seconds, he put it down and reached for his notepad. "Okay, let's say our friends at the CIA wanted you to see inside that bunker. They might have flipped Arbuckle years ago or approached her recently. Either way, their stink is all over what happened."

"How can you be sure?"

"Harrison is the senior agent, and he didn't possess access to that bunker. Therefore, her security card should not have opened that hatch. There's no way in hell she would have been granted special permission unless she was working for another agency."

"Wouldn't we know about it? She's one of ours."

"How naïve are you? Didn't I train you better than this?"

I shrugged, but the dig hurt. "So she's working for us and working for them. They must know we'll figure that out."

"They don't care. They'll disavow recruiting her. There won't be a paper trail. Even if we could prove it, what would that accomplish?" He shook the thought away. "The point was to make sure we knew someone might have been held inside that bunker. That might feed into the motive, so we need to determine if anyone was being kept on base." He removed the USB from his pocket and twirled it between his fingers. "We know the bomber was caught on the footage. He gained access by manipulating the base security systems. We also suspect someone was being held in an underground cell inside the server room. This entire situation screams black ops espionage. The real question is was the IED meant to take out the base computer systems or was it planted as a diversion to free the prisoner."

"How would a prison break relate to the explosion in the

Branded Telecom building?" The thought went through my mind before Jablonsky could say a word. "The CIA uses that building for interrogations. They probably have holding cells too."

"Bingo."

"Any idea who they might be holding or what high-value targets we've captured lately?"

"HVTs are rarely publicized until we've gotten whatever intel we can out of them and move them to a secure location. It's possible whatever op DCS is running has been compromised. Based on what we know, I'd say that op has moved from the middle of the desert to our shores, and they need our help to clean up their mess. That's why they wanted you to see what was behind the curtain."

"And they couldn't tell us about this directly because it would implicate the illegal activities of the agency, which would garner additional scrutiny and trigger congressional hearings and oversight committees," I surmised.

"And it would gain a lot of public attention. They can't afford that, which means we're in the midst of some serious black ops shit."

"What are we supposed to do about it? We still have no idea what's going on."

"As if that weren't bad enough, they're in a position to hang your ass out to dry." He pressed his lips together. "Let's hope these complaints die away because if they don't, we might be looking for new careers."

"After this shit, I wouldn't necessarily object."

"Yeah, just as long as they don't decide to paint us as scapegoats and blame the bombings on us." Jablonsky leaned back in his seat. "There's no use worrying about it now. We can't do much until we land. Once we do, I'll turn over every rock and call every contact I've ever had to find out who was inside that bunker at the time of the detonation. That will get us one step closer to determining what these company men have dragged us into."

"Do you think that'll work?"

"It has to. We were meant to see this for a reason. They wouldn't have given us a glimpse inside if it was just another dead end, and up until now, we've hit nothing but dead ends. This will lead to something. I'm just not sure I want to know what that something is." He flipped the USB around in his hand. I could tell when Mark was worried, and at the moment, he was scared shitless. "At least we have some footage of the bomber. When we get back, I want you to run this through facial rec and dig up everything you can on the base bombing from four months ago. Are you certain there were no attacks prior to that one?"

"As far as I know. Then again, we've been in the dark for so long, it's possible there have been other incidents, and the CIA or DCS brushed them under the rug."

Jablonsky took a long slow inhale, tucking the USB safely back in his pocket. "We're dealing with some serious shit."

"I don't like the possibilities that are running around inside my head. Dirty bombs, wide-scale panic, potentially hundreds of thousands of casualties. Am I just letting my imagination run wild?"

He focused on the blue sky outside the window. "I don't know." He turned back with a grim smile. "I'll need you sharp, and if I've learned anything in the last twelve hours, it's that you don't function well when you're tired and jetlagged. Try to get some sleep. With the time difference, we should land and get back to the office by mid-morning. We're going to have a full day ahead of us, so seriously, get some rest. That's an order."

"I don't follow those particularly well."

"Try, Alex. I need you."

Nodding, I dropped my seat into a reclining position and pulled the shade on the window. It didn't do much to dim the cabin, so Jablonsky got up and closed the rest of the shades. Then he took a seat across the aisle from me. Since he had slept last night, he picked up the stack of files we'd brought with us and the copies of the ones we'd gotten from the base and began to piece everything together to fit with our newest theory. Perhaps by the time we touched down, he'd have identified the captive or have some inkling of what type of top-secret op was being conducted. Frankly, I didn't think we were any closer to finding an answer than we were before we left home a day and a half ago.

After two hours, I managed to calm my racing thoughts and fall into an uneasy sleep. My dreams were a mix of random images and emotions, and when I opened my eyes again, we were landing. It was time to get to work.

TWELVE

"Some detective left another message for you," Agent Davis said when I entered the bullpen. "The note's on your desk."

"Thanks." Taking a deep breath, I needed a couple of minutes to decompress. After leaving a quick voicemail telling Martin that I was home safe and sound, I leafed through the memos and various post-its. Jacobs had phoned twice, leaving cryptic and urgent requests for a return call. Whatever he wanted had something to do with the black site. Maybe he identified the bomber. Dialing Jacobs' private line, I leaned back in my chair. I needed to come off relaxed, even though I was pretty tightly wound after being in a war zone and getting reprimanded by base command, not to mention the long flight afterward.

"Where the hell have you been?" Jacobs asked.

"That must have been the least friendly greeting I've ever gotten."

"Parker, stop. You took over our case, which is fine, except I want to know where the hell the case went."

"What are you talking about?"

He sighed dramatically. "I went to perform a quick follow-up. There was a problem with some paperwork, so I tried to get a hold of Dutch. I figured he'd be at the office, except the entire place was cleared out. They must have had a fire sale. Even the doorknobs and keypads were ripped out. He's gone. His line's been disconnected. His house emptied."

"Okay."

"No, it's not okay. What the hell happened? Who are these people?"

"You're the detective. Shouldn't you figure that out?"

He let out a very long and creative string of expletives. "Get your ass down to the precinct, or I'll send officers to escort you." He slammed the receiver down.

I pulled the phone away, my ear ringing from the force of his hang up. Reluctantly climbing out of my chair, I went to Mark's office and knocked. The door was shut tight, and I knew the reason. Cracking it open, I stuck my head inside. "We have another problem."

"What?"

"Branded Telecom cleared out. From what Jacobs said, the building's been gutted. Dutch disappeared, along with everyone connected to the fake telecom company. The PD wants answers. How much am I allowed to disclose?"

Mark swore a few times, although not as creatively as Jacobs. "Are we certain they're gone?"

"I don't know."

"Go find out. At this point, I don't give a shit about the limitations those CIA douches placed on our investigation. We need answers. I don't want this city to turn into a war zone." He lifted the phone off his desk. "Get me, Kendall. It's urgent." He placed his palm over the mouthpiece. "If the Director agrees, I'm sending a hoard of our crime techs to analyze every inch of that building. We need to know everything that happened inside and who might have been there." He waved his hand at the door. "Go. For all we know, the police are already poking around and contaminating our evidence."

I dashed to the car and drove with the lights on. Swinging the car into a reserved space at the rear of the building, I dialed Jacobs, hoping he'd meet me at the front desk. Instead, the call went to voicemail. I couldn't help but think he was screening. After flashing my credentials and giving my name, I was allowed entry upstairs.

Jacobs' desk was empty, so I marched purposefully to Lt. Moretti's office. I had no earthly idea what I was going to say to the man. Probably something along the lines of *please stay away from Branded Telecom and everyone related to it because Jablonsky said so.* Yeah, that wasn't going to work. Before I could knock, someone grabbed my shoulder.

"Parker," Detective Derek Heathcliff pulled me away from the door, "you're here to see Jacobs, right?"

I nodded.

"Branded Telecom?"

"Yeah."

"Good." He led me toward his desk, pointing at an empty chair. "Take a seat."

"Derek, I don't have time to catch up with you right now. The OIO's in the middle of this clusterfuck of a case."

He gave me a hard look. At one point we'd been good friends, but I wasn't sure if that friendship had survived the fallout from our last case. "Sit down, Alex. I've been assigned to help Jacobs. Apparently, he would prefer not having to deal with you." He sat, waiting for me to follow his lead. "You took the case from us, so I understand what we've done is step on your toes. Be that as it may, we each have jobs to do, so don't make mine any harder."

I dropped into the chair. It was no secret I'd made Derek's life a lot harder in recent years. He lost someone recently, and despite the fact I knew it wasn't my fault, I wasn't sure if he realized it. It wouldn't kill me to play nice for a few minutes. "What can I do for you?"

He stared into my eyes. "Why did the OIO take over the case?"

"I can't tell you."

"Do you know why the Branded Telecom employees have gone AWOL?"

"Not exactly. I have a few suspicions, but I'm not at liberty to share them."

His fingers itched to pick up a pen and jot down some notes, but he resisted. "Okay, let's try this another way."

"I need to interrupt for a second. Do you have officers or techs inside the telecom building?"

"The last I heard, we had officers outside. We're waiting on a warrant before we tear the place apart. We didn't get the opportunity when the bomb went off, so we're not going to miss our second chance. Frankly, I don't believe we need the piece of paper. The building's unlocked. Everything is in the open, but we're being cautious."

"Can I persuade you otherwise?" My eyes pleaded with him. "Does it make a difference if I say it may be a matter of national security?"

"Is it?"

"I just got back from one of our military bases in Turkey."

He worked his jaw for a moment. "What are we dealing with?" I didn't answer immediately, and he leaned forward, his eyes intense. "Are we talking about another terrorist attack? Was the explosion a mistake or a dry run? How much damage should we expect?" His eyes narrowed. "Why haven't you alerted us about the imminent threat?"

"There isn't an imminent threat. At least, I don't know if there is. We are operating under the assumption this is not terrorism, and we have no intel suggesting a future attack." Although that was technically true, Jablonsky seemed just as freaked out about the possibility as Heathcliff. Perhaps I should have been more frightened and less annoyed. Damn the jetlag. It must be screwing with my rationale and priorities. "I can't tell you much." My eyes darted around, but no one was nearby. "You know my darkest secrets, Detective. Can I trust you with another one?"

He nodded. "Go on."

"We believe Branded Telecom was a front for a clandestine operation. That's all you need to know, but the OIO will need full, unadulterated access to the building. We're cleaning up the mess, so to speak, and we need to tear apart the building without the risk of it being compromised further. That's why I'm here. I need to get the police department to stand down."

"Why doesn't your office make it official?"

"Jablonsky's working on it."

His mind ran through the possibilities. "You're not supposed to be looking into this matter either." He flopped backward in the seat, making the chair rock. "Why the hell not?"

"It's complicated."

"Everything with you is. No wonder Jacobs is pissed you've been lying to him. He doesn't understand why we aren't investigating a bombing, why the victims aren't cooperating, and why the OIO said they were taking over but only in a half-assed way."

"Moretti signed off on it."

"Yeah, until Jacobs went back to get a signature for the report and discovered everything was cleared out. Now Moretti wants back in on this. Tell your office to balls up and do something. If not, we'll conduct a thorough search and open a wide-scale investigation into the matter."

"Fine." I pulled out my cell phone. "Let me make a call."

When Jablonsky answered, I filled him in on the PD's stance. However, Director Kendall still believed we should play nice with other government agencies. It was nothing more than politics, but there wasn't much we could do about it. Instead, we were going to step back and let the police do the work.

Disconnecting, I looked at Heathcliff. "I guess the case is yours again. Congratulations."

"In all seriousness, how bad is it?"

"Honestly, I have no idea. Mark and I are attempting to determine what kind of op is in play, but we've been hitting roadblock after roadblock." I gestured at the desk between us. "This case is nothing more than a ping-pong tournament. One minute we don't want the case. The next, we do. Then the assholes grabbed me off the street and the lesbian OIO agent set me up." I shook my head. "Don't even ask." Biting my lip, I knew I ran out of favors a long time ago. "Do you think I can check out the building while your teams rip it apart?"

He nodded. "I'll drive."

The outside of the building was surrounded by police vehicles. Several forensic vans dotted the spaces between the half dozen patrol cars. Jacobs was leaning against the front door when we pulled up.

"Is Parker taking over again?" he asked Heathcliff, as if I

were invisible.

"No. You wanted the case back, so it's yours," I replied. "Can we please call a truce? I didn't mean to deceive you."

Jacobs narrowed his eyes. "Yes, you did, but we're not children. So what the hell are you doing here?"

"She wants to look around," Heathcliff piped up. "I said it was okay. Did we get the warrant yet?"

"Five minutes," Jacobs replied.

"Okay, boys, I'll meet you inside." Pulling open the unlocked office door, I wondered why Dutch hadn't bothered to lock up. Jablonsky's words came to mind. They wanted us to find something. Now I just had to figure out what that something was.

The explosion occurred on the fourth floor, so I started there. Donning a pair of gloves, I did a quick search of the rooms, the desks, and anything else that appeared suspicious. The shattered glass had been swept away. The charring and burn patterns from the IED seemed less pronounced, as if someone had tried to clean them up.

After finding nothing on the fourth floor, I went down to the third. I was met with more empty office space and not a single clue, so I moved on to the fifth floor. From the growing din inside, I knew the police had begun their search. They'd work level by level, so I had a bit more time. After searching the main area, I went down a narrow corridor. Three rooms previously had high-tech security, but the units had been ripped from the walls.

"Son of a bitch." I entered what had once been the white room. It smelled of fresh paint, and the walls were now a muted grey. A couple of area rugs had been tossed inside, but the white metal chairs made it obvious this was where they had brought me.

I took a few photos and moved on to the second previously locked room. This one was much bleaker, but something about it made the hairs on the back of my neck stand on end. Now all I needed to do was figure out why.

When Heathcliff and Jacobs found me, I was crouched down in the corner of the room, staring at the floor. The IED had gone off beneath us. I couldn't help but think some of the tiles had buckled. But the damage wasn't clearly discernible. Maybe I was imagining things.

"Do you feel that?" Heathcliff asked.

"Tingling," Jacobs said. "What is that?"

"So I'm not insane." I jerked my chin at the center of the floor that looked a bit lower. "The bomb went off beneath us. Are we sure this room is structurally sound?"

"That's what we were told." Heathcliff crouched down to get a better look. Removing his pen, he tried to pry up a piece of the tile, but it didn't budge. "There's something under here." He held his palm over it. "I'd say whatever's causing that tingling sensation is coming from right here."

Without a word, Jacobs left. I moved closer to Heathcliff. He was correct. The tingling felt almost like a low-level electric current. Perhaps the power lines had been damaged, explaining the slight scent of ozone in the air.

"Fun tidbit," I volunteered, "there was a similar detonation at one of our FOBs. It was strategically placed to knock out the power and computer systems. The base was blacked out for hours. I bet whatever lines run beneath here are the same ones that the IED knocked out."

"Something must be damaged. If there's an active current, it could be what's causing this static discharge." Heathcliff stood, offering me a hand up. "It'd probably be best to stay clear until the techs investigate. One puddle of water and we could turn into fried chicken."

"I'll mark that off the dinner menu." We cleared out of the room, lingering in the doorway and observing the rest of our surroundings. "What do you think they used that room for?"

"It looks like a tech hub." He pointed to several jacks and outlets on the wall. "They had hardwired LAN cables coming through those ports. Maybe it was a server room. That goes along with what you said about that other bombing." He put a hand on my shoulder. "If this is number two, how can you be certain there won't be a number three?"

"Actually, this might be number three. I'm just not sure yet."

THIRTEEN

After the techs cleared the room and turned off the electricity, they pried the tiles from the floor. That move might have gone beyond the scope of the warrant. But damaged electrical wiring posed a danger to public safety, and the warrant was purely for show, seeing as how the building was vacant. So there was that.

Beneath the tile, they found a thick braid of wiring. Some of the wires had nicks and damage that might have been due to the blast impact on the level below. Working under the assumption the electrical discharge was causing the tingling in the air, they decided it was best to leave the power off for the time being.

I crept back inside and examined the wiring. "Any idea what most of this is?"

"Someone was running a heavy-duty computer here. They wanted instantaneous internet access." The tech separated a few of the wires. "A lot of power went in to making this happen. From the number of hookups, I'm guessing they were operating several powerful systems."

"They wanted to create a supercomputer," another tech said, glancing toward us from his spot near the wall outlets. "By hardwiring enough processors together with enough memory, it can be done. At least it looks like what they were doing." He wiped his hands on his coveralls and stood up. "Then again, this is a telecom company. They need a lot of operating and processing power. It's not surprising."

"Parker," Jacobs called from the doorway, "I need to ask you something."

Leaving the techs to their work, I went into the hallway. There was no hard evidence, and a bunch of networked computers and drives wasn't out of the ordinary for a telecom company, even if they were just a CIA front. Too bad the actual computers had been removed. The leftover wiring and jacks were useless. "What?"

"It's probably just an urban myth, but didn't the NSA convince telecom companies to route their customers' calls and data through some big government machine as part of a program to prevent future terrorist activities?"

"Yes, and they also experiment on little green men inside Area 51."

"Fine. Clearly, I must be crazy. So you don't think this building is a front the government is using to spy on us?"

I laughed. "Unfortunately, I do, so if you get abducted by the men in black, be careful because they carry tasers." I headed for the stairs. "Good luck, Jacobs."

"You're ready to leave?" Heathcliff asked. He had been studying the epicenter of the explosion.

"I've seen everything there is to see. Unless the techs can pull data from the power cords or discover a hidden hard drive, I'm pretty sure this place was wiped clean."

"That's what I've been hearing." Heathcliff led the way down the steps and back to the lobby. "What are you going to tell Jablonsky?"

"That the PD was nice enough to take a dead end investigation off our hands."

"Don't be catty."

"You don't happen to have any other ongoing investigations that deal with bombings or telecom companies in the works, do you?"

"No."

"What about government cover-ups? Jacobs was talking conspiracy theories."

"You'd be the expert on those." He unlocked the cruiser and waited for me to get inside. "And you're going to let me know if anything comes to fruition. I don't care if it's the CIA, DHS, DCS, or the NSA. If anyone has intel that another bombing is going to happen, I want to know about it. It was sheer luck no one was hurt this time. I doubt we'll be that fortunate a second time."

I stared at the building. Only one thought ran through my mind. It wasn't luck.

*　　*　　*

Returning to the office, I checked in with Agent Lawson and our tech department. The USB footage from the base was being analyzed against the image of Vega. It would take time, especially since the few images of the bomber weren't conducive to the software. The techs were still playing the video files and scooping out screenshots, which they were enhancing before running them through facial rec. Even the photo ID we had of Vega wasn't working well with the program.

"It looks like this image was doctored to fall within the parameters of a vast amount of profiles. The software uses certain key features to make a connection, but this photo ID is skewed. It's almost as if the guy was wearing tactical makeup in order to fit a more general profile. Even the angle of his face makes it more difficult to determine the length of his nose or the distance from his lips to his nostrils, and with the thick-framed glasses and reflection on the lenses, we can't even accurately pinpoint the distance between his eyes," Lawson sighed. "This bastard is one lucky son of a bitch."

"Could it be a computer image that he doctored?" I asked.

Lawson set his jaw. "I've never seen anyone do something like that. How could he? This was an ID taken on the base."

"Maybe it's a fake ID." Our bomber might have the ability to hack a military base and reupload an image they originally had taken, or the entire ID was faked. "I don't know. Just don't assume that anything we know is true."

"That'll make coming up with a positive identification more challenging."

"Do the best you can."

I went downstairs and looked through the files again. Then I went into an empty conference room, closed the blinds, and got to work. Now that I'd visited the last two crime scenes, for lack of a better term, I could draw on the commonalities. First and foremost, both bombings occurred near a computer hub. The device used was of a similar construction, possibly the same, and the CIA had their stink all over the two scenes.

Assuming Mark was correct in believing we had been granted access deliberately to these areas because there was something to find, my mind circled back to the holding cell inside the bunker and the interrogation rooms inside the telecom building. However, neither explosion resulted in casualties as far as we knew.

Grabbing the phone, I dialed Hartley's extension. "Kate, come downstairs and bring all the shipping records and manifests you have on Branded Telecom."

"I thought we weren't doing that anymore."

"Yeah, well, you're not. I am."

"Alex, you're going to get in trouble."

I laughed. "You're starting to sound like my last partner. Are you going to call Lucca and rat me out?"

I could hear the eye roll through the phone. "I'll be there in a sec."

Internally scoffing at Director Kendall's insistence to keep this investigation on a need to know basis, I flipped the whiteboard over so Kate wouldn't see my musings, closed the file folders, and placed them on the seat of one of the office chairs. Deciding that was sufficient to protect the secrecy of the investigation, I nodded to myself and waited for her to appear.

"Thanks." Taking the pages, I placed them on the table. "IIow large were the shipments? Is it possible Branded Telecom was sending or receiving something besides phone cords or whatever it is we think they were shipping?"

She shrugged. "Package weight was several hundred pounds. The containers were large enough to hold a few refrigerators, so I guess they could have been sending pretty much anything."

A stray thought crossed my mind. "How were they sent?"

"What?"

"They were flown over." I pointed to the delivery method. "Is there any way of figuring out where the cargo was kept on the plane? Was it in the hold, or did it have some kind of special handling instructions?"

She stared at the pages for a long moment. "I don't work for UPS. You do understand that I'm a forensic accountant. I can tell you how they paid the shipping costs. I'm not sure I can tell you how it was shipped." She jerked her chin at the blank board. "What are you doing? Why the sudden interest?"

"It might be important. I don't know yet."

Before she could say anything, Jablonsky entered the conference room. "Agent Hartley, I believe Davis was looking for you."

She gave me another look. Holding up her hands in defeat, she stepped away from the table. "It's your ass, Alex."

"Yep."

Nodding to Mark, she left the room. Jablonsky crossed the room to the boards and flipped them around. Snickering, he pulled the stack of files off the seat and placed them on the table next to the documents Kate had procured.

"How are the police doing?" he asked.

"They're tearing the place apart. It appears the IED detonated on the level below the building's nerve center. We found a ton of wires. Some were damaged in the blast. The techs think Branded Telecom had a supercomputer."

Mark nodded, not saying anything. "What are these manifests for?"

"I've been considering the possibility someone might have been kept at these locations. Perhaps the explosion is a way to target an individual."

"Or orchestrate a prison break."

"What do you know?"

"I'm not sure yet. As soon as I have something solid, I'll tell you. In the meantime, continue chasing whatever rabbit you have in your sights." He moved toward the door. "Just be careful who you involve."

"I thought our office was clean."

"It should be, but I don't trust the spooks not to have a few aces up their sleeves to keep us in line."

After several calls and banging my head against the wall, I was ready to throw in the towel. The jetlag never went away, and it was rearing its ugly head. I wanted to go home and sleep for a week. My body didn't know where it was or what time it was supposed to be. All it knew was that it didn't want to be in this conference room any longer.

I copied down the few thoughts I had put on the board and wiped the slate clean. Taking the files and the documents to my desk, I locked them in the bottom drawer. After checking my messages a final time, I turned off the computer and knocked on Mark's office door.

"Enter." He looked up, offering a grim smile. "We have a problem." Getting up, he perched on the edge of the desk. "A little bird told me one of the special ops teams picked up a blackhat while conducting recon in an old Eastern Bloc country."

"Personally, I would have gone with an ushanka."

Jablonsky looked utterly confused. "A blackhat is a computer genius. It's my understanding he can hack absolutely anything."

"I know. Go on."

He shook his head, realizing it was too late in the day to bother trying to understand my sense of humor. "He's been detained and moved periodically to several of our outposts and bases. Two of those bases were bombed."

"Southeastern Europe and Turkey."

"Apparently, he possesses knowledge and abilities the United States government highly values, but the group he worked for prior to his current detainment wants to make sure he can't share that information with us."

"Why does this sound like a sick version of capture the

flag? Do they want to kill him or rescue him?"

"I don't know. My buddy in the state department isn't sure either. I'm guessing the point of the bomb is to destroy our computer systems in order to destroy any intel we receive from the blackhat."

"I guess that makes sense."

"I've made several calls to Agents Harrison and Arbuckle. No one has called back, but I'm hoping that will change." He checked the time, remembering they were eight hours ahead. "I should hear something from them soon."

"Have you spoken to our spy friends about this?"

"I tried, but they're denying everything. We're going to need proof to fire back if we don't want them to feed us more bullshit."

"I still don't see a connection between some mystical blackhat we're holding hostage on military bases and what happened in a local office building a few days ago. But," my mind went back to the shipping manifests, "if Branded Telecom was transporting live cargo, it'd be easy enough to smuggle an asset out of a country and into another one. Any idea how to determine if that's the case?"

"Were the shipments made using military aircraft?"

"Maybe. They were sent directly to and from the bases."

"In that case, they would have used military cargo planes. I'd bet my ass they had our blackhat and a few spooks onboard. Can I see the manifests?"

Running back to my desk, I grabbed the files from the drawer and returned to Jablonsky's office. He skimmed them again, highlighted a few numbers, and checked the time. He let out a huff and pushed the pages toward me.

"Branded Telecom had a shipment from the southeastern European base to Turkey right after the first bomb went off, and they had another shipment leaving Turkey after the second bombing."

"Damn, I completely missed that."

He brushed my blunder away. "It happens. I'll look through these and see what I can dig up. You look like shit. Why don't you call it a night?"

"That's what I stopped in to tell you."

He smiled. "I'm sorry if this was such an inconvenience."

"Don't let it happen again." I grinned. "Now if you'll excuse me, I have a hot date."

"I thought you weren't seeing Marty until this weekend."

"I wasn't talking about him. I was referencing my pillow and sleeping in my own bed. If I'm not here in the morning, don't bother calling. It just means I'm getting my beauty rest."

"Have a good night, Parker."

Keeping my eyes open on the drive home took more effort than I imagined. Luckily, I made it to my apartment without incident. Yawning as I unlocked the door, I lugged my bag inside and flipped on the lights. The answering machine blinked. I hit play and went into the bedroom to change while a telemarketer left a message. The second one was a courtesy call from the real estate office, congratulating me on the apartment. I was certain Martin received a similar call. The next message was from my co-homeowner. He had gotten carried away while shopping for a bed and cookware. However, he insisted the living room was my domain.

I double-checked that I locked the front door, turned off the lights, and climbed into bed. Closing my eyes, I sunk into the mattress, letting the tension seep out of my body. My mind went blank, and I fell asleep in record time. That would probably explain why I didn't hear the scratching creak when my fire escape was jimmied open or wake up when two men entered my bedroom.

The room remained in utter darkness. No matter how much I struggled to open my eyes, I couldn't see anything but pitch blackness. I wasn't even sure I was in bed, let alone awake. "Who's there?" I asked.

"We're not here to hurt you, but we need to talk."

"Who are you?" I asked, while my mind fought its way through the sleepy fog and tried to remember if the backup in my nightstand drawer was loaded. I had no idea, but that meant they wouldn't either. Unfortunately, I didn't think blindly aiming a gun was a great plan. "What do you want?"

"We just want to talk," a man said.

"About what?" The disembodied voices in the darkness added to my dreamlike state. "Show yourselves," I insisted.

"Sorry, we can't do that. We're here because we don't have a choice. Things got away from us. Without your help, this country could be facing a serious threat."

"Why me? Why now? I've been at the office all day. I'm sure you could have found the phone number or called the main line and had the call rerouted."

"We said this is a secret. We only want your help," the man berated. "Pay attention."

I started nodding off again, and someone shook me. "Wake up, Agent Parker. The clock's ticking," the second voice urged. "Our asset was nearly killed in the explosion, but he decrypted a transmission just in time to escape. He disappeared, and we can't locate him."

"Who?" I mumbled, blinking in and out.

"Our blackhat."

FOURTEEN

I woke the next day exactly how I'd fallen asleep. My head hurt, and my body ached from being in the same position for so long. A sense of unease settled over me. Something didn't feel right. My dream hit me like a ton of bricks. I scanned the bedroom for signs that someone had been in my apartment. My nine millimeter remained on the nightstand, my cell phone in the charger, and my luggage haphazardly dropped in the middle of the room. Nothing was disturbed.

Grabbing my weapon, I slowly got out of bed and caught my reflection in the mirror. Even I looked the same. Cautiously, I crept into the living room. No one was there. The front door was locked and bolted, and the fire escape was shut tight. Everything was as I left it.

I rubbed my face and scanned the room again, hoping to notice footprints or some sign that my dream had been real. Picking up my landline, I listened for a dial tone and phoned Mark.

"You weren't kidding when you said you'd be late this morning," he teased. "Are you on your way?"

Blinking, I glanced at the clock. It was almost one p.m. "I just had a hell of a dream."

"Oh yeah?"

"Actually, I'm not entirely convinced it was a dream." I peered out the window, checking for evidence that someone had been on the fire escape, but it was covered in the usual layer of dirt from the air and the rain. "But it must have been." I sighed. "I dreamt a couple of men broke into my apartment to give us a message. I think they were CIA."

"What was the message?"

I wasn't sure if he was playing along or if he thought that weird disembodied conversation actually happened. "The blackhat was specifically targeted. He escaped the explosion, but they lost track of him."

"Huh." He inhaled loudly. "You should probably get to the office soon."

That wasn't a reassuring response. After a quick shower, I rushed to the federal building. My hair was still wet when I arrived, so I put it in a ponytail during the elevator ride to the OIO level. Foregoing my usual office routine, I barged through Mark's door.

"What's up?" I asked.

"I thought you didn't give a shit about this case."

"Things change. Fill me in."

"After you left last night, I ran through those cargo manifests. It appears our captive needed some powerful computer gear. Branded Telecom shipped the equipment to the European base prior to the first detonation. The company had sent several other shipments in the past to other bases and American strongholds without incident, but that was before we had a blackhat in custody. One of the civilian employees must have seen the amount of processing power being brought in, said something to the wrong person, and that's what led Vega to detonate the first explosive. Another heavy-duty shipment was sent to Turkey prior to the explosion there. If the bomber isn't tracking our captive's movements, he's tracking the computer gear."

"Makes sense. Why didn't we know this sooner?"

"One hand doesn't know what the other is doing. Agent Arbuckle phoned this morning but didn't say much other than to acknowledge the base had recently received new computer equipment before the explosion, and it had to be replaced afterward."

"I'm guessing they haven't made any progress determining the identity of the bomber or how he accessed the file room above the bunker."

"She said one of the teams discovered a civilian employee dead. They suspect he might have assisted the bomber, but they don't have any hard proof."

"Why couldn't they have told us that four days ago and saved us a trip?"

"Torture violates the Geneva Convention, but so do several of our enhanced interrogation tactics. If the man died while being questioned in our custody, the United States would be facing severe political and humanitarian repercussions. So maybe that's why we found him already dead." He sighed. "I don't want to think too much about it, and you shouldn't either."

"I already have too much on my conscience. I don't need to worry about anyone else's crimes. Do we know anything for sure about the blackhat?"

"When Arbuckle called, she said a Branded Telecom shipment was sent out as soon as power was restored to the base the day of the explosion. One of the elite teams accompanied the package. She didn't say what the package was, and when I asked, she pretended not to know. However, after another dozen calls and selling my soul to the devil, I discovered the cargo plane landed at a local military base to refuel and load up on supplies."

"When was that?"

"About a week ago." He licked his lips. "Actually, it was two days before we were called to the Branded Telecom building."

"Have there been any odd shipments since then?"

Mark shook his head. "I've assigned several agents the task of checking passport records after the cargo plane landed to see if anyone suspicious entered the country. We're flagging anyone from Turkey, but I might be jumping the gun."

"You really believe the CIA smuggled a blackhat into the

country despite his known terrorist affiliation?"

"Anarchist," he corrected. "We aren't talking Jihadists. We're talking anarchists."

"And that's better?"

"Not necessarily, but it might mean they're more selective about who they kill. I don't believe they're violent. They're just antigovernment. And the fact that we captured or turned one of theirs and intend to use his skills to strengthen our government doesn't sit well with them."

"So they're here to liberate him."

"Or kill him if he turned."

"You just said you didn't think they were violent."

"In terms of planning a massive strike on our soil or targeting our bases with the intent on inflicting casualties."

"Fine, so where is the computer hacker? Shouldn't those CIA agents have him stashed someplace safe? How do we know he isn't in their custody? For that matter, how can we be certain any of this is even true?"

"The anarchist group is comprised of several skilled hackers. They've repeatedly breached our intelligence databases and have discovered a list of our safe houses. They also accessed the records and databases we've scoured, so they knew precisely where their abducted comrade would be. So he did the only thing he could do. He ran."

"How do you know this?"

"The NSA verified the intrusions into our system and flagged the compromised data."

"It's just like my dream."

"Apparently, your subconscious was working over time." Jablonsky rubbed his cheek. "This is why we have to keep our investigation secret. This anarchist hacker group is monitoring our policing agencies, hoping to get a lead. We have to find this blackhat quickly and quietly and without using our normal resources."

"Do we know his name or have a description? What do we know about the anarchist group that's after him?"

Jablonsky picked up a manila envelope and held it out. "This was inside my car when I left work last night. It should answer the rest of your questions. Keep it confidential." His phone rang, and he answered. After a few words, he hung up. "I have to speak to Director Kendall. Read that, and we'll strategize when I return." He went to the door. "I hope you didn't burn too many bridges at the PD. We might need them to be on the lookout for our hacker."

Unclasping the metal hooks on the envelope, I wasn't entirely sure what intel Jablonsky received. I also didn't understand exactly why he believed it. I was taking everything we'd learned with a grain of salt. After sliding out several sheets of paper and a few surveillance photos, I decided to give our mystery informant the benefit of the doubt.

The anarchist hacker group, Anarkhos, formed over a decade ago. Even then, the world didn't make much sense, but with the current climate, its membership had skyrocketed. There was unrest across the globe and not just in the United States. Like every other anarchist group throughout time, they didn't believe in government. This group, in particular, believed in an entirely free society. Every individual would have the right and means to do and act as he or she pleased. In order to empower these sovereign individuals, Anarkhos wanted complete disclosure and unlimited access to all knowledge. This included everything from secret recipes to nuclear launch codes. They believed if we each had equal footing and power, no disparities would exist regardless of wealth, gender, race, etc. It was fucking lunacy.

In order to achieve their goal and make all information available, they'd been scouting the dark web and recruiting the best and most talented computer hackers. A single sheet of paper contained a list of several dozen suspected hackers who had already joined Anarkhos' ranks. A few of them were on our most wanted lists. These hackers were so infamous, the cybercrimes division would get a hard-on at the thought of taking any one of them into custody. Yeah, we definitely had a problem.

On the last page was a photo and brief bio of the man we suspected the CIA had captured and turned, Stavos Kiter. He was just shy of six feet, slender build, wore glasses, and credited with remotely breaching sensitive government databases. The actual details of that breach were redacted, and I couldn't help but think if I found Kiter, I'd ask him about it. He was recruited by Anarkhos eight months ago and allegedly opened several backdoors into Russia, China, the United States, and England's intelligence networks. He then took the data and broadcast it throughout the dark web. It took almost twelve hours before the U.S. recognized the breach and stopped him. I wasn't sure how long it took the other countries or what secrets we lost, but it wasn't good.

Jablonsky returned and took a seat behind his desk. "What do you think?"

"We're supposed to find this guy and protect him despite his crimes against our country?"

"We turned him, allegedly." He jerked his chin at the bottom of the page. "Once Kiter was captured, he agreed to assist in tightening security and preventing future intrusions in exchange for protection."

"Are we certain he didn't broadcast his location to his friends so they could come and save him?"

"It's possible. We won't know anything for certain until we find him and figure out what's what." He stared at the photo. "And we can't put his picture over the wire because they'll pick it up. He'd probably just hack the feed and change it anyway."

"So how are we supposed to find him? We don't have the manpower or resources to search every inch of the city on the off chance he hasn't already fled to some tropical island. This guy is a genius. He can fake everything, ID, money, whatever, and get the hell out of Dodge. If DCS and the CIA can't find him, I don't think we'll be able to either."

"Maybe we don't look for him. Maybe we make everyone think we are, and when his buddies make another attempt to rescue him or silence him, whichever the case may be, we stop them."

"Great," I replied, nonplussed. "Practically everything is computerized from traffic lights to the power grid. These Anarkhos assholes could probably cripple the entire city if they choose, and from what we've seen so far, I bet they'd go to those lengths to get to Kiter. Planning a sting could lead to a lot of damage and fallout, and there won't be any guarantees we'll even be able to arrest them, let alone keep them in custody." Sighing, I leafed through the intel again. "How many of these anarchists were sent to find the traitor?"

"I don't know. Like I said, we have people checking recent travelers."

"Right, because they didn't hack those databases." I couldn't even think about reining in the sarcasm. This was a ridiculous assignment. We were up against a group we couldn't fight against. "Shouldn't we get cybercrimes involved?"

"No. That's fighting fire with fire, which will lead to more destruction. We need to keep this secret, and we need to do it the old-fashioned way."

"By beating up the computer geeks with phonebooks?"

"In a manner of speaking, yeah. That's exactly what we're going to do. As of this morning, Director Kendall outlined the parameters of our mission, along with our goals. He's coordinating with DCS to make sure our play fits in with their operation and that they'll be onboard. This is no longer some secret they can keep off the books. They shit the bed, and we're rubbing their noses in it." He looked at me for a long moment. "There will be repercussions. I don't know how severe. I don't even know exactly what they can do to us, but based on what they've already done or tried to do, I don't imagine they're going to take kindly to our interference."

"But they asked for our help."

"It doesn't matter. This op was unsanctioned. The agents who screwed up will face some sort of punishment, and they'll seek some form of retribution in order to throw dirt onto us and salvage as much of their careers and reputations as possible. I want you to be prepared for whatever shitstorm might be headed our way."

"So it's just another day at the office then." I leaned back in the chair. "In that case, we might as well get started on the plan."

FIFTEEN

Now that I had my assignment, my focus shifted to identifying the bomber or bombers. The bomb techs had been analyzing the materials and blast pattern since they received the intel from the police department. Based on what we knew and a few educated guesses, they were in the midst of reconstructing the bomb. While it was directional, like a claymore, its main purpose wasn't to cause physical destruction. The charring and property damage were side effects. The real point of the blast was the emission of an electromagnetic pulse that fried or shorted out anything electronic. Scarily enough, most WMDs also produced electromagnetic pulses as a byproduct.

"We haven't identified the signature yet," the bomb tech said. "I'm guessing we're dealing with someone new. I've never seen anything like this." He pointed to the pieces of tape he'd placed on the floor and walls. "The blast zone is limited. However, the force would be enough to wound or possibly kill anyone within the area. We're lucky it didn't go off in the middle of the workday."

Surveying the tape marks, I estimated it to be roughly the same sized expanse that had been affected inside the telecom building. However, the explosion at the military base had been larger.

"Theoretically, how big could you make one of these?" I asked.

He chewed on a toothpick and reached for a calculator. "The bigger the blast, the stronger the electronic distortion. If you wanted to maximize damage, this isn't the device to use. Now, if you want to completely shut down a city, strategically placing one of these would do it."

"How big?" I repeated, a cold chill traveling down my spine.

"Off the top of my head, I'd say the sky's the limit. To take out this city, you could probably make one that would fit inside the back of a van. Maybe you'd need one of those small moving vans, but that'd be about it. You wouldn't even have to remove the device from the van. Just park it as close to the power grid as possible, and that's all she wrote. The vehicle would be destroyed, but the wave it generated would be able to penetrate through the shell and possibly through a building. It'd take out the power grid, probably some cell towers, and the effect could possibly cascade throughout the region. It'd be lights out, at least until the backup systems took over."

"Providing they weren't compromised."

"What?"

"Nothing. Is there any way to stop it or deactivate it?"

"I'll let you know. Right now, this is just a lot of guesswork. It might be possible to rig some kind of shield that would prevent the EMP discharge, y'know like how microwaves screw with wi-fi signals, but that's just a theory. The local bomb squad might know more than we do. They recovered the original pieces. We just have copies of their work."

"Thanks."

Returning to my desk, I picked up the phone to call Jacobs but thought better of it and replaced the handset. The best way to stop a bomb was to stop the bomber, but this wasn't about a bomb. This was about a hacker.

After checking on the progress that had been made to screen recent visitors, I went back to the drawing board. Since this was nothing more than a game of capture the flag, the only thing I needed to do was figure out where the flag was. I knew where our team had put it, and I knew it wasn't there anymore. Did it move by itself? Or did someone take it?

"If I were a computer genius, where would I go?" Too bad my computer didn't have an answer to that question. Being on the run required certain things. I was personally aware of what those were—untraceable assets, a safe place to hide, transportation, and a plan to escape. Cash was easiest, but Kiter would probably use someone else's credit card or identification. He was a techie. He wouldn't go low-tech. He wasn't hardwired to think in those channels.

Picking up the phone again, I spoke to someone in fraud and requested any reports they received of stolen identities and credit cards since the time of the explosion. Then I called Heathcliff and asked that he pull the reports the police department received during the week and pass them along. Hanging up, I sifted through the FBI reports flooding my inbox. Somewhere in this mess was our blackhat. He would have used a credit card to secure a hotel room, plane or bus tickets, possibly a rental car, maybe a burner phone or laptop, and whatever other computer gear he thought he'd need to erase himself and disappear. And if he was really smart, he would have used several different cards registered to several different people.

I made a few calls to some underworld contacts. I knew people in paper, and our guy would need a new ID fast. I wasn't sure he'd know where to go to find the right people, but the dark web was supposed to be the yellow pages for illicit activities. So someone might have heard something.

After seven phone calls, all of which ended with my insistence that they let me know if anyone matching Kiter's description showed up at their shops, I returned to my analysis of the FBI records. Could there really be this many people who reported fraudulent credit card activity or stolen identities in the last week and a half? No wonder cybercrimes always had their hands full. I missed the old days when our biggest problem was Nigerian princes offering millions of dollars in exchange for a small fee.

Mark crept up to my desk and leaned over my shoulder. "How's it going?"

"I'm going to find him. Did anything shake loose on your end?"

"Not yet. It's ridiculous how many people come into this country every day. You were right. It's a fool's errand, but it's the best we can do."

"What are our ghost friends doing?"

"As far as I can tell, not a damn thing. They claim to be monitoring the area for possible future activity and promising to pass all actionable intel to us. It's nothing but lies. Kendall's pissed. He's certain they cleared out after they lost the asset. From what the PD said, that building is completely empty. Dutch's apartment was cleaned and wiped. They're long gone."

Another possibility came to mind. "Do you think they have Kiter and are using us as a smoke screen to distract Anarkhos?"

When Jablonsky didn't offer an immediate answer, I turned in my chair to look up at him. He cocked an eyebrow and shrugged. "It's not beyond the realm of possibility."

"Since when do you say crap like that?"

"That's a direct quote from our boss, followed by some very specific instructions. Let me make sure I get this right." He cleared his throat. "Do the best you can under these fucking circumstances."

I laughed. "That sounds more like something you'd say."

"Where do you think I learned it?" He tapped on my desk. "Finish up as much as you can, but try to get out of here sometime tonight. We shouldn't have to pull all-nighters when we aren't positive this isn't a waste of our time. Kiter could be across the world by now."

After Jablonsky left, I made my way through the fraud reports. Over two dozen met at least some aspect of my search criteria, so I left them on the side. Placing another call to the fraud unit, I let out a sigh when it went to voicemail. Apparently, our FBI colleagues had called it a day. Resigned to leave a message for any additional intel they had on those select cases, I told the responding agent to check his inbox and sent the detailed request with all twenty-six case numbers. It was a start.

Staring at my blank computer screen, I absently tapped on the keyboard in the hopes of coming up with my next plan of action. I could find the records on those cases myself, but that didn't hold much appeal. None of them fit enough points to convince me they would yield positive results. Sure, a bus ticket was purchased with one or a plane ticket with another. Someone had even decided to be glamorous by staying in a hotel suite and racking up quite the room service bill, but unless I found a common thread connecting all of them and used that thread to track our blackhat's movements, this was just another steaming pile of worthless crap.

"Shit." My eyes darted to the clock. Grabbing my phone, I dialed Martin's cell. Hopefully, his workaholic tendencies were firing on all cylinders.

A ringing sounded from the end of the hallway. I leaned over my desk to see if I was imagining things. One of the probationary agents who manned the front for walk-ins was escorting him to my desk. At least he didn't look angry. Actually, he looked rather amused.

He answered his phone just as they reached me. "Hey," Martin said, pressing his phone to his ear and holding his finger up to keep me from disturbing him, "I was just thinking about you."

"Thanks." I nodded to the agent, who quickly disappeared.

"What are you wearing?" Martin grinned as if he found this routine incredibly clever.

"Martin," I hissed.

"Sorry, sweetheart, I'm on the phone. This will only take a few minutes," he said, covering the mouthpiece.

Playing along, I pressed my phone back to my ear. "A hotel robe and nothing else. I've been waiting for you for hours. Are you working late?"

"I just left the office. I need to pick up something, and then I'll be on my way. Go ahead and fill the hot tub. I'll be there soon." He hung up his phone and smiled at me. "Sorry about that. My girlfriend and I have standing plans, and I know she'd never forget or lose track of time."

"Did you really just leave work?"

"About an hour ago. I went to the hotel, but you hadn't checked in. We never worked out our logistics this week, so I figured I'd meet you at the office for once. Is this okay?" He looked around the empty bullpen. "I don't want to get in the way of the hustle and bustle. I can see how incredibly busy everyone is." He glanced at my desk. "Tell me the truth. Are you the only OIO agent in the entire building? Is that why you are always so swamped with work?"

"No," I jerked my head toward Jablonsky's office, "there are two of us." I got out of the chair, bypassing Martin's attempt for a hello kiss. Somehow, being inside this building made me feel the need to keep professional boundaries. "I'm just going to tell Mark good night, and we can get out of here."

Martin followed me down the hall, standing behind me while I knocked on Mark's open office door. "I'm heading out," I said. "My escort arrived, and it'd be rude to keep him waiting. Plus, I believe I have to pay by the hour."

Jablonsky glanced up, smiling at Martin. "Did you come to spring her?"

"Yep. You do realize there are labor laws in this country. I needed to make sure they weren't being violated." He winked at his friend. "We're going to grab something to eat. Would you care to join us?"

"Not tonight, but you two have fun." Mark pointed a finger at me. "I'll give you a call in the morning. Don't turn off your phone."

"I wouldn't dream of it."

"Hey, Parker," he called before we made it two steps from the doorway, "did you finish reviewing the fraud reports?"

"Yeah, I sent a request for more details on several of the files, but nothing struck me as solid."

He sucked in his upper lip and nodded. "It's the best we can do for now." He saw Martin lingering close by. "Go on. Get out of here."

I grabbed my jacket and purse from my desk and made sure my drawers were locked. "Wow, you've been in the federal building twice in two weeks. Let's not make this a habit." I pushed the button for the elevator. "Is your car out front?"

"My driver's waiting, but I'll send him on his way if you don't believe you'll be abducted from our date night again."

"I hope not. This is supposed to be our time."

The elevator doors closed, and he let out a breath. "Alex, I'm not mad. I know how work gets. You're human. You forgot. It's okay." He stared at the doors and not at me. "How was your trip?"

"Pretty terrible. I'm still jetlagged. I lost a day somewhere. I think it happened on the plane, but I can't be certain. With the eight hour flight and the eight hour time change, I feel like I should have gotten the time back when I returned, but it didn't seem to work that way."

"It's the sixteen hours on the plane that you're not accounting for," he offered, waiting for a real response. "Did you think it was Thursday?"

"Maybe." The doors opened on the main level, and we stared out at the agent manning the desk. "Listen, I can't guarantee anything, so if you'd rather have Marcal drive you to the hotel, I can meet you there."

"I'll take my chances." He pushed the garage button and turned to face me. "Jablonsky expects you to work this weekend. Weren't we supposed to go furniture shopping?"

"We will. I promise."

He raised a skeptical eyebrow. "Yeah, okay."

"No," I shook my head, leading the way out of the elevator and to my parked car, "don't be patronizing. I gave you my word. I wouldn't just do that when we're trying to rebuild trust. We're going furniture shopping tomorrow, even if that means we are online shopping at 11:59 p.m. from inside a government vehicle while executing a bust."

"You're going to take me for a ride along?"

"Why not? You went through advanced weapons and tactics training to prove you could handle yourself in any situation, and if those are the lengths that I have to go in order to keep my promise, then so be it."

We got into my car, but before I could even put the key in the ignition, he leaned over the center console, grasped my face in his hands, and kissed me hard. "I love you."

SIXTEEN

Instead of hiding out and ordering room service, we decided to enjoy dinner at the hotel restaurant. They recently hired a chef who only served farm to table, sustainably sourced foods. Since this was basically Martin's wet dream, he ordered the tasting menu which was an endless parade of food that seemed to take forever. It was delicious, but I wasn't in the right mindset for the feast or intimate dinner. Thankfully, Martin was an excellent conversationalist. He could probably talk to himself for hours and be perfectly content. For the last two courses, he had droned on about our new apartment, moving in next weekend, the bedroom furniture he bought, and the kitchen appliances, cookware, and place settings he picked out.

"Are you sure you didn't forget something?" I teased. "What about a giant serving dish in case we want to host a dinner party for fifty people?"

"Fifty people won't fit in our apartment. Actually, I was hoping we'd be the only people in our apartment."

"What about the O'Connells? Nick and Jen drag us out for double dates periodically. At some point, they'll realize we're part-time cohabitating. Nick is a detective. And

Jablonsky's already seen the place. One of them might just show up."

"That doesn't mean we have to invite them." He moved his napkin so the waitress could place another dish in front of him.

"When did you become so inhospitable?" I joked, knowing how cordial and diplomatic Martin was.

"Did you want to throw a housewarming party?" The possibility that I might want to invite guests surprised him, and he studied me closely. "I didn't think you'd enjoy that, but there's no reason we can't do it. We can get it catered and rent some extra chairs and those little round tables. We could probably host fifteen, not fifty." He rubbed his jaw. "Maybe I should have gotten a larger serving dish."

I laughed. "I was kidding. This is for us. It's our bubble away from the world. I don't want anyone invading our little haven, at least not yet." I took a bite and chewed thoughtfully. "Are you sure this isn't too exorbitant? We could have found something more reasonably priced."

"Don't worry about it. The waitress knows to add dinner to the room tab."

"That's not what I was talking about."

"I know." He took my hand and kissed my knuckles. "You can buy the couch."

The server returned to see if we needed anything else, and while Martin asked several questions about various courses, my phone buzzed. I glanced at it, seeing Heathcliff's name on the display. My fingers itched to grab it, but I saw the flash of disappointment cross Martin's eyes. Answering now would be rude and violate date night etiquette. I put the phone on the table, staring at it and hoping he'd leave a message.

"Who is it?" Martin asked when the server disappeared to ask the chef one of his questions.

"Heathcliff. It's probably about our case."

"So answer it."

Not needing to be told twice, I hit the green button and held it to my ear. "What's up?"

"I pulled those reports you asked about. They're at my desk, but I am on my way out. If you want to look at them,

I'll be here in the morning. I just have one quick question."

"Shoot."

"What do stolen credit cards and wallets have to do with a bombing?"

"Can I answer that in the morning?"

He didn't respond immediately. After a few seconds, he said, "Are you tracking the bomber?"

"Not exactly."

"Then what exactly? I'm not waiting until tomorrow."

"I'm trying to track his target. It's a long shot, but I don't know what else to do. I need to have a word with the bomb squad. I thought about asking Jacobs to arrange that, but I chickened out."

"You can ask him tomorrow. And you better bring us something solid. I'll see you in the morning."

"Night, Derek."

I hung up and looked around the room, checking to see that none of the nearby diners appeared interested in my conversation. They didn't seem to care, but Martin was a different story. However, he knew better than to press the matter when we were in public.

"Are you ready to go upstairs?" he asked.

I pretended to be offended. "Do you really think I'm that kind of girl?"

He smiled. "I hope so."

*   *   *

My phone buzzed, and Martin reached for it. "It's Jablonsky."

"Let it go to voicemail." I opened one eye. The clock wasn't in sight. "What time is it?"

"It's almost eight." He brushed my hair from my face.

I buried my head under the pillow. "Tell me it isn't morning." My head was pounding, and my back, neck, and shoulders ached. I'd spent too long at my desk yesterday. The phone stopped buzzing, letting out an annoying chime to announce a waiting message. "Press play," I muttered from beneath the pillow. Martin did as I asked, and I blindly held out my hand, pulling the phone underneath the pillow with me.

Jablonsky must have stayed at the office all night. He went through the bulk of the fraud cases I thought might have been relevant and ruled out twenty-three of them. The three that appeared suspicious were flagged, and we'd be alerted if any of the names or cards were used. Maybe we had something. Thankfully, he did the work, so I didn't have to report in unless something pinged.

"I'll make coffee and order breakfast," Martin said when I surfaced from beneath the pillow and leaned over to put my phone back on the nightstand.

"Don't you dare." I dropped onto his chest and shut my eyes. "I'm exhausted. I need two more hours." I shifted and groaned until the pinching in my shoulder stopped.

He sensed my discomfort and gently rubbed my back while I drifted off. When I woke up again, he kissed my forehead. "How are you feeling? Any better?"

"I'm fine. Just tired. Remind me again why so many people like to travel."

"Vacations can be nice. Relaxing. Exotic. A warm sandy beach. No work calls at eight a.m. No trips to the precinct. No bomb threats."

"Where do I sign up for that?" I asked. "You can be my travel agent any time." He grinned and pulled his arms away as I sat up. "My last travel agent tossed me into the middle of a war zone." I gave him a quick peck. "But I can't talk about that or my current case. So the things you overheard when I was on the phone or you forced out of me while I was in an orgasm-induced haze need to be forgotten. I don't want that to interfere with us, but I hope you understand why I have to work this weekend."

He nodded. "To save time and water, perhaps we should share a shower."

I rubbed my neck. "Since we want to save the planet, I don't think we have any other choice."

While I went through my morning routine and stepped into the shower, Martin called for room service, requesting delivery in an hour. A few minutes later, he joined me. When we were finished, I stepped out and dried off. Martin came up behind me and kissed my neck while I squeezed the excess water from my long hair.

"What's that?" He pushed a fingertip against my hip. "Did you have to get vaccinated before your trip?"

I spun to look at my back in the mirror. "Fuck." I stared at the puncture mark. There was only one way that got there. Apparently, my dream from the other night wasn't a dream.

"What is it?" he asked, concerned by the outburst.

Shaking my head, I wrapped a towel around me and returned to the bedroom to grab my phone. After sending a text to Mark, I dropped onto the bed. Those assholes abducted me off the street, broke into my apartment, and apparently sedated me, and they still expected us to fix their mistakes. I was livid.

"Alex?" Martin asked from the doorway.

"I'm okay. I'm just tired of being played. It doesn't matter. It isn't important." I kept repeating this while I returned to the now empty bathroom and closed the door. After dressing and drying my hair, I tucked the resentment away and joined Martin for breakfast, but my appetite disappeared with my good mood. After a few sips of coffee, I grabbed my purse. "Stay here, okay? Maybe give Bruiser a call. Your bodyguard probably can't do much, but when I get back later, I'd like to know that he's around."

"What's wrong?"

"Those jerks who pulled us off the street decided they should mess with me again, and until you pointed it out, I didn't even realize it. How screwed up is that?" I shook my head. "I need to get to the bottom of this before these assholes decide to make our lives a living hell." I forced a smirk onto my face. "Plus, I might need a second opinion on the sofa. I don't trust your taste in couches."

"Since when?" Martin asked, feigning hurt. "I thought you loved my couch."

"Yes, but it's not a good color. And the backrest could be higher."

"Fine. We'll be waiting." He grabbed my hand and pulled me onto his lap for a long, passionate kiss. "Be careful."

"Always."

On my way to the precinct, I picked up a tray of fancy coffees and an assortment of breakfast items. Perhaps I'd been jerking the police around the same way the CIA had been jerking me around, but at least I was nice enough to bring them breakfast to make up for it. It was after eleven by the time I arrived. Heathcliff had already started reviewing the reports, even though he wasn't entirely aware of the situation. Taking a seat beside him, I put the drink carrier and bag down and reached for a blank notepad and pen.

"Jablonsky phoned late last night, requesting the same information you did." He snatched a folder out of my hand. "I already went through that stack." He slid a pile over. "You can start with these." He waited until I picked up another folder before speaking again. "Your boss didn't say why he wanted these reports either, but he gave us some criteria." He dropped his pen and read off the list of notes he made to determine relevancy. "Did I miss anything?"

"Those are the same guidelines I've been using."

"Good." After reviewing another report, he added it to the unrelated pile and reached for the bag. "These aren't donuts." He pulled a pumpernickel bagel out and reached for one of the cups. "I knew there was a reason I told you to stop by in the morning." He took a bite and wiped the cream cheese from his mouth. "There's just one more thing I need from you, Parker."

I smiled. "Sorry, Martin called dibs."

Derek blushed ever so slightly, his gaze dropping to his desk. He cleared his throat and gave me a stern look. "I need to know what's really going on. You know you can confide in me about anything." He stared into my eyes. He was one of the few people who knew my darkest sins. Trust was never an issue between us. But I wouldn't divulge anything that would jeopardize his life or career, and he knew that. "It's time you start talking."

Leaning close, I lowered my voice. "Another agency's op went awry. The OIO was already involved due to a similar bombing overseas, so I guess they decided they had no choice but to bring us in. Truthfully, we haven't been given much information. Everything we've learned is purely coincidental or what they wanted us to find. I don't even know how much of it is true. Most of it has come from unofficial sources, and the agency keeps screwing us over every chance they get. I know I'm guilty of doing the same to you, but suffice it to say, a valuable asset was in custody. The bombing was either meant to aid his escape or to permanently silence him. As far as I'm aware, that asset is in the wind. He has mad computer skills, so I'm assuming he'll use those to try to go to ground."

"And he'll use stolen credit cards and IDs to do it." Heathcliff narrowed his eyes. "Why haven't you issued a BOLO or put his description out over the wire?"

"We can't risk the bomber using that to his advantage. Plus, I did say he has mad computer skills. He could alter the intel, create fake reports, or realize we are on to him and change his appearance. I don't think it's our best move, and I'm absolutely certain the other agency won't take kindly to having the details broadcast."

"Who screwed up? U.S. Marshals?"

I shook my head. "Don't concern yourself with that."

He didn't look pleased, but he dropped the topic. "What did you need from the bomb squad?"

"Any additional details they may have about the device used in the explosion."

"Jacobs spoke extensively to them when he first caught the case. He just needed to run a quick errand, but when he gets back, I'm sure he'll be thrilled to assist in any way possible."

"Yeah, right."

Heathcliff snorted, hiding a smile. "Maybe I told him to give you a second chance on account of all those hours spent in the federal building messing with your brain and sense of decency. Also, I explained to him the fact of the matter."

"Which is?"

"That you aren't capable of working a case without our help."

I stuck my tongue out and reached for another report. "Just so you know, I spit in one of those cups, and I'm not telling you which one."

"It's good to have you back, Parker. But as usual, the circumstances could be better."

SEVENTEEN

"Y'know, if we didn't get the 9-1-1 call, we never would have known about the blast. We never would have investigated the Branded Telecom building or spoke to anyone from the company." Jacobs chuckled. "And we wouldn't be in the middle of this fucking mess right now. Sometimes ignorance is bliss. I wish I hadn't seen behind the curtain."

"Tell me about it," I muttered.

The computer model of the IED was basically the same design as what the FBI bomb techs drafted. However, this one contained more accurate information about the detonator. It had a timer but was remotely triggered. The bomb was placed inside a box. Once the parcel was planted in the proper location, someone flipped the switch on a remote, starting the countdown timer. When the buzzer dinged, everything went boom.

"Is there any way to estimate the timer length?" I asked.

"No, ma'am," the tech replied. "It could have been anywhere from seconds to minutes. Based on the pieces of timer we found, I'd say it would have maxed out a second shy of an hour and forty minutes, but that doesn't mean it couldn't have been set for only a few seconds."

"The bomber only needed enough time to get clear of the blast zone," Jacobs said.

"But he had to deliver the bomb in the middle of the night." I considered the possibilities.

"Not necessarily," the tech replied. "The package could have been delivered at any point. All the bomber needed to do was get close enough for a remote detonation."

"No, our bomber planted it himself," Jacobs insisted, beating me to the punch. "The blast was directional. He placed it in order to make sure it blew in the right direction, and with the cover of night, he would have had plenty of time to get away before detonating the IED. Maybe the explosion was meant to cover up another crime."

"I wouldn't doubt that. What distance are we talking about for a remote detonation?" I asked.

"Maybe fifty feet since the telecom building has a lot of interference," the tech said.

"What would cause that?" I glanced at Jacobs who appeared lost in thought.

"It could be from the building materials or the wiring in the walls. It's hard to pinpoint exactly. Some areas just have crappy service for no apparent reason."

"Fifty feet. We can work with that. Thanks." I headed out of the room with the detective at my heels. "Did you uncover anything else of interest inside the building after I left?"

"Forensics didn't pull any prints or DNA. The building was scrubbed clean. There was no surveillance equipment, and the computer lines we found didn't hold any data. It's like no one ever stepped foot inside prior to the explosion, and we can't exactly question anyone from BT since they vanished into thin air."

"Or they never existed." I shook my head. "So fifty feet from that office. Let's figure out where the bomber could have been to set off the explosion."

"He was either inside," Jacobs said, realizing how limiting the parameters were, "or in the neighboring building. The explosive was placed in an outer office, and the blast went inward. Someone on the fourth floor of the nearest building might have been within the fifty foot radius."

"Let's find out." I reached for my phone. "I need to check in with Jablonsky. Go find your measuring tape. I'll meet you at your desk." After Jacobs left, I phoned Mark.

"Got anything?" Mark asked, his voice thick and gravelly from sleep.

"Jacobs is getting curious. He's piecing a lot together. The police need to know the truth."

"Parker," Mark warned.

"I already gave Heathcliff the cliff notes version." I snorted at the wordplay. "It's their case too, and we need the help."

"Fine, but when they get abducted in the middle of the night, that's on you. What are they doing now?"

"Heathcliff's analyzing stolen credit card activity, and Jacobs is checking to see where the bomber might have been positioned around the time of the explosion. But that got me thinking. If Kiter fled the building, he had a very narrow window in which to do it. The bomber would have been waiting for him. The CIA must have had agents responding, assuming there weren't any on the premises, so how did Kiter escape without detection?"

"The bastard called the cops and used them as a distraction." Jablonsky reached the same conclusion I had. "The spooks would have scoured the city for him, but they didn't get the chance because they had to clear out of the building and make sure everything was locked up tight before the police arrived. That's how the bomber slipped away. The CIA was duped by their own asset."

"I'll see what Jacobs and Heathcliff come up with, but our new priority should be finding some way of tracking down the 9-1-1 caller. My gut says it was Kiter. If we can find footage of him leaving the adjacent office building, we might be able to pick up his trail."

"See what overlaps with the stolen credit cards and spending. Maybe he left some breadcrumbs."

After disconnecting, I jogged up the steps. Jacobs and Heathcliff were discussing their progress. Sidling up to the desk, I stood on the opposite side, watching Jacobs spread out the map of the area. He pulled out a ruler and took a couple of measurements before consulting the legend.

"It's close, but the neighboring building should fall within our radius. We've been operating under the assumption the anonymous 9-1-1 caller was involved, but we don't have enough evidence to suggest he's the bomber. And since we weren't able to determine which phone inside the building was used, the bomb specs might be enough to get a warrant to examine the interior surveillance tapes from the adjacent building and their phone records. I'll make a call." Jacobs disappeared from sight.

"Didn't your office pull the nearby CCTV feeds?" Heathcliff asked.

"We didn't find anything. If something had been there, it was wiped. In order to catch this bastard, we need to think out of the box."

"No wonder they called you."

"Too bad I'm running low on ideas." I leafed through the paperwork on the desk, hoping some random tidbit would trigger something in my brain, but it didn't.

Finally, Jacobs returned. "We got the search warrant. Do you want to take a ride?"

"Sure. I need to talk to you about something." I nodded to Derek and followed Jacobs out of the precinct.

On our way to serve the warrant, I told him what I had told Heathcliff. No more. No less.

"So that's what Branded Telecom's been hiding and how they managed to disappear. The escape was covered up by the explosion. I knew there was more to the story than what you had told me," Jacobs said.

"I don't know if the explosion was used to free the asset or to silence him. I've been led to believe it was a botched assassination, but I have my doubts. All we know for certain is the IED messed with the electronics. You saw the security measures in place during the initial walkthrough. The blast should have caused the locks to disengage, allowing the asset to escape."

"Then why were the doors locked when we responded to the call?" Jacobs asked. "Are you sure the interference didn't seal the doors?"

Had I been thinking about this all wrong? "I don't know."

"You need to find out. If some asset was being detained inside that building, shouldn't there have been guards?"

"I don't know."

He let out a disgruntled scoff. "Right."

"I'm serious, Detective. I don't know. They're keeping me in the dark too, and they removed the locks when they abandoned the building. So we can't test that theory."

"Fine, then I'll tell you what I think. Your bomber isn't working alone. He has a team. They overpowered whatever law enforcement agents were present, and they took the asset."

"Or he ran during the commotion."

"That could be." Jacobs tapped against the steering wheel. "How come there isn't a manhunt to find this asset? Since we had him in custody, we should know everything about him. We could plaster his mug all over the media. It wouldn't take long to bring him in."

"We can't. His identity is classified. No one can know that we had him or were holding him."

"Someone knew. What do you think the bomber and his buddies are going to do once they find him, if they haven't already?"

"I don't know."

"You don't know much of anything. Do you know what we're going to do if we find him?"

"He'll be taken into federal custody and relocated to another secure facility." I wasn't positive of that, but I imagined DCS or the CIA would magically reappear and take over.

"What about the bombers? Do we know anything about them? My priority has always been identifying and arresting them, but you and your pals don't seem to care one way or the other."

I let the snide comment go. "We don't have any usable intel on the bomber," I lied, not at liberty to disclose intel on Anarkhos. Kendall had made that clear by following the mandate set by Clandestine Service, who deemed details on the anarchist group classified. They were just another threat we didn't want the public to find out about.

"All right. I guess we'll continue to work this case ass-backward."

Jacobs found a metered spot and parked on the street near the building. I surveyed the area, wondering how many cameras caught the incident on tape. Surprisingly, the blast hadn't been powerful enough to interrupt anything outside the walls of the telecom building. The building must have been shielded somehow.

"Detective," I said, "the bomber was inside the building when he detonated the bomb."

"How can you be sure?"

"The blast didn't cause any distortion to any exterior electronics. I don't think a signal would have penetrated inside the building."

"So the warrant for the adjacent building is pointless?"

"The warrant isn't pointless. The 9-1-1 call came from somewhere inside." I still believed Kiter had escaped from the telecom building, sought refuge inside the neighboring building, and alerted the authorities in order to aid his escape. "Either the bomber or our missing asset was inside at some point."

"Then keep your mouth shut and let me do the talking."

I followed Jacobs past the telecom building and into the lobby of the adjacent building. The metal detector blared when we went through. Jacobs pointed to his badge and handed the warrant to the security guard standing nearby. I flipped open my credentials and held them out before a different guard could get close enough to pat me down. He seemed a little too excited by the prospect, so I gave him an icy glare.

"We need access to the third, fourth, and fifth floors." Jacobs nodded at the paperwork. "We also need to review your security footage from a week and a half ago, and we need copies of your phone records from that same night. Someone inside this building phoned 9-1-1. We'd like to know who that was."

The guard read the limitations on the warrant. "I need to call the office manager. Follow me please."

We followed the man into a back office, past the four

receptionists seated behind a long counter. As we went through the building, I read the placards on the wall, hoping to figure out what went on inside this building. From what I gathered, it was a company office building, not that dissimilar from the Martin Technologies building. They had a customer service center, a marketing department, research, online processing department, accounts, billing, and human resources.

"Mr. Weir and a member from our legal team will be down momentarily. You can wait over there." The guard pointed to some chairs and couches that appeared to have never been used.

"Sure." Jacobs gave me another glance and led the way to the reception area. "Do you think Branded Telecom looked anything like this before they ran for the hills?"

"I doubt it." I took a seat on one of the stiff couches and wiggled around a bit. My feet didn't touch the floor. I tucked one leg underneath me and leaned against the arm. Nope. This sorry excuse for a couch wasn't doing it for me.

Jacobs' brow furrowed. "What the hell's wrong with you?"

"Just practicing for later." I got off the couch and sat in the chair next to him. "No wonder the furniture appears pristine. You'd have to be out of your mind to sit on it for more than a few seconds."

"You can wait in the car."

"That won't be necessary." I perched on the edge of the chair, feeling my nine millimeter shift forward against my ribs. "How much access are we granted?"

"We can explore the areas of the building that fall within the fifty foot radius of the IED, and the company has to hand over their phone records from the time the 9-1-1 call was placed and any internal surveillance footage taken during the two hour window surrounding the explosion. It isn't much, but it's all we need. We have no basis for believing anyone inside this building was part of the plot. However, that doesn't mean this building wasn't used as a staging ground."

When two men in high-end tailored suits appeared before us, I knew we were dealing with the big guns. Jacobs spoke to Mr. Weir, the office manager, while I remained silent, sizing up the attorney who had yet to speak but was raptly listening to the exchange.

"We'd be more than happy to cooperate and allow you access to those areas for your investigation," Weir said, glancing at the attorney. "However, I'd prefer if you keep this discreet. You've already questioned us about the phone call, and we were compliant then. We would have provided you with the records without your presence drawing so much attention."

"I apologize for the inconvenience," Jacobs said in that bored rehearsed tone I'd heard him use in the past, "but it's imperative we examine these areas for any signs that someone broke into the building and made the call. It's possible you suffered a break-in and didn't realize it."

"Very well." Weir gestured to one of the guards to escort us to the third floor to begin our search. "But you won't find anything. The janitorial staff keeps everything spotless. Any evidence that might have existed is surely gone by now."

"It can't hurt to look," Jacobs said, and we followed the guard.

Glancing behind me, I saw Weir and the lawyer go to the guard station. Weir issued orders for a thorough security sweep while the lawyer placed a call. I had no reason to believe they were involved, but I couldn't help but think Weir was afraid there had been a breach, which made me curious as to what he had to hide.

EIGHTEEN

Jacobs examined every nook and cranny we were allowed to access. After a cursory check, I felt confident the bomber hadn't been inside the building. If he had, whatever evidence he might have left behind was long gone. Instead, I focused on how Stavos Kiter gained access to the building in the middle of the night.

"Are there any emergency exits? Rear doors? Freight elevators?" I asked the guard who had shown us to several offices on the third, fourth, and fifth floors.

"Of course, ma'am. The building is up to code. Do you need to see our latest inspection?"

"That won't be necessary," Jacobs said from his spot near the window. He peered into the street. He couldn't actually see the Branded Telecom building from here on account of it being right next door, but he could see any action below us. Assuming the police approached from the front of the building, someone could have watched for their arrival before sneaking away. "Do you recall any issues a week and a half ago. It would have been that Wednesday night or Thursday morning?"

"None." The guard waited patiently while Jacobs stared out the window. "As far as we know, there's been no unauthorized access to the building."

"The 9-1-1 call was placed from inside this building on the time and date in question," Jacobs insisted. "How do you explain that?"

"We have twenty-four hour security. It's possible one of the guards heard something and called the police."

Jacobs turned around and scrutinized the security guard. "I need the names of everyone inside this building at the time." He waved his hand at the guard. "Go get them."

"Sir," the guard began, and Jacobs glowered at him, "you'll have to ask Mr. Weir about that."

"For the love of god, if you or one of your pals knows something about the bombing next door, you better tell me. Now."

The guard shrugged and remained silent. Jacobs glanced at me. I knew damn well the police already questioned the guards on duty about the call, and they all denied placing it. This was a ploy to buy me time to look around. Jacobs marched out of the room and back to the elevator. The guard looked torn between staying with me and following Jacobs but finally relented and dashed down the hallway to catch up with the detective before the elevator doors could close.

"Works for me," I muttered, giving the room a final look and heading down the corridor. An emergency exit sign illuminated a doorway at the back of the building, so I went to check it out. Pushing the door open, I found a staircase that ran down the back of the building. Deciding to see where it led, I went down the five flights of stairs, noting the lack of security cameras. At the bottom was another door. I pushed it open. It led into an alleyway on the other side of the building, farthest from Branded Telecom.

No alarms blared. I held the door open while I checked the alley for security cameras. I didn't find any. Releasing the door handle, I listened for the emergency exit to lock in place. Once it did, I donned a pair of gloves and jiggled the handle, but the door didn't budge. On the wall beside the door was an electronic card reader.

Leaning in close, I examined the plastic weatherproof casing, noticing deep scratches on the bottom. "Why, hello there." I removed my phone and took a few photos and dialed Jablonsky. "I need a crime scene unit to dust for prints." I told him where I was and what I was doing.

"Jacobs has a search warrant?" Jablonsky asked.

"For the offices, phone records, and interior feed. This is outside."

He mulled it over. "Do you think we'll get a usable print?"

"We might. I doubt Kiter had time to pick up gloves while he was running for his life."

"And if the PD runs it, they'll use IAFIS. We can't afford Kiter's identity getting dinged if your assumption's correct." He sighed heavily. "Isn't this what I told you we were trying to avoid?"

"What do you want me to do? Wipe off any prints?" I stared at the card reader. "I'm not willing to do that. We aren't even sure Kiter was here. This is speculation. If you want to pick up his trail, we need to know where to start. Send one of our teams down here, and we'll do a side-by-side manual comparison. If we rule Kiter out, we'll run whatever prints we find through the databases, but if it's a match, we might be able to determine where he went next."

"Do you think the CIA is going to give us a copy of Kiter's prints in order to see if they match?"

"So what the hell are we supposed to do?"

"Keep Jacobs occupied. I'll grab a team and be on my way."

Returning to the lobby, I went inside and smiled at the security guards as I walked through the metal detector, inevitably setting it off a second time. Jacobs turned around, his hand on his weapon, and gave me a bewildered look.

"Sorry. I got turned around." I joined him at the guard station. Weir was gone, but the attorney was overseeing the fulfillment of the warrant. "What'd I miss?"

"Nothing." Jacobs bumped against my shoulder. "These people have been kind enough to turn over their employee roster for the evening in question, and they're providing us copies of the phone records and interior security footage for the date and time we asked."

"Excellent." I smiled warmly at the attorney. "Do you happen to have any exterior security cameras?"

"We don't. If any crime were to occur, we believe the perpetrator would have to enter the building in order to commit the crime. That's why we have building security and interior systems."

I nodded. "What exactly do you do here?"

"We're the main office for an internet company."

"What kind of internet company?" Jacobs asked, finding this fascinating.

The attorney reddened slightly. "We sell custom made sexual health aids. The manufacturing and shipping are done at a separate facility. We run the website and provide customer service support." The man sniffed indignantly, and Jacobs glanced around the lobby. "We don't like to advertise that fact outright."

"I see." Jacobs jotted a note in his pad. "I believe that's all we need for now."

The attorney handed him a card. "If you have any other questions, I'd be happy to answer them."

"All right." The detective focused on me. "Anything you wanted to ask?"

I shook my head. "We'll be in touch."

Jacobs and I returned to the car. Surreptitiously, I tried to keep an eye on the alleyway, hoping no one decided to use the emergency exit as an entrance. With any luck, Mark would arrive soon.

"Parker," Jacobs said, and my eyes shot to him, "what's on your mind?"

"Nothing."

"Did you find anything upstairs?"

"No."

"I guess you were right." He flipped through the security guard roster and the phone logs. "I'll send some uniforms back here tonight to question the guards who work the night shift. Maybe with their boss gone, they'll be more accommodating than they were the first time we talked to them. I don't know. The building manager was being cagey. And did you see how squirrely the attorney got when I asked what they do inside that building?" He frowned.

"Sexual health aids?"

"They probably sell pornography and sex toys. Depending on precisely what they're selling, it could be illegal."

Lifting his radio, Jacobs requested a background on the company while we waited in the car. After a couple of minutes, he received a response that they appeared legit.

"Guess that answers that question." He tapped his fingers against the USB drive that held the security cam footage. "Phone logs don't indicate who placed the call. It was the main line, so it could have been one of several extensions. Everything comes down to the security footage."

"Shouldn't we get back and check it out?" I wanted to get away from here before Jablonsky and a crime scene unit rolled up. I needed Jacobs to trust me, and having my team investigate behind his back wouldn't accomplish that.

"In a minute." He tapped the drive against the steering wheel. "How'd you end up at the front entrance the second time? The elevator's in the rear."

"I took the stairs."

"I didn't see a sign for that in the lobby."

"It doesn't lead to the lobby. It lets out in the alley. It's an emergency exit. Obviously, it didn't trigger any alarms, but the door locks from the inside. So it'd be difficult to gain access to the building from there." I bit my lip. "I phoned Jablonsky to send a team to print the door since your warrant didn't cover it."

"That was a good idea." He opened the car door. "When were you planning to tell me?"

"I just did."

"Uh-huh." He glanced back into the car. "Show me this emergency exit."

While we examined it, a dark SUV pulled up, and Mark and two techs stepped out. He nodded to us and pointed the techs at the door handle and card reader. Jacobs stepped back, and Mark pulled him aside.

"What'd you learn, kid?" Mark asked.

"Not much." Jacobs gave him a rundown of what we'd just gone over. "We were just about to head back and run through the surveillance cam footage."

"You still think the bomber was inside this building?" Mark asked.

Jacobs looked pointedly at me. "Parker decided that wasn't possible. The telecom building has shielding preventing outside radio frequencies from penetrating the interior. It would have made it nearly impossible for the bomber to have been elsewhere when he triggered the remote detonation."

"Which means the asset might have made the 9-1-1 call." Mark looked at me. "Go back to the precinct and see if you identify anyone on the footage. I'll call if we get a hit on those prints."

After we got back in the cruiser and were on our way to the station, Jacobs let out a laugh. "Doesn't Agent Jablonsky realize I don't work for him?"

"You don't? Why didn't you say something sooner?"

Jacobs rolled his eyes. "And you wonder why the PD can't stand you guys. Feds are nothing more than entitled, pompous assholes."

"Present company included?"

"Only some of the time."

When we returned to the precinct, Jacobs took his newly acquired toy to the tech department to scan the footage. I insisted on getting a copy, but if we didn't spot Kiter or someone else inside the building, the USB would be useless.

"Wouldn't the guards have noticed someone sneaking in?" Heathcliff asked as soon as he joined us.

"Only if they were paying attention," I said.

"But we've spoken to them several times since the call was placed. They would have examined the footage to avoid a scandal. We're more likely to get a hit if..." Heathcliff's voice trailed off as an unrecognizable illuminated blob made its way across the screen. "What is that?"

"Dammit." I slapped my palm against the table and turned away from the screen. "This guy is unbelievable. Where did he get an infrared light?"

"And the security guards didn't think to report this?"

Heathcliff asked.

"They probably thought it was a glitch."

Jacobs pressed his lips together, following the guy with the glowing blob for a face from camera to camera. When the man stopped moving, Jacobs zoomed out and hit pause. "He made the 9-1-1 call from a second floor office." He hit play, and the glowing blob hung up and disappeared out of camera range. Twenty minutes later, we caught a glimpse of him entering the emergency exit. "We don't know how he got in, but we know how he got out. Call your office and find out if they found anything else at the exit."

Not bothering to argue, I dialed Mark and relayed what we just observed on the screen. The card reader had been wiped, and Jablonsky didn't want to pursue getting a separate warrant to print the handrails in the stairwell or the phone in the office. He was sure we wouldn't find anything. If Kiter or whoever was on screen had rigged an infrared light to hide his face, he wouldn't have left prints.

"That's it?" Jacobs asked. "We know someone involved in the bombing was inside the porno building, and you're not going to do anything about it?"

"It won't help."

Jacobs looked like he wanted to argue, but Heathcliff cleared his throat. "Parker's right. We know someone was there nine days ago. He isn't there now. Even if we arrest every single person inside that building on whatever trumped up obscenity charges we can find, it won't get us any closer to preventing another bombing. It'll just be a lot of paperwork and a waste of valuable time." Heathcliff gave me a look. "While you were gone, I pulled several reports that might be relevant. Let me give you the information to track. I went ahead and flagged them, but they might coincide with the FBI reports you're already monitoring."

NINETEEN

"We're just supposed to wait for something to happen?" I asked.

After Heathcliff gave me the relevant information on recently stolen credit cards and IDs, I dropped it off at the OIO and had it added to the list we were tracking. So far, there hadn't been a blip on any of the accounts, and I feared Kiter must have ditched those cards for new ones. I was also convinced he was long gone.

"We can only speculate that he placed the 9-1-1 call after the explosion, and he hid inside the other office building until the police arrived. He's hiding from the bomber," Mark said.

"Or maybe just the CIA. They might have taken him into protective custody, but they'll never willingly let him walk free again."

Mark let out a lengthy exhale. "So the guy has every reason to avoid us and the people who want to kill him. The problem is he's dangerous, and Anarkhos is dangerous. The longer he's running around free, the greater the chances are we'll end up with a body count."

"It's been over a week. Maybe they're gone."

"That's just wishful thinking. Anarkhos is here, and they

know Kiter a lot better than we do. They know what he'll do and where he'll hide. If the threat was removed, the CIA would have called us off the case by now."

"Sure, they would, and pigs fly." I shook my head and grabbed my jacket. It was getting late, and I had a couch to buy. "Make sure I get notified if we get a hit. In the meantime, I have a promise to keep."

"You think making Marty happy is more important than this?"

My expression soured. "I would stay here and do something if there was something to do, but there isn't. And we both know it. I don't know what game you're playing, but the fact that you didn't even want to dust for prints or investigate the building where the 9-1-1 call originated makes me think you're keeping something from me, just like these CIA assholes. And I'm tired of it. I'm tired of doing things half-assed, and I'm tired of the limitations that have been placed on this agency and the police department." I stared at him for a moment. "But maybe I'm crazy."

"No, you're not." Something moved behind his eyes, but he didn't share the thought, further irritating me. "I'll call if I need you or if something shakes loose."

"Great." I would have preferred being called crazy, but Jablonsky didn't deny my allegations, which meant they were true. He was hiding something, and I didn't like it.

I made it back to the hotel in record time. Leaving my car with the valet, I returned to our suite and let myself in. As promised, Martin's bodyguard, Bruiser, was positioned on the couch. He was watching a war documentary while Martin remained buried in spreadsheets. I closed the door and nodded to Bruiser. Martin glanced up from behind his laptop and offered a shy smile.

"Who wants to buy a couch?" I asked, rubbing my palms together.

Martin saved his files and closed the lid. He checked his watch. "I guess we have time to do that. When are you expected back at work?"

"Bite your tongue. After we pick out our new furniture, I want to come back here, put on one of those fluffy robes, and not leave this room for the rest of the weekend."

Bruiser turned off the television. "No one told me to bring my pajamas."

I laughed. "Sorry, we'll do better next time."

He glanced at Martin, who ducked into the bedroom to get his wallet. "Ms. Parker, would you mind telling me why I'm here?"

"We had an altercation with several government agents last weekend. Those same agents broke into my apartment while I was sleeping, so I wanted to make sure they didn't try anything like that again." After checking to make sure Martin wasn't returning, I moved closer to Bruiser. "Look, I'm doing my best not to flip out whenever things get dicey, but you're on the payroll to protect him. That's your job now. Not mine. Whatever he says, goes, but I feel better knowing you're around."

"Very good, ma'am."

"You know I hate that."

"Yes, ma'am." He winked. "And for the record, I have his back. You don't need to worry."

"Thanks, Jones." It was rare I used his real name, and Bruiser smiled.

"I just phoned Marcal to pick us up. He should be here in ten minutes," Martin said when he returned to the living room as if he hadn't come up with some excuse so I could have a heart to heart with his bodyguard. "I figured it'd be easiest to take my town car."

"Sounds great," I replied.

The ride to the furniture store was uneventful. Marcal had been Martin's driver for over a decade, and the two were pretty close. Martin had given Marcal and his wife a gift for their anniversary, so Marcal spent the ride telling us about the Venezuelan restaurant his wife absolutely adored and how wonderful the play was. Martin's generosity and charm knew no bounds. He would do something equally special for Bruiser to show his appreciation for having his bodyguard work on his days off.

"Charmer," I whispered in his ear. "You really have them fooled into thinking you're a nice guy."

"I am." He gave me a playful look. "Nice guys finish last.

It's the gentlemanly thing to do." I smacked his arm, turning away to hide my blush. "Don't dish it out if you can't take it," he teased.

We bickered quietly for the rest of the ride to the furniture store. When we entered, Martin shook hands with one of the salesmen and introduced me. The salesman led us to the section for living room furniture and disappeared. I liked that he didn't hover, but I had a feeling Martin had something to do with that.

After testing out a dozen different couches and sectionals, I moved on to the next display. My mind wasn't on furnishing our new apartment. It was on the case. Stavos Kiter planned his escape. He knew how to get out of the building. He knew where to hide. He knew how to get inside the porno building, and he was acutely aware of their security measures. I wasn't entirely sure how he managed to rig an infrared LED light to mask his face from the cameras, but I was positive it was him. He probably knew how long it'd take for the police, the fire department, and the bomb squad to respond. Maybe there was no hit squad from Anarkhos coming to kill him. Maybe it was just one anarchist who got scooped up by the CIA who wanted to make a run for it. He could have probably made the IED out of tinfoil and some salvaged wires for all I knew.

"Sweetheart," Martin sat on the chair across from me, "what do you think?"

"I don't know." I blinked a few times. "Maybe you're right. Maybe a couch is just a couch. You pick." I looked at the vast array in the showroom. "My head's not in this."

"I noticed."

"Man, I suck at keeping promises." I shook my head and climbed off the couch.

He came up behind me and rubbed my shoulders. "Let me help you with this." He scanned the displays. "What features do you want?"

"Something we can sleep on."

"Then we should buy a futon," he said, exasperated. "We are not sleeping on the couch," his eyes lit up, "but I know what you want." He led me toward the back of the room. "You want something long enough to stretch out on."

My eye caught a beautiful suede sofa in slate grey, and I dropped down onto it. The fabric was ridiculously soft. I wriggled against the backrest, trying to see if I could be comfortable and if it supported enough of my upper back and neck.

"Get up," Martin insisted, and as soon as I did, he stretched out on top of it. "Come here." He pulled me down against his chest.

"I don't think we're supposed to lie down on the furniture."

"It's the only way we can test it out."

I looked around, realizing the entire room was empty. "Did you slip the salesman a bribe so we could browse at our leisure?"

"It wasn't a bribe." He rubbed the back of his neck. "It needs throw pillows. The arm's not cushioned enough. He blindly reached behind him toward the next display and snagged one of the pillows. "That was an easy fix."

I found my eyes closing as I tucked myself against his side. "This could be ours."

"Yes, it could."

"Ours," I repeated, feeling the magnitude of the word. We had an apartment. It was our apartment. And this might be our couch. My insides clenched.

"Yep." He ran his fingers through my hair and kissed me. "Unless you want to test out another twenty or thirty couches." He sensed my trepidation. "I want to make sure you don't have buyer's remorse." The brilliant green of his irises burned into my soul. "Do you need more time to think about it?" We weren't talking about couches anymore.

"No." I gave him a reassuring smile. "I like this one."

"Me too." He pointed lazily to the matching chair. "We should get one of those to go with it."

"And a coffee table and a side table but not these. I like that black glossy set we saw. Or is that too monochromatic?"

"It's perfect," Martin insisted.

We remained on the couch, picking out various pieces from our position. I didn't think we needed much. Just the coffee and side table, the chair, and the couch. I hadn't looked at the price tag, but given how much Martin had already invested, the price didn't matter. Hopefully, my credit card would agree.

When the salesman stepped back into the showroom, he smiled at us. "It looks like you found a winner."

"I have," Martin said as we sat up. "The lady will take this sofa and chair and those tables." He pointed across the room. "And I want to add the bar set we talked about the last time I was here but in the same finish as the tables to my order."

"Let me buy it for you," I said.

"It relates to the kitchen, and we both agreed that was my domain." He pecked my cheek. "You already give me so much."

The salesman smiled at us. "You two make such a gorgeous couple. Is this your first home?"

"More or less," Martin replied. "Can you make sure everything is delivered at the same time? We need it by Thursday."

"Absolutely," the salesman said. After making sure everything would be delivered to our place on Thursday, I gave the man my credit card to swipe. "Thanks so much for your business. If you need anything else, please let me know." He handed each of us a copy of his card, and we collected Bruiser on our way out.

Martin opened the car door, and I slid into the back. "See, you kept your promise," he said. After telling Marcal to return to the hotel, he put up the privacy window. "This time next week we'll be in our apartment. You never even really got to see the place, and with the way things have been, we haven't had the chance to talk very much about it."

"That's my fault."

"That's not why I said that. I want you to know how much this means to me. The fact that you're trying so hard, despite the craziness. I love you for that. I want this to work. I hope we'll be okay. That we'll make it."

There were no words. I wanted things to work out, but the universe never seemed to be on my side. This week, it was the CIA and anarchists ruining my plans. Who knows what it'd be next week. Or the week after.

Finally, I found my voice. "We better because we'll end up having one hell of a fight over who gets that sofa."

As soon as we got back to the hotel, Martin's phone rang. It was a nice change of pace, and I allowed him the same courtesy he had given me the night before. At least my job wasn't the only one getting in the way.

While he dealt with whatever issue had arisen at his company, I did some internet browsing. My search began with simple ways to become unrecognizable to a security camera and ended with a thorough examination of what Jacobs dubbed the porno building. Whatever public information I could find on the building or the company might lead to how Kiter determined it was a good place to evade the authorities.

Eventually, I ended up on the company's website. Martin crept back into the room and leaned over my shoulder. He was through with work and wanted to see what had caught my interest.

"Are you looking to buy something for the bedroom?" he asked. "This is because I picked out the bed and furniture, isn't it? Maybe I should have done that a lot sooner." I rolled my eyes, but he ignored it. "Ooh, that looks interesting." He pointed to an item on the screen.

"I'm not even sure what it does."

"Finding out could be fun."

"That's a hard pass." I gave him a look. "You do realize these are supposed to be sexual health aids. Are you having trouble performing?"

"You didn't seem to think so last night."

"I was jetlagged. I wasn't paying that much attention. My entire sense of being was off."

"That had nothing to do with how many times I got you off."

I slapped his arm. "Don't be crass." I closed the website after finding plenty disturbing but nothing illegal. "Do you think we need something to play with in the bedroom?"

His lips brushed against the shell of my ear. "You're the only thing I want to play with."

"Good answer."

He smiled, pleased with himself, and dropped into the chair beside me. "Why were you looking at sex toys?"

"Would you believe it was for work?"

He snickered. "You should say it's for research purposes. That's a bit more convincing."

"It is for work." I sighed. "Someone used the company's office building to evade the cops. I was hoping to find information on the building layout, security measures, or something useful, but all I found was the catalog."

"Did this guy disguise himself as a giant dildo?"

I laughed. "I didn't notice that on the security footage."

"Then your browsing wasn't work related." He winked. "How about we order dinner and then I'll take you into the bedroom so you can continue your research with a live specimen?"

"I told you it wasn't research."

He smiled. "Whatever you say."

TWENTY

"Seriously?" I glared at my phone and dropped my fork.

"Don't answer it," Martin suggested.

"I have to." I recognized the number as belonging to our fraud unit. Pushing the room service cart away, I got up from the couch and answered on my way to the bedroom. "Did we get a hit?"

"Two of the credit cards are showing recent activity. They were used to purchase train tickets less than ten minutes ago."

"Where?" I stowed my nine millimeter in my shoulder holster and grabbed my jacket.

"At the two southeastern kiosks near the central transportation hub."

"How long ago?"

"Seven minutes on one. Three on the other."

"Send teams to intercept, but keep this quiet. I want people on the platforms. Did you notify Jablonsky?"

"He didn't answer."

"Try him again and keep trying until he gets his ass down there. I'm on my way." I hung up the phone. Our hotel was only two blocks from the hub. I was the closest agent. "I'll be back later," I yelled over my shoulder, dashing out of the suite and into the waiting elevator.

When I hit the lobby, I broke into a run. The two blocks flew by. I slowed when the transportation hub came into view. From here, a person could take a bus, the subway, or a long distance train. That didn't take into account the dozens of taxis and private ride-share vehicles that idled nearby. Kiter was executing his escape plan. I just didn't know what it was.

Slowing my pace to a brisk jog, I remained across the street, watching the pedestrians milling about. It was early evening. The streetlights had come on, but the sky hadn't gone completely dark yet. Visibility wasn't great, but with the number of lights outside the hub, Kiter would surely be picked up on the security cameras.

"Where are you?" I narrowed my eyes while I headed for the kiosk. Once I was close enough to avoid making a scene, I pushed my way to the front of the line and held out my badge. "Federal agent," I announced to the disgruntled customers, "step aside." The ticket agent waited, knowing what I was about to ask. "Sir, you just sold a train ticket to someone named Randolph Kramer. He paid with a credit card. It happened less than ten minutes ago. Do you have any idea where the man went?"

"Sorry."

My eyes scanned the vicinity, noting the security cameras. "He probably had a hat or glasses. Something large and gaudy. Did anyone like that buy a ticket?"

"I don't remember."

"Okay. I need you to pull up the credit card transaction and tell me where this guy is headed. Randolph Kramer," I repeated. "It's extremely important."

As soon as I knew the destination, I phoned it in. Before I could go in search of the second kiosk where the other ticket had been purchased using a different credit card, two dark SUVs pulled to a stop in the no parking zone. So much for keeping things under wraps. If Kiter was here, he'd see them and run.

I scanned the area, looking for our target, but I didn't spot him. Hopefully, he was already inside or not in a position to see the government vehicles. Our teams needed to be positioned on the platforms in case Kiter used one of the tickets, but my gut said this was a smoke screen. He just wanted us to think he was catching a train.

I nodded to one of the agents, recognizing him. "Until Jablonsky gets here, this is my op." I pointed to two of the men. "A second ticket was purchased at that kiosk under the name Benjamin Cowland. Find out where he's going and get to that platform. You've all seen photos of our suspect. You know what he looks like. He's jumpy, so blend in. Don't announce. Sneak up and grab him. I need a radio."

One of the men grabbed a handheld from the SUV, and I tucked it in my pocket. After the first team moved toward the kiosk, I sent the second team to stake out the second platform. The agents were wired with comms, so they'd be able to communicate much less suspiciously than I could. Where the hell was Jablonsky? I didn't think Kiter was going to hop a train, but we didn't have enough manpower to cover the metro lines and the buses.

Turning around, I evaluated the area. Think, Parker. If I were running, where would I go? Kiter could have gone in any direction, but he would have wanted to avoid detection. That meant staying away from DOT and security cameras. If he were to catch a ride, he'd do it someplace he couldn't be spotted.

Dialing Agent Lawson, I asked about blind spots in the vicinity. This was a highly trafficked, commercial area. Cameras were everywhere. Unfortunately, it'd take a lot of time and resources to gain access and scan them all. Still, our blackhat would be wary and avoid them if he could.

My eyes zeroed in on a nearby restaurant. Several tables were outside with large red and white striped umbrellas. The umbrellas were large enough to prevent detection. If Kiter waited under one of them for a taxi or ride-share, he could conceivably slip away and catch a plane or drive out of town. It's what I'd do.

I jogged toward the restaurant. A couple of people were eating on the patio. The only illumination came from the small candles on the tables. They called it ambiance. I called it a security threat. The last table in the row was occupied by a single man. He wore a hoodie pulled over his head, and his back was to me. I slowed my approach, waiting until I was beside the table before making a move. I'd seen Kiter's photograph, but I had no idea if the hoodie at the table belonged to him.

What the hell. "Stavos?" I asked.

The man turned, probably out of habit. For a split second, I saw his face. I located our blackhat. I grabbed his forearm, a second away from cuffing him, but he batted the lit candle at me. It caught the front of my shirt. I released his arm to pat out the fire. In that split second, he jutted away from the table and across the street at a dead run.

Shoving his chair out of the way, I gave chase. This guy was fast, but I was faster. Pulling the radio from my pocket, I relayed the coordinates and requested backup. Kiter zigzagged across the street, turned down the next one, and crossed again. By the time he made it to the curb, I was only two feet behind him. I stretched forward, moments away from pouncing, when a bike messenger clipped me.

I hit the asphalt hard. The bike and its rider went down, and the sound of screeching brakes and car horns cut through the stinging pain in my side. Son of a bitch. Kiter didn't turn to see what caused the commotion. Instead, he jutted out of sight. Grabbing the radio, I notified our teams of his last known location.

"Do not lose him," I snapped.

Someone in a suit dashed down the street, but I didn't get a good enough look to figure out which of our agents was a track star. We should have Kiter in a matter of minutes.

"Miss, are you okay?" a passerby asked as a crowd congregated around the scene of the accident. "You're bleeding. Stay there. I called 9-1-1."

"I'm all right." I winced, pulling myself off the ground. My palm and forearm were scraped from hitting the pavement, and my right pant leg was cut open, revealing a nasty gash on my calf from the bike pedal. I couldn't feel either of them. The only thing I felt was the searing sting in my side from where the handlebars impacted. Clicking the radio again, I said, "Roll an ambulance to my location. A civilian's down."

Gripping my side, I knelt next to the downed bike messenger. At least he had been smart enough to wear a helmet, even though he was speeding through the parking lane without any lighting or reflectors after dark. He didn't look so good, but he was in better shape than the bicycle. The tire and handlebars were bent and at odd angles. The accident had caused traffic to back up. Angry honks blared in the background. My eyes kept darting back to the last place I'd seen Kiter. I should have had him. I would have had him if it weren't for this reckless jerk and his bike.

"Try not to move." I crouched closer to the messenger. Since my palms were scraped and bloody, I didn't touch him. "An ambulance is on the way. Hang in there."

"What the hell were you doing, lady?" the bike messenger snapped.

Before I could answer, the second team of agents ran up on the scene. "Parker?"

"I'm fine. Don't lose our suspect. He turned down that alleyway. I haven't heard anything since. Someone's in pursuit." They hesitated to move, and I shouted at them, "Go."

An SUV pulled up with flashing lights, blocking oncoming traffic. Jablonsky and three other agents stepped out of the vehicle. Mark barked orders, and one of the agents offered assistance to the civilian casualty.

"Parker?" Mark asked.

I pointed toward the alleyway. "Stavos was right there. Probably three minutes ago. Maybe you can catch him. Dark hoodie. Jeans. Black tennis shoes with white stripes. We need to get this son of a bitch."

"You heard her," Jablonsky said, and the two agents raced toward where I pointed. "Are you okay?"

"No. I should have had him. I was practically on top of him." My unintentional glare burned through the bike messenger who was being treated by the third agent. "If this jackass didn't ram into me with his bike, Kiter would be in custody now."

"You got here fast."

"I was at the hotel. I ran over. Literally."

"Okay."

The ambulance pulled up, followed by a patrol car. I told the cop what happened while the messenger squawked and bitched, blaming me for the accident. Thankfully, the noise stopped when the EMT loaded him into the rig. The police officer dragged the wrecked bicycle to the curb and turned back to Mark and me. "Anything we should know?"

"We have it handled," Mark said. "Just make sure that guy learns his lesson. The parking lane is not for biking."

"We'll take care of it." The cop looked at me. "Are you okay? I can call a second ambo."

"I'm fine."

"Suit yourself."

Mark took the radio from my hand and requested additional information on the pursuit. The response he received was less than stellar. They'd lost the trail. The blackhat was in the wind.

"Fuck," I swore. "I shouldn't have stopped. I should have gone after him."

"Graham," Mark ignored me and spoke to the other agent who had been assisting the messenger, "grab the first-aid kit from the glove box and patch up Parker. I don't want her bleeding in the car."

"Yes, sir," Agent Graham replied.

I leaned against the hood while Graham bandaged my calf and arm. His eyes homed in on the way I cradled my side. I shook my head, and he backed off. After relaying orders to rendezvous back at the federal building, Mark opened the door.

"Get in," he said to me. Then he focused on Graham. "Make sure everything is handled here and grab a ride with Bravo team."

Once I was fastened into the passenger's seat, Mark put the SUV in gear, flipped the lights, and cut into the flow of traffic. After a few blocks, he killed the flashing lights and cast a curious look in my direction.

"You diverted the teams to the platform, so you were the only one in a position to pursue. Was that in order to ensure this op remained on a need to know basis?"

I shook my head. "We go where the intelligence points. It pointed to the trains, but I didn't believe it. You wouldn't have either, but the agents you sent were briefed on the suspect. They would have spotted him in the event I was wrong."

"They only know his name and face. They don't know the entire reason why we want him. I need you to tell me exactly what went down and everything that happened."

"Fine, but first, I want to know where you were and why you didn't answer when the fraud unit called with the notification."

"I was speaking to Director Kendall."

"So what took you so long to get here?"

He huffed like a wolf trying to blow down a house. "I don't need to explain myself to you, but someone had to assemble the teams and give them a quick briefing so they could respond. It's not like you were at the office." I didn't say anything in response. It was no secret Mark was miffed I left early. "Did you and Marty get a chance to buy a couch?" His tone was much kinder than it had been.

"Yeah. It took some looking, but we found one." And then I filled in Mark on every detail concerning my pursuit of Kiter. "It looks like we have a manhunt on our hands."

"Are you sure the man you saw continuing the pursuit was one of our agents?"

"Who else could it have been?"

"I don't know." Mark pulled into the garage and killed the engine. "We'll figure it out. In the meantime, we're going upstairs. I'll conduct a briefing and share what you've told me. If there are any questions, you'll answer them. As soon as that's over, I'll have someone take you to the hospital to get checked out, and then you'll get dropped off at the hotel. Is that clear?"

"I'm okay. That's not necessary."

"Yes, it is." He reached for the door handle. "And don't protest about it upstairs or tell anyone that you're fine. Pretend you're not. Got it?"

"Why?"

"Just do as I say."

TWENTY-ONE

When I got back to the hotel, I found a note.

Since you went to the office, I thought it was only fair that I do the same. Your dinner is in the fridge, or call the kitchen and have them make whatever you like. I'll be back soon. ~ J.M.

Unsure if that note was passive-aggressive or just Martin being a workaholic, I decided to give him the benefit of the doubt. After all, I was the one who literally ran out in the middle of our meal with barely a goodbye. We probably needed another therapy session to address those underlying issues. On the bright side, we bought a couch. Maybe the therapist would make a house call, and I could nap on the soft suede during our session.

Stripping out of my burnt, ripped, and bloody clothing, I put on one of Martin's shirts and eased onto the sofa. The ER nurse cleaned and bandaged my cuts, but the jury was out on whether my ribs were broken. There was too much swelling to get a clear picture, but since there wasn't much they could do about it either way, I was sent home with the usual care instructions. I reached for the hotel phone, ordered a bucket of ice water, and hung up.

By the time Martin returned, I was halfway through a

pay-per-view movie. He entered the suite, announced himself, and bid Bruiser goodnight. He had gotten his bodyguard a room across the hall. When I didn't surface, Martin called my name.

"I'm right here." I raised my right arm in the air.

"Did you eat?" He opened the fridge, finding my food untouched.

"Not yet, but if you feel like bringing my plate over, that'd be nice." After chasing Kiter through the streets, I wasn't very hungry. Too much activity and stress always suppressed my appetite, but now that it had been a few hours, I could eat.

"Sure." His voice sounded odd. "How long have you been back?"

I hit pause on the remote to see the play counter. "About an hour."

"I didn't know how long you'd be gone. You didn't say much before you left."

"It was time sensitive. Our suspect had been spotted. I had to move."

"Did you catch him?" Martin heated my leftovers in the tiny hotel provided microwave.

"No. I got in an altercation with a bicyclist instead."

He placed the plate on the coffee table and turned around to look at me. "Shit. What happened?"

"A bicycle plowed right into my side. I'm okay. Just a few cuts. The ribs might be busted. Jury's out on that one. Mark made me go to the ER. If he hadn't, I would have gotten back sooner. Not that it would have made any difference since you were probably gone by then. Did you deal with your work snafu?"

"Yeah. It wasn't that big of a deal."

I saw the look on his face. I'd seen that look more times than I cared to count. It was that angry, worried expression. A cross between wanting to put his fist through a wall and holding me in his arms and never letting go. But this time, there was something else in his eyes. It was the understanding that this couldn't keep happening.

"Hey," I said quietly, sitting up, "it was an accident. It could have happened to anyone, at any time. You know how insane bike messengers are. They're practically homicidal."

"Yep."

"I shouldn't have run out during dinner. I'll try not to do it again." I picked up the plate and balanced it on my lap. "We can have dinner now, if you want to share my leftovers." I skewered a piece of steak and held out the fork. "C'mon, you know you want to."

He smiled. "How about I order dessert, and we'll split that instead."

"I can be persuaded." I ate a few bites while he ordered more room service. When I was finished eating, I put the plate back on the table and sunk against him. "You know what I'd like?"

"Hmm?"

"To spend the rest of the weekend right here with you."

"You keep saying that."

"I mean it."

"If you can make it happen, I'll be here."

Based on Jablonsky's instructions, I was certain I was benched for the next twenty-four hours in accordance with doctor's orders. I had no idea why, but regardless, that didn't mean I couldn't take advantage of it. After the last week and a half, I was convinced Martin was having buyer's remorse about the apartment. Perhaps I was too. But we both wanted our relationship to last. The only problem was figuring out how, and that had always been our problem.

* * *

The next day, I was sore. The constant stinging had morphed into a throbbing. Instead of my typical insistence that I was fine and Martin need not take care of me, I let him. He crushed the ice and wrapped it in one of the bathroom towels since the cubes were too hard against my bruises. We ate in bed, watched several movies, and made out a little.

When the phone rang that evening, I wanted to fling it out the window. Sighing, I climbed out of bed. Duty calls.

"Are you leaving again?" Martin asked, not bothering to hide the annoyance from his voice.

I turned, hoping to convey everything with my eyes. "I don't want to."

He pressed his lips together, his expression grim. "Okay."

After stepping out of the room, I answered the call. It was Mark. He didn't waste time on pleasantries or asking how I felt. A copy of my medical report had been sent back to the office with the agent who escorted me, so my boss already had a rundown of my injuries.

"Kiter eluded us, but we know he's ready to run. Kendall spent all night debating some things with DCS. We've been granted more leeway, and he's briefed every FBI agent in the office. It's a manhunt now. We're not sharing this with anyone else, and we're not issuing the usual reports. We're keeping this off the books. We've been hacked before. We don't want Anarkhos to target us and screw with our systems. The OIO can't afford that," Mark said. "I expect you'll be here in the morning."

"Of course."

"Okay. I want you to know Kiter getting away wasn't your fault. You did the best you could. We're going to find him, lure out these anarchist assholes, and make sure our city's safe."

"Rah rah."

"Parker."

"It sounded like you were giving a pep talk. I thought you might want a cheerleader." I waited, but he didn't respond with a snappy comeback or a disparaging growl. "Why did you send me home last night? The trail was warm. We could have continued pursuit. Maybe we would have found him. What about the agent tracking him?"

"Whoever came up behind you wasn't one of our people."

"So who the hell was he?"

"Probably a CIA operative. I have a feeling they've been monitoring us. Maybe they tapped into our radio communications. All I know is we didn't find that guy and we didn't find Kiter. From what Kendall was told,

Clandestine Service doesn't have the blackhat in custody."

"Great. No wonder they call these guys spooks. They just sneak up on people. They might as well yell 'boo' while they're at it."

"Is it possible that in the commotion you left out a few details?"

"No." I didn't like being second-guessed.

"Too bad. I was hoping you'd have some sixth sense on how to track Kiter or some inkling of where he might have been going. You normally have some sort of intuition about these things."

"Yeah, when we get to work the case through the normal channels. How am I supposed to determine anything when the only evidence we have is intel provided to us by an agency known for lying?"

"Fair point. Tomorrow, I need you to go down to the precinct and make nice. See if the responding officer took any statements or found anything in the vicinity of the accident that might connect to our case. After that, I'll see you at the office. You can help coordinate the teams. We've already established a search grid based on the locations where the credit cards were reported stolen, but it hasn't yielded any results yet."

"I'll see you in the morning. I'll bring the coffee." Hanging up the phone, I went back into the bedroom and snuggled against Martin. "I'm here for the night."

"Good. You know, I'd be happy to get you a doctor's excuse so you can stay home for the next few days. I'm sure I can find someone who will take a bribe." His hand brushed against the wet towel at my side, and I knew a part of him was serious. "I'll get some more ice, and we can finish our movie." He went to the doorway. "Tonight's our last night here, and since you're not leaving anytime soon, we should make the most of it. Champagne, strawberries, and I'm thinking hot fudge sundaes."

"With champagne?"

"Why not?"

"Fine by me, but it sounds disgusting."

The rest of the evening was a blur, lost in a haze of alcohol and sugar. Somehow, I managed to keep my mind off work. Or rather, Martin kept me distracted. Normally, I would zone out during a movie and find myself dwelling on a case, but that didn't happen on account of our constant conversation and snack interruptions. Either I was figuring out how to focus on the moment, or his charm and wit were working overtime to prevent me from running for the nearest exit. Last night had been a wake-up call. So today was spent proving that yesterday was just a fluke. I believe they call it denial.

But once the lights went out and he fell asleep, my mind went into overdrive. I'd barely had time to process how I'd lost Kiter before Mark showed up, asked me what happened, and ordered me away. I couldn't help but dwell on that fact. Our conversation this evening was odd. Come to think of it, Mark had been acting strangely ever since we returned from Turkey, and it seemed to be progressing as we closed in on catching Kiter.

I hated that I let the anarchist slip through my grasp. I should have had him. I should have seen that bike and slowed down. Or I should have been faster. If I'd just been a second faster, I wouldn't have been in front of the messenger. Perhaps I screwed up by sending the two teams to the platforms. I knew Kiter wasn't going to take a train, so why did I tell them to look? Maybe this was my fault. Mark must have realized it, and that's why he asked all those questions. The one thing I knew for certain about my boss, he'd do anything to protect me.

"Dumbass," I muttered.

Martin stirred, and I closed my eyes, hoping he wouldn't wake up. After his breathing returned to a slow, steady rhythm, I climbed out of bed and went into the other room. I needed to do something. I needed to figure out where Kiter was going and how we could track him, and I only had a few hours to do it. Unfortunately, I didn't have any ideas.

The blackhat knew we were looking for him. It was the only reason he wasted the time buying the train tickets and sacrificing two stolen identities. He was smart. He shouldn't have been hanging around so close to the train depot.

Snorting, I rubbed my eyes. He was waiting for us. He wanted to see if we were tracking him and if we realized he was using stolen credit cards. By showing up, we tipped our hand. Now he'd be even more careful. I doubted he'd risk using any of the other cards or identities he had taken. He'd need clean cards.

I scanned the contact list on my phone. Fraud had busted a few money men. Their informant list would be far more substantial than mine, but I might be able to squeeze a few names out of some of my underworld contacts. I checked the time. It was early enough for black market dealers to be awake. Shit, it was probably prime business hours. After several calls, I hit the same dead ends as before. This wasn't working.

Going back to the drawing board, I thought about my conversation with Mark. How would we work a normal case? We'd be tracking the bomber, not the victim. We'd determine the items used to assemble the device, figure out where they were purchased, track the orders, and get an ID on the bomb maker. If that didn't work, which I was certain it wouldn't since I didn't believe the items were purchased locally, we'd check for a signature and review similar cases. Check and check.

The similar cases led to detonations on overseas military bases. The commonality was Stavos Kiter. If we found him, we'd find the bomber, or we could string him up like bait and use him to lure out the bomber. However, I didn't think the CIA cared about Anarkhos. They wanted Kiter for his computer skills. They probably wanted to use him to hack the Russians or do something equally moronic. Anarkhos wanted to prevent that from happening by any means necessary. So who did Kiter fear more? Us or them?

Convinced that determining that would give us the edge in locating Kiter, I choreographed several different scenarios, hoping to stumble upon one that might yield results. However, the longer I spent working on our options, the more convinced I became that nothing would work. The only way we were going to find Kiter was through luck, and the only way we'd get Anarkhos would be through more detonations.

That thought burned through my brain like lightning. How many bombs did they bring with them? Would they have to make a local purchase to build another device? Would they even need another device? If we broadcast that we had Kiter in custody, it might convince them to strike. If we could detain them and interrogate them, they might turn over some valuable information that would allow us to determine where Kiter would hide or how he might be planning an escape. It would solve the problem on both ends, appeasing the PD and the CIA. Plus, I didn't have any better ideas.

"Alex?" Martin called.

I turned off the living room light and returned to the bedroom. "I'm here. I just couldn't get comfortable."

"What can I do?"

"Nothing. Go back to sleep." I leaned over and kissed him, deciding that I should do the same.

TWENTY-TWO

The next morning at the precinct was business as usual. From the looks of Heathcliff and Jacobs, I imagined they'd worked the entire weekend. I felt guilty for having yesterday off, but if I had spent every waking moment on this case, like I should have, I had no idea what that would have done to my relationship with Martin. Damned if you do, and damned if you don't.

"I heard you almost caught our guy," Jacobs said.

"Not the bomber. The asset."

"But you lost him." Jacobs folded his arms over his chest and shook his head. "We could have sent additional units to assist. We might have been able to box him in."

"Should of, could of, would of."

He stared at me. "How many cases have we worked together?"

"You keep asking me that. Why does it matter?"

"I'm just trying to figure out when you burnt out."

"Are you planning to bust my balls the rest of the morning, or are you going to do what I asked?"

"Fine. I'll grab a hold of the responding officer from Saturday night."

He walked away, and I swiveled in the chair. Heathcliff

had gone to grab additional reports of stolen IDs and credit cards, and he was going to make a few calls to some detectives in the other units to see if anyone knew where to go for clean credit cards and IDs. The more intel the OIO collected, the more rocks we'd be able to overturn.

While the two detectives were occupied, I snooped through the files on their desks. They were still intent on tracking the bomb materials and had been doing their due diligence on the items needed and places that sold them. Quickly copying down the list of retailers they were checking out, I dropped my pen just as Jacobs returned with the officer at his side.

"Agent Parker, this is Officer Barry," Jacobs said.

It was the same guy who responded to the accident Saturday night. "I just need to ask you a few questions and get copies of your report," I said.

"Sure." He had the stink of rookie on him, coming off nervous and overeager. "That was around eight o'clock." He flipped through his notepad. "The pedestrian hit by the taxi cab, right?"

"No. The bike accident, remember?"

He focused on my face. "That's right. The messenger blamed you for the whole thing." He laughed. "When I got around to doing my follow-up, I met the guy at the hospital. He had to get like eighteen stitches. He was pissed."

"Not the point," I said.

Jacobs hid his chuckle.

"I need to know what you remember from the accident. Did you notice anyone suspicious or remember finding something odd in the vicinity?" I asked.

Officer Barry turned to Jacobs, expecting the detective to provide him with answers or a clue as to what I wanted. "Um...I picked up the bike. It was trashed. He's going to need a new one."

"No," Jacobs corrected, "she's asking about anything odd. Did anyone come by after the accident and ask questions? Did anyone mention a man being chased or see who was following him? Anything like that?"

"No, sir," Barry said. "It was a crazy busy night. By the

time I cleared the scene and spoke to the EMTs, I got another radio call. A jaywalker was hit by a taxi a few blocks away. The guy hit so hard, he broke the windshield. That was a fucking huge mess. I got there before the ambulance did. We had to call in additional units to reroute traffic, and we had to get the road cleaned up. By the time fire and ambulances responded, a third radio call came in. A couple in a crosswalk was hit by a bus. That wasn't nearly as brutal, but it was a damn bus. Who gets hit by a bus?"

"Barry," I interrupted, "did anyone else show up at the scene of the bike accident?"

"No, ma'am. Patrols were pretty thin that night. I didn't even have a partner. I followed protocol, took statements, jotted down necessary information, cleared the scene, and responded to the next call." Barry gave Jacobs another look. "Did I do something wrong?"

Jacobs shook his head. "No. I think you've answered Agent Parker's question."

I offered a polite smile. "That was it."

Barry remained, unsure what to do. Jacobs clapped him on the back, thanked him again, and sent him back to his division. I grabbed my jacket and the copy of the accident report and headed for the door, lost in thought. If Kiter had dropped anything, it might still be on the street or at the outdoor table, but our people probably would have noticed it. At least now I had the name of the bike messenger. It was a long shot, but it wouldn't hurt to run his background and make sure the accident was nothing more than bad luck and even worse timing.

"You're welcome," Jacobs called to my retreating back.

With a million thoughts running through my mind, I barely remembered to grab coffees on my way to the office. After a quick stop, I pulled into the underground parking garage, grabbed the files and the tray, and took the elevator up. When I emerged on our floor, the place was alight with activity.

"What's happening?" I asked Davis who darted to his desk to grab the phone.

"You didn't hear? Your case just became our top

priority. The bomber phoned in a threat of another attack."

"What? When?"

Davis ignored my questions, concentrating on the phone pressed to his ear. Not wasting time, I went straight to Jablonsky's office. He wasn't inside. Spinning on my heel, I searched the area for someone who could provide answers. Finally, I zeroed in on Mark's back as he rushed past several desks. Sprinting across the bullpen, I caught up with him before the elevator doors closed.

"What's going on?" I asked, shoving my way inside.

He looked up from the buttons. "The shit's hit the fan. This morning, the FBI received a phone call from someone alleging to be the bomber. He issued a list of demands. Unless we comply, he's threatened to detonate more devices and cripple the city. Our best people are doing what they can to identify the caller and determine where it originated."

"Are we certain it's Anarkhos?"

"That's yet to be determined, but my money's on the man we know as Vega."

"What does he want?"

"Kiter." The elevator doors opened, and Jablonsky stepped out. "Come with me. We're meeting with Kendall. Since the threat came in, he's been conferring with our intelligence counterparts to determine the legitimacy of the threat and figure out why Anarkhos is convinced we have Kiter in custody."

"Are you sure we don't?" A flash of the man continuing pursuit after I was mowed down shot through my mind. "Maybe the CIA captured him."

"We're about to find out."

Jablonsky led the way down the corridor to the director's office. Kendall was waiting for us. As soon as the door closed, he said, "I've spoken to DCS. The assistant director swore to me they did not take Stavos Kiter or anyone else from Anarkhos into custody. Presently, they are still searching for leads to recapture the blackhat. They were unaware of the threat we received this morning and are sending an agent to help us determine the legitimacy of the call. At the moment, we cannot be certain Anarkhos is holding the city hostage. It could be anyone. We don't even know how real the threat is." Kendall placed his palms on his desk. "That being said, hoofbeats are normally horses. We've seen two bombings overseas and one here, so far. Intelligence suggests these three events are linked to Anarkhos. I doubt this is a coincidence. Until we hear otherwise, we need to take this threat seriously."

"I agree," Jablonsky said. "The caller didn't name any targets or provide much of anything. Even if we want to meet his demands, he didn't give us instructions on how to do that. I'm assuming that means he will make another attempt to communicate. I've already assigned several teams to a task force. Right now, we're determining potential targets and will increase security. But sir, we need to notify the locals, so they'll be ready to mobilize."

"I'm aware. The assistant director at DCS asked that I hold off until his agent arrives. Reluctantly, I agreed. We don't know what we're facing, and if we act hastily, we risk forcing these anarchists to make a move. Our focus should be on finding them and stopping them without turning this into a massacre."

"Sir," I piped up, "the devices used aren't designed to inflict a mass number of casualties. In fact, aside from the danger associated with being in the immediate blast zone, the damage is mainly geared toward electronic disruption. I don't think Anarkhos wants to hurt people. At least they haven't so far. But the power grid, cell towers, computer hubs, those would be perfect targets. By knocking out those things, the city would be crippled. The infrastructure would be decimated. There would be pandemonium."

"Total anarchy." Kendall licked his lips. "I imagine that's precisely the type of action they'd take." His eyes went to Jablonsky. "Make sure our people assess those possibilities, if they aren't already doing so." He reached for the phone. "Get me a list of targets ASAP. I'll call the police commissioner and ask for increased patrols. We don't have to tell the PD why, and if it comes from within their chain of command, it'll be less suspicious. That should be enough to keep DCS off our asses."

"Yes, sir," Jablonsky said. On the way to the elevator, he

updated me on what was already being done. As soon as we were stuck in the privacy of the metal box, he turned to me. "I need you to brief the task force and stay on top of this. I have a hard time believing a group of computer hackers is suddenly misinformed when it comes to Kiter's whereabouts. I'm going to shake the tree and find out if one of our agencies has him. Maybe it isn't DCS or the CIA, but that doesn't mean he didn't get scooped up elsewhere. If someone has him, we need to know. We can't proceed or attempt a negotiation when we're fumbling around in the dark."

I took an unsteady breath. "Okay."

"It's all right, Alex. You can handle this."

"Sure." The last time I was left in charge, my partner was killed. I didn't want to lead a team, which always made life interesting since I didn't want to be told what to do either. "Is anything to be left out of the briefing?"

"No. Kendall greenlit the sharing of intel. This is a high-priority case. We no longer give a shit what DCS wants. Preventing domestic terrorism is our job, and we're going to do it to the best of our ability. That means every single one of our people needs to be aware of the situation and be on alert. If some other agency has a problem with that, they can fuck off."

The elevator doors opened, and Mark barked to everyone in the bullpen that I would lead the briefing in the conference room before disappearing into his office. I grabbed one of the coffees and a notepad and waited for everyone to congregate inside. A minute later, I stood at the front of the conference table. The room was full of OIO agents waiting for instructions. Under different circumstances, this might have been fun, but today wasn't the day for fun.

"Okay, people, listen up." I gave them the rundown of what I'd just been told, even though I was sure they were already well-versed in it. Next, I got progress reports on how things were going. I handed out assignments, making sure our focus was on determining the location and identity of the caller and narrowing down the list of potential targets. "Get to work. If you find something, come tell me or Jablonsky."

The room cleared quickly, and I took a moment to stare at the ceiling and breathe. Once the overwhelming feeling abated, I grabbed the nearest files and updated the boards with relevant information. While I worked, several agents came in to provide updated intel or ask questions. For the first time since I was assigned this case, progress was being made. There was finally something for us to do. Too bad it took such a serious threat for the OIO and FBI to stop allowing DCS to keep us on a leash. We weren't their bitch, and they were about to learn that the hard way.

"Agent Parker," a familiar voice said from the doorway, "I was told you were coordinating our intelligence."

The hairs on the back of my neck stood on end. I rolled my shoulders back before turning around to face the newcomer. The man before me was the same man who conducted that pointless interrogation in the white room. I had half a mind to shoot him.

"I didn't catch your name."

"Reece." He gave half a nod while he put a messenger bag on top of the table and took out some files. "Stavos Kiter is not in our custody. We do not know where he is."

"And I'm supposed to believe that?" I folded my arms across my chest. "You didn't even have the decency to provide a name the last time we met. You've done nothing to help us or this investigation, and now it's *my job* to prevent the anarchist group that your team pissed off from blowing us all to kingdom come. So unless you have something to say that isn't another blanket denial, get the hell out of my conference room."

He opened a folder marked classified and pushed it toward me. "Aside from exchanging gunfire during the raid in which we originally captured Kiter, Anarkhos has no history of violence. Their actions lead to violence. There is no denying it, but they themselves have not taken up arms. The previous explosions that we credit to them resulted in zero casualties."

"You can't be that naïve. These are desperate times. They've tried to play nice, but it hasn't gotten them anywhere. You can't assume they won't change their tactics." I flipped through the paperwork. It contained profiles of several Anarkhos members without the redacted bits. I pulled out a page with a photo of a man I recognized—Guillermo Vega. The CIA listed that as his known alias. They made sure not to give us anything we didn't already have. "He's responsible for the first bombing."

"And the second." Reece pumped his eyebrows up and down. "And the third."

"You're certain he's here?"

"Every man inside that folder is here."

"You son of a bitch." I pushed back from the table, coming to my full height. "What else haven't you told us?"

"That's it." He nodded down at the folder. "That's everything we know. We've been scouring passport records to determine which Anarkhos members entered the country. This is what we found."

"Funny, we've been doing the same thing with zero results."

Reece didn't speak. He stood his ground, turning his attention to the intel we'd been compiling concerning the caller, target locations, and the like. "This hasn't yielded the results we intended."

"No shit. It's not like you've done anything but fuck this up and fuck with us."

For a full minute, he scanned the boards, his lips moving as if he were silently repeating everything. When he was finished, his pupils focused on me. "Do you need reminding that those who live in glass houses shouldn't cast stones?"

"What the hell is that supposed to mean?"

He crossed to my side of the table, coming to stand six inches from me. "You've done nothing but screw around and screw with us. When you weren't botching the capture of our asset, what exactly were you doing?"

"Working my ass off on this case."

He raised a skeptical eyebrow, a smug, superior look on his face. "I don't doubt you were working your ass off while on your back." His grin was cruel. "But haven't you started to wonder why your boyfriend won't let you near his place?

It doesn't matter how nice the hotel is. An affair is still an affair."

"My personal life is none of your business."

"I bet his girlfriend wouldn't feel the same way. Why don't we call her and find out?"

The words barely had time to process. I didn't believe them. I didn't believe this pompous prick. Until Mark grabbed my arm and pulled me away from CIA Agent Reece, I was unaware of the fact that I was a split second away from hitting him. I was also unaware of anyone else in the room.

"Parker, upstairs. Now," Mark growled in my ear. "Go see how Lawson's doing."

My breathing was harsh, expelling itself in ragged exhales. The blood pounded in my ears. This asshole shouldn't have been able to get under my skin like that. How did he know how to push my buttons? And how did he know where I'd been all weekend?

TWENTY-THREE

Storming upstairs, I went into the tech's lair, past the equipment and agents assembled, and into the office. Shutting myself inside, I paced back and forth, rubbing my eyes and running my hands through my hair, effectively ruining my bun. A timid knock sounded at the door, and Lawson asked if everything was okay.

"I'll be out in a minute." Removing my phone from my pocket, I tapped it against my lip. Calling Martin to ask if a known liar just lied to me would be stupid, but the accusation bothered me. Every word from Reece's mouth bothered me. He blamed me for not doing my job when he was the one who couldn't do his. It was nothing more than an ad hominem attack designed to focus my thoughts on the misdirection. I would be damned if he derailed this case.

The same thought from earlier crossed my mind again. How did Reece know I was in a hotel? That wasn't in any of the reports. That was private. It wasn't relevant.

"Hey, Lawson," I poked my head out of the office, "can you come in here for a sec? I need your help." When he came into the room, he closed the door. "Sorry, I barged in and took over your office."

"Mi office et su office. Is everything okay? Besides the obvious, I mean."

"I need a bug check. I think the CIA's tracking me, but I'm not sure how."

"They could have pinged your phone."

"Yeah, I guess." Those hazy, dreamlike memories came to mind. "Can you do a quick scan to see if I'm emitting any radio frequencies? It'll make me feel better."

"Sure." Returning a few seconds later with the scanner, he powered it on and instructed me to remove my phone and any other devices. When he wanded me, the bells and whistles went off. "Did you forget something in your pocket?"

"No." A sick feeling traveled through me. "There was a weird puncture at the top of my hip a few days ago." I undid the button on my pants in order to slide the waist down an inch. "Is that anything?"

He frowned, checked the equipment, and ran his fingers over my skin. "I'm guessing it's a subdermal GPS tracker."

"Like a lowjack for dogs?"

"Maybe. I won't know until we remove it."

"Then cut it the hell out." I leaned over the desk. "C'mon, I don't have all day."

He cleared his throat uncomfortably. "I've never done this to a live specimen."

"Pretend I'm dead."

"Yeah, well, on the few odd occasions I've seen something similar to this, the ME usually does the cutting." Lawson was a computer geek by trade. Blood wasn't part of his job description. "I'll get the medic to do it."

"While you're at it, get Jablonsky. I need to talk to him, and I don't want that CIA twat anywhere near us."

Just as Lawson opened the door, Jablonsky reached for the door handle. The two practically collided, but Jablonsky righted the tech, pushing him off to the side while he entered the room. He gave me an odd look, wondering why my shirt was untucked.

"I barely had time to stop you from hitting him," Jablonsky said. "What the hell were you thinking?"

"That he deserved it."

"I don't doubt it, but that would have been a career ender. You can't do it."

"We'll see." I took a deep breath, holding up my hand before he could continue to berate me. "Those assholes stuck a tracking chip in my hip, like I'm a dog that might run away." An ugly smile crept onto my face. "He tipped his hand when he started spouting out shit about how I haven't been doing my job and how..." I closed my eyes.

Jablonsky put a steadying hand on my shoulder. "What?"

"It's stupid." I opened my eyes and looked at him. "It isn't even worth repeating."

"Humor me."

I sighed. "Will you tell me the truth?"

"Yeah, what is it?"

"I feel like a moron for asking, but does Martin have another girlfriend? We were apart for three months. I told him to move on. I can't fault him if he did. I just need to know."

Jablonsky snickered. "Marty wouldn't buy an apartment if you were a side piece."

"Isn't that what wealthy men do to keep their mistresses separate from their wives?"

"Maybe, but he's not married. And if you were just a piece of ass, he wouldn't be investing in a future together. Believe me when I say you're all the woman he can handle. Some days, you might be a bit too much to handle. Hence the apartment." His expression soured. "Is this nonsense what that putz said to you?"

I nodded. "He's supposed to be in the intelligence business."

"Intelligence my ass." Jablonsky stepped back at the sound of footsteps. When the medic and Lawson came inside, he turned to them. "Get that tracker out of Agent Parker. Do your best to keep it intact. I want a full workup on it, and send the device and info to Director Kendall. Whoever did this isn't going to get away with it." He took a deep breath. "After that's done, I want a sweep of the entire building and all of our agents to make sure no one else is compromised. I want a complete report by the end of the day."

After a quick slice and dice and a purple band-aid, I went back downstairs. Until I knew I had plenty of ammo to fire at Reece, I chose to ignore him. He hung around the conference room, sipping the sludge from the coffeepot and studying our maps and charts. Several of our agents came in with additional background information. I pinned it to the board and scribbled a few notes beside it.

"I'm here to assist," Reece said, breaking the tense silence. He pointed a pen at the notations I just made. "Why are you scouting locations? We shared a list of potential targets with you when you first began the investigation."

My lack of response further irritated him, and he got up from his chair and tapped the board emphatically. I turned, conveying with my eyes that he should back off. Instead, he locked eyes with me in a confrontational manner.

"Anarkhos wants Kiter. We have two options here. One, we locate Kiter. Two, we locate the source of the threat. At the moment, we aren't certain Anarkhos is the source of the threat." I spoke slowly so the words would process through his pathetic pea brain.

"Is that a joke?"

"No. It's along the same lines that you've been feeding us for the last two weeks. Anarkhos hasn't taken credit. They haven't identified themselves. We have to rule out other possibilities."

"Who else would want Kiter?" Reece asked, exasperated.

"You."

He exhaled, spinning around and slamming the chair beneath the table. "You think we called in a threat? Why would we do that?"

Before I could answer, Jablonsky stepped into the room. His eyes flicked the unspoken question to me. In response, I gave a barely perceptible headshake. No, I wasn't about to smack some sense into this guy, even though I wanted to.

"Is there a problem?" Jablonsky asked.

Reece turned to him. "No. Agent Parker was simply enlightening me as to how other entities might be after Kiter."

"Good." Jablonsky leaned against the table. "Since we're on the subject, are you positive Kiter wasn't snatched up by some black ops group or rogue spies? Whoever called in the threat was pretty damn adamant about having Kiter released, and since we're just lowly FBI agents, we had no idea what he was talking about. We still don't. As far as we know, Kiter's in the wind, but the caller was positive some agency has him in custody. Do you think you might be able to make some calls and get verification that isn't the case?"

"I already have. We don't have him."

"So you say," I replied, "but hypothetically, whoever demanded Kiter's release would be in a position to access sensitive, classified intelligence. Do you know anyone like that?"

"They're fucking blackhat hackers. Our best people have been unable to stop their intrusions. They get what they want. They do what they want. That's why we need Kiter. We need to turn one of them to build a decent defense system," Reece spat.

Jablonsky glanced at me before turning back to Reece. "Since these anarchists are omnipotent and have skills far beyond our capabilities, why would they need us to free Kiter? Couldn't they do it themselves? Why threaten us? They used the bombs to scramble our systems to bust him out, so why would they warn us about another detonation? It doesn't make any sense."

Reece's eyes darted back and forth. "Do you think Kiter made the threatening call? What would be the purpose? To throw us off the scent?"

Jablonsky shrugged. "It's a possibility."

"I need to make some calls." Reece left the room.

My shoulders slumped, and I exhaled. "Is that what we really think? It doesn't sound particularly plausible. I don't buy it."

"Neither do I, but it bought us some time." He stared at the boards. "Our task force triangulated a four block radius from where the call originated. It's a large area to canvass, but I sent a few teams to get started. We'll see what we find. In the meantime, I made some calls to other agencies. They swear Kiter wasn't picked up. Did you get the police report from Saturday's accident?"

"It's on my desk."

"Drop it in my office when you get a chance." Jablonsky headed for the door, but something went off in my brain.

"No one knows who Kiter is. We haven't issued his photo or profile over the wire. It's all hush-hush. The only thing we know is he's using fake IDs and credit cards, or he was Saturday night." I shoved some files aside, finding the list of cards we were monitoring. "If he was picked up with a fake ID, no one would know who they had in custody." Grabbing my phone, I started dialing.

Jablonsky nodded. "I'm picking up what you're laying down. I'll have the other agencies check to see if any of those names were brought in."

"I'm calling the PD. Perhaps they'll be able to help," I said as Jablonsky went out the door. "Hey, Derek, I need you to check something for me." I updated him on the situation and waited while he ran the extensive list of names we'd pulled.

"I'm not seeing anything. I'll keep checking periodically. Sometimes, the system is slow to update."

"Thanks." Hanging up, I felt like there was something to it. That, of course, relied on two things. First, that the caller wasn't full of shit. Second, that the CIA wasn't lying to us. So far, they'd provided nothing but a bunch of whitewashed lies and zero truths. It was hard to believe them now. "Dammit, Parker. Think."

Detouring to my desk, I grabbed another coffee from the carrier. It was now cold, but it would do the trick. Then I picked up the accident report and brought it into Jablonsky's office and placed it on his desk while he worked his angles. I didn't spot Reece anywhere and hoped the spook vanished into thin air.

I turned on my computer, figuring I might as well use the downtime to check my messages and see if there were any updates. When I opened my e-mail, I found a waiting message. It was from an anonymous account that had been created the day before. Wondering how anyone had gotten my work address which was used strictly for office purposes, I hit the preview button, paranoid enough not to open it for fear it was a virus or worm designed by the blackhats.

It was a message from one of my contacts. He didn't want to phone, but he provided a list of fake identities that had recently been created. It wasn't exactly what I had asked for, but it might lead to something. I ran the names through the database, but I didn't find any arrest records. Copying down the list, I dropped it off on Jablonsky's desk for the other agencies to evaluate and dialed Heathcliff again.

"I have some more names for you." I read the list and waited.

"I'm sorry, Alex. Nothing's coming up."

"It was worth a shot. Did you hear about any increased patrols?"

"I did. Should I be worried?"

"Only if we don't find the bomber's next target."

"I'll take that as a yes. When's the FBI officially going to tell us what's going on?"

"As soon as we figure that out. Listen, get Jacobs and that rookie who reported to the scene of the accident on Saturday night and meet me at the train depot. That's Kiter's last known location. If he dropped something or left something behind, we might be able to find it."

"Okay. Just promise me you aren't going to blab everything to some rookie cop, especially when it's been tough as nails to get you to open up about anything relevant."

"I just want him around in case he remembers picking something up or seeing something. He seemed flustered when I spoke to him earlier. Maybe a field trip will calm him down and jog his memory." I grabbed a photo of Kiter, a set of keys, and made sure my desk was locked. "I'll see you in a few minutes."

TWENTY-FOUR

I spoke to the two ticket takers from Saturday night. This time, I showed them each the photo of Kiter. They didn't remember him ten minutes after he purchased the train tickets, so they didn't remember him now. Sighing, I scanned the vicinity. Jacobs had taken the rookie to ask about locker rentals from Saturday night, so Heathcliff stuck by my side like gum on a shoe.

"What's wrong?" he asked, reading my mood.

"This case is getting under my skin. Pun intended." Quickly, I filled him in on the subdermal GPS tracker.

"If your suspicions are correct and clandestine government agents chipped you, why wouldn't they have put a chip inside their asset?"

"Maybe they did. The electromagnetic wave caused by the detonation would have shorted it out. Hell, a quick jolt from a taser would probably do the same thing."

"Still, it seems weird they were tracking you. Wouldn't there be easier, less invasive ways of doing it? Your phone. The government vehicle you drive. Calling and asking where you are."

"I don't know. All I can say for certain is that after the bicyclist took me down, I saw a man in a suit running down the street in the direction Kiter had just gone. I don't believe that's a coincidence."

"All right, take me through it."

We took the same route I had Saturday night and stopped outside the restaurant. Most of the umbrellas were closed. It was early in the afternoon, and from the sign on the door, the place didn't open until four. Heathcliff removed his badge and knocked, holding the shield against the pane of glass. A second later, someone in chef whites opened the door.

"Is there a problem?" the cook asked.

"We need a minute of your time." Heathcliff remained stiff and stoic, and I heard Joe Friday's voice in my head saying, 'just the facts, sir.' He held out his hand for the photograph of Kiter. I gave it to him, but Heathcliff didn't offer it to the cook. "Who was covering the outdoor patio Saturday night between seven and eight?"

"Karina and Pablo." The chef narrowed his eyes. "What's this about?"

"Are they here?" Heathcliff waited for the man to nod. "Can you get them?"

The cook gave Heathcliff a hard stare. "Look, this is my restaurant. They are my waiters. I would like to know what this is about." The cook's eyes shifted to me. Until now I hadn't spoken a word, but it was time I said something.

"Special Agent Alexis Parker." I held out my credentials. "A fugitive was seen near your establishment Saturday evening. We just want to know if anyone noticed him."

"Yeah, okay. No prob. I'll go get them." The cook stepped away from the door. "You can come inside if you want."

Heathcliff waited for me to make the first move. I entered the establishment. There wasn't much to see. It had a full service bar, a few dining rooms separated by partitions, and a bustling staff preparing for the late opening. While we waited for Karina and Pablo, Heathcliff clicked his radio to tell Jacobs where we were.

A few seconds later, the cook led the servers to the front door. Once we verified they had been working the outdoor patio at the time and date specified, Heathcliff showed them the photograph we had of Kiter. Karina studied it before shrugging.

"What about you?" I jerked my chin at Pablo. "Do you remember this guy? He might not have been a customer. Maybe just someone who took a seat at an empty table."

Pablo scratched his head. "I remember somebody in a hoodie. I told him to scram, but he kept hanging around under the umbrellas. I thought it was weird. It was dark though, so not that many people wanted to sit outside. While I was putting in some orders, he must have left. He wasn't there when I came back."

"Was it the man in the photo?" Heathcliff asked.

"I have no idea. It was dark. I just wanted to make sure he wasn't a mugger or graffiti artist. Other than that, I didn't really give a shit what he was doing."

"You didn't happen to see where he came from or where he went, did you?" I doubted Pablo had seen the chase. I didn't remember any wait staff outside during the encounter.

"Nope." After a moment, his face brightened as if a light bulb had turned on over his head. "Actually, I remember one couple saying some girl approached him. They must have had words or gotten into it because he threw a candle at her. It sounded like bullshit. But the candle was on the ground, and a couple of chairs were overturned."

"Do you remember who said that?" Heathcliff asked.

"Just one of our customers," Pablo replied.

Heathcliff focused on the cook again. "Sir, it would really help us out if you could pull your records from that night so we can get into contact with the witnesses."

"You can look through our receipts all you want, but there's just one problem. Our credit card reader went down Friday, and it wasn't repaired until this morning. We were cash only all weekend."

"Of course you were." I rubbed my eyes and stepped toward the door. "That's just how it goes."

Heathcliff thanked the cook and his staff for their time, took down their names and numbers, and escorted me out of the restaurant. "Don't fucking lose it, Parker. We don't have time for one of your meltdowns or temper tantrums."

"I'm not. I'm just frustrated."

"Now you know how we feel," Jacobs said from behind. His voice caused me to jump. "I take it you didn't find anything either." He looked up, reading the sign. "Or were they just not serving dinner yet?"

"I tracked the target to that table." I pointed to the one on the end. "From there, he darted across the street. I pursued until I got clipped." I glared at the rookie. "Did you check anything besides the immediate scene of the accident?"

"I did my job," Barry insisted.

"We're not going to find anything out here," Heathcliff said quietly. He had moved down to the table and was checking the seats, umbrella, and candle holder. "If there was something to find, it's gone now." He looked up. "It was worth checking."

"Did you two have better luck?" I asked.

"No one rented a locker during that time period. I don't think your target had anything to stow." Jacobs flipped through his notes.

"I'm just trying to find him." I took the photograph out of my pocket and unfolded it on the table. "Too bad no one spotted him."

The rookie leaned over my shoulder. "That's the guy you're looking for?"

"Yeah."

"What was he wearing the last time you saw him?" Barry asked.

"A dark hoodie. Jeans. Black sneakers." My eyes locked onto his. "Don't overthink it. Just tell me what you know."

"You said his name was Stavos Kiter," the rookie replied. "The guy they peeled off the asphalt wasn't Stavos Kiter. His ID said Joseph Rourke."

"Rourke. Shit." I recognized the name from the list my contact had e-mailed.

Heathcliff's gaze went electric. "Where's Rourke now?"

"The dude was taken to the hospital. I told you about him this morning, right? It was the second accident I had to respond to that night. It was like," Barry spun around, "four blocks that way."

"Rourke's our guy?" Jacobs asked, and I nodded. "Okay,

I'll take junior back to the station, pull the reports, and find out what we can. The two of you, go to the hospital and see if he's still there."

Heathcliff and I raced back to the car. On the way, I phoned Jablonsky, relaying the message through my labored breaths. For once, CIA Agent Reece hadn't lied to us. I just hoped the rookie cop was right and Kiter's collision with a taxi cab had been severe enough to warrant an extended hospital stay. We needed Kiter to use as leverage to stop Anarkhos from unleashing another IED on the city. If they decided to target a hospital, there would be casualties. A lot of them.

Hitting the lights and siren, I zoomed through traffic. "I can't believe this."

Heathcliff didn't say a word. He clung to the overhead handle as I made a sharp turn. Switching lanes, I slid into the turning lane and took a side street, hoping to get away from the lunchtime crowd. Unfortunately, we hit a crawl. Smashing my palm against the horn, I hoped someone would move, but we were gridlocked. I checked the mirrors, slid partially into the bike lane and partially onto the sidewalk, and continued at a reasonable pace.

"This is why we have accidents," Heathcliff mused.

"Shut it." I tossed him a playful look before slamming on the brakes when someone stepped in front of the car. Jerking the wheel to the left, I got back onto the road and into the turning lane. After another couple of blocks, I pulled into the hospital parking lot. Leaving the car at the end of the fire lane, I stepped out, daring Heathcliff to mention my parking was a violation, but he had his priorities in order—finding the blackhat.

We went straight to the information desk. Heathcliff took lead, seeing as how the police had jurisdiction over the accident. The woman at the reception desk lifted the phone and made a call. I tapped my foot impatiently. Medical records were confidential. HIPAA violations were serious, and getting a hospital staffer to disclose anything was like pulling teeth. After several minutes, she hung up the phone and shifted through some paperwork.

"Mr. Rourke is no longer being treated," she replied.

"Where did he go?" I snapped, but Heathcliff lifted his hand in the hopes I'd back off.

"Ma'am, the patient was a victim of an accident. Other police officers have already spoken to him. It has just now come to our attention that he is a person of interest in an ongoing investigation. We need to locate him." There was no question to his words.

She sighed. "I understand. All I can tell you is he isn't here. He was discharged Sunday evening. I don't know where he went after that."

"Thanks for your time," Heathcliff rubbed a hand down his face and reached for his phone. While he dialed the precinct, we returned to the car. Amazingly, it wasn't ticketed or towed. "Who took Joseph Rourke's statement?" He waited a few seconds. "All right. We're on our way back. Have the records pulled from that night, and call in the officer who made the bust. We need to talk to him."

"What bust?" I asked.

"When they brought Kiter to the hospital, the ER staff had to remove his clothing and personal belongings. They placed them in a bag. When an officer came in to take his statement and check on his condition, he noticed several IDs under different names. Since his belongings were in the clear plastic bag and in plain sight, the officer got curious. He also found several credit cards in various names, figured the victim was a pickpocket or mugger who was running away when he was hit by the taxi. So as soon as Kiter was cleared to leave the hospital, we arrested him."

"No fucking way. We had him and didn't even know it? That's crazy." A less pleasant thought crossed my mind. "Don't tell me he's been released on bail."

"I don't know. I had the records pulled. Jacobs is on it. As soon as we find him, we'll lock him down. Do you mind if I ask what we're supposed to do with him once we locate him?"

"We figure out how to leverage him in order to get the bombers to back off." A sick feeling developed in the pit of my stomach. Hitting speed dial, I waited for Jablonsky to answer. "I have a lead on Kiter. The PD's assisting. If I find him, what should I do?"

"Sit on him," Jablonsky said. "Three minutes ago, we received a demand from Guillermo Vega. Anarkhos has planted a bomb somewhere in the city. He'll give us the location and a method of disarming it as long as we do exactly what he says."

My breath caught in my throat. "What do they want? Are we certain it was Vega?"

"Yeah. Anarkhos has decided to take credit for the bombings. Vega wants Kiter out of custody and booked on an international flight. They gave us the flight number and departure time. After the plane is in international airspace, they'll tell us how to stop the detonation."

"How can we trust them?"

"We can't, but they can't trust us either. It's a flight. I don't care if it's with a non-American airline. We could have it redirected and rerouted, and Kiter could be taken back into custody. Anarkhos must know that. It's a smoke screen. They want us to focus our attention there. Reece has already made several calls to ensure his people are on that flight and positioned throughout the airport. But like I said, I think it's a bluff. They are trying to force us to react. They'll probably follow our movements, figure out where Kiter is, and spring him themselves. Or kill him. I don't know which."

"Do you think the bomb is a bluff too?" I asked as a pang of fear coiled through my insides.

"I have no idea."

TWENTY-FIVE

"Parker," Derek's voice was gentle as he put a cautious hand on my back, "you okay?"

I shook my head. Since our arrival at the precinct, I'd been authorized to provide details on Anarkhos and Kiter to the major crimes unit, and after that, I read the riot act to the arresting officer, the dumbass rookie, and the desk sergeant who had sent Kiter to central booking. The police arrested the man for possession of stolen property. They ran his prints through the system, but they didn't find a match. He refused to provide a real name, so they booked him with nothing more than a number and a photograph and sent out the usual 'can you identify' notice. And now they fucking lost him.

I brought my eyes up to stare at every man assembled inside Lt. Moretti's office. "The OIO received word that a bomb has been planted. The group responsible knows you arrested the man we know as Stavos Kiter. They want him released from custody and on a plane by midnight, or they'll detonate another explosive."

Moretti bristled, his angry glare rivaling mine as he scanned the room. "He should be awaiting an arraignment since we arrested him. How did we lose him? Have we checked the holding cells in the courthouse?"

Jacobs nodded. His arms remained crossed over his chest. The bulk of his resentment was focused on the rookie officer who had responded to the accident, but some of it dribbled onto me. He didn't say a word, but I knew what he was thinking. If I had been upfront from the beginning, this wouldn't have happened.

"Given the computer acumen of the anarchist group, we've printed hard copies of Kiter's photograph. Right now, we're circulating them around. Based on the current demands and our own assumptions, we're guessing Kiter is still in custody. He probably assumed someone else's identity to mount another escape," Heathcliff said. "We have people in the courthouse and at the prison performing visual sweeps. We will find him."

"We better." Moretti zeroed in on me. "Do we have any idea where the bomb might be?"

"The OIO's working on it. The CIA is assisting in gathering additional intel, but based on previous experiences, we're guessing the target will be technological in nature with the ability to cripple most of the city."

Moretti sucked in his top lip. "Let's hope it doesn't come to that." He looked around the room. "Need I remind you that none of this bears repeating? We're on high alert, but until we know something definitive, we don't want to cause a panic." His angry glower found its way to the rookie. "Keep a tight lid on this, and go find that asshole."

The arresting officer, Harkavy, held back while Jacobs dragged the rookie out of the room. Once they were gone, Harkavy cleared his throat and spoke. "I followed procedure. The IDs he had all contained his photograph. We had no way of knowing what was real and what was fake. He didn't talk. He wouldn't. He didn't even ask for a lawyer. What was I supposed to do?"

Moretti blinked a few times. "You did the right thing. This isn't your fault." His eyes met mine for a second. "After we fix this, we'll have plenty of time to point fingers, but for now, round up everyone who saw or spoke to Kiter. Perhaps someone noticed something."

Nodding, Harkavy pushed his way out of the room.

Moretti set his jaw and continued to stare. "Would you tell me if we needed to plan an evacuation?"

I hadn't even thought that far ahead. Things were just happening, and I didn't have the luxury to process them. "If we identify the target, I'll let you know what it is."

"I'm assuming it's a soft target."

"Probably." My expression remained grim. "Hopefully, they'll stick to their M.O. Anyone in the immediate blast radius will be in danger, but we're betting the zone won't be that large."

"I hope you're right."

Without another word, I went out the door. Heathcliff was already at his desk, the phone held in one hand while the other worked the keyboard. He shot a look in my direction.

Jablonsky wanted me on top of this. Since I was already at the precinct and had the best chance of locating Kiter, I was to work this angle. In the meantime, my boss was doing his best to track Vega and any other members of Anarkhos who might be stateside, all while keeping Reece and the CIA busy with thwarting the exchange. I just needed to figure out how a man arrested for possession of stolen property was literally lost in the system.

"Thanks." Heathcliff hung up the phone. "It looks like Kiter might have switched with someone else awaiting arraignment. I ordered the records from the jail to be sent over so we can see who the newly incarcerated are, but it takes forty-eight hours for the system to update and process."

"We don't have forty-eight hours. What makes you think he switched?"

"What else could he do? It's not like he could crawl out the bathroom window, and since we didn't have a name assigned to him, it'd be easy enough to go by something else. If I were facing a murder or sexual assault charge, I'd gladly switch with the guy caught with stolen property."

"Good point." I took a breath. "We need to get down to the jail and physically go through the fish."

"Jacobs, Harkavy, and Barry are on it. Two of them know precisely what Kiter looks like, and Jacobs has seen his photo enough to figure it out." Heathcliff rubbed his palms together. "They'll find him."

"Two more sets of eyes wouldn't hurt." I palmed my keys.

"It's a men's prison, and you're a Fed. That's two strikes already. If you show up, it'll be like feeding time in the zoo. We don't need to rattle the cages when we want to get this done as quickly as possible. Do you hear me?"

There was truth behind his words, so I dropped my keys. "I can't just stay here and do nothing."

"We need to figure out how Anarkhos knew we arrested Kiter. If we determine that, we might be able to determine where Kiter is. They tracked him somehow. Conceivably, we should be able to do the same." Pushing away from the desk, Heathcliff grabbed a stack of case files. "C'mon, let's see what the guys in the AV club can do for us."

The techs in the police department were no slouches when it came to computer programming. While we briefed them on the situation and circumstances, they set to work. Two of them began running the list of recent arrestees, hoping to find Kiter, while another two tirelessly clicked through screen after screen, checking for signs of intrusions into the police department's internal systems.

After almost an hour, they found something. Exchanging a glance with Heathcliff, I leaned over the desk. The numbers and symbols were a foreign language I didn't speak or understand, but they meant something to the techs. The woman behind the screen copied a file or address on to a separate drive and slid her chair over to another computer. She uploaded the data, entering code faster than I could type.

"What do we have, Bex?" her male counterpart asked. He slid his chair closer. After a moment of studying the screen, he diligently keyed in the same entry she had just typed.

"What's going on?" I asked.

Bex didn't look up from the display. "They're still here," she said.

"What?" Heathcliff edged closer. "Here, as in inside the building?" His hand moved involuntarily toward his hip.

"No." She didn't elaborate.

The male tech stopped typing. "They're monitoring activity on our servers at this very moment. The connection remains open. We're trying to get a location before they realize they've been discovered and pull out."

"Then do it." Heathcliff took a step away from the computer, putting his hands on top of his head as he waited anxiously for the results.

I stepped out of the room, not wanting to distract them from their jobs, and phoned the OIO. "Anarkhos is inside the PD's computers as we speak. We're trying to get a location. Is there anything we can do remotely?"

"Hang on," Agent Lawson replied.

A commotion in the background ensued, and Jablonsky grabbed the phone. "I'm preparing units to mobilize. As soon as you have that location, I'm gonna need it."

"I don't know if we'll get it." I stuck my head back into the room, watching as the techs typed at lightning speed. "Do you think Reece or his pals might be better equipped to track the hacker's location via their internet connection?"

Jablonsky swore. "Probably, but he left. And he isn't answering his damn phone."

"Parker," Heathcliff bellowed, and I returned to the room, "they're wiping our system."

Forgetting the phone, I returned to the computer. While Bex and her partner were tracking the location, the other two techs remained focused on finding Kiter. The screen in front of one of them appeared blank. The other monitor still held data, but the photos had been erased. The intake numbers were gone.

"They know where he is or where he's supposed to be." Remembering the phone, I lifted it to my ear and updated Jablonsky.

"We have to find Kiter before they do." Heathcliff reached for his radio. "I'll warn Jacobs of this new hiccup."

"Holy shit," Bex cursed. "No. Come on, baby." She stabbed at the keys furiously. "Dammit all to hell." The screen jumped and blinked, changing the colors on the display to orange and green before blacking out. "No." She slammed her palms on the keyboard.

"Hang on," the other tech said, continuing to type. "They're pulling out. I'll try to follow them."

"How are you doing that?" Bex asked.

A grin crossed his face. "Instead of using our servers, I created a hotspot with a separate IP. I used the same backdoor they did. Hopefully, they'll leave a trail since they're using so many proxies and bouncing their IP across the globe that they can't just unplug."

I held my breath, feeling Heathcliff press closer. One of us should probably cross our fingers. It couldn't hurt.

For a split second, something flashed on the screen. It was gone a moment later. The tech rubbed a hand down his face and clicked a few more keys. The data that had been scrolling on the screen replayed. He tapped a key when the final number flashed, and it paused. Copying it down, he opened a new window, typed in a few things, and waited.

"Here's the address," the tech said, pointing to the street number.

Reading it off to Jablonsky, I heard Derek repeat the same thing into his radio. The OIO teams were ready to move. By the time I hung up, they were en route to the location. The PD wasn't taking any chances and was sending its own squad to the address in question too.

"Let's move," I insisted, not waiting for Derek as I beelined out of the precinct. He caught up to me by the time I unlocked the car.

We didn't speak on the way. Instead, we mentally prepared for whatever was to come. We were facing an unknown group of anarchists with bomb making capabilities. The address on the screen didn't provide any clue as to what we might be walking into. Heathcliff keyed the address into the onboard navigation system and scanned the maps.

"Take a right," he insisted. "Pull in around back."

Without questioning his judgment, I executed the turn and parked in an alleyway. The area was mostly commercial. The address on the screen led to a building undergoing construction. The windows were papered over, except for one on the second floor. If Vega had brought a team with him, like Reece insisted, a lookout might have seen our approach. Heathcliff radioed in our position and waited for an affirmative. The police units arrived before us and were parked out front. No one had breached yet, but a team was waiting outside each door. I didn't know where my team was, but they couldn't be far behind.

We waited for the location to be scouted, and the entrances secured. No one was leaving without us noticing. Heathcliff and I were poised at a side door. Over the radio, someone asked if we should wait for the bomb squad. Heathcliff quirked an eyebrow but remained pressed against the wall to the left of the doorway. I was on the right, gun in hand, awaiting the order to breach. My phone buzzed, and my breath caught.

"Easy." Heathcliff chuckled.

I removed the phone. "Where are you guys?"

"We're in pursuit of Vega. He left the location and got into a waiting cab. Have the police arrived on scene yet?" Jablonsky asked.

"We're preparing to breach," I replied.

"Let me know what you find. As soon as Vega gets out of the car, we'll take him down."

"Affirmative." I disconnected and tucked the phone back in my pocket. "Vega's not here. I don't know if anyone else is."

Heathcliff relayed the intel over the radio, waiting for orders. The bomb squad was on the way with thermal gear and sniffers, but the brass was getting itchy. Vega was on the move, which meant he could be on his way to plant a bomb. Even if the OIO took him down, whatever intel we needed to locate the device might be inside this building.

"Check the doors, make sure there are no tripwires, and prepare to breach." The order came over the radio.

Heathcliff's grip tightened on his weapon. "I'll crack the door," he offered. Glancing around the alleyway for any signs of enemy movement, he holstered his weapon, removed a lock pick gun from his belt, and jammed it into the lock.

"Cheater," I quipped, hoping to break some of the

tension.

He held the knob in one hand and squeezed the trigger. It popped, and he slowly edged the door open half an inch. "Do you see anything?"

I leaned in, checking the space between the door and the frame. He pushed it a little wider, and I checked the top and bottom. "We're clear."

Nodding, he pulled the door back. From the tiny glimpse I'd gotten of the interior, there wasn't much inside. This would probably turn into another dead end.

"Clear," he reported. A minute later, we received additional reports the other doorways weren't booby-trapped. "On my count."

I nodded. He pushed the door open, and I went in first, muzzle aimed in front of me.

TWENTY-SIX

The ground floor didn't even have walls yet. It was a large cavernous area. The ceiling was incomplete, exposing large beams and the skeletal structure of what would inevitably become another department store. The upper levels didn't have walls either, but thick broad beams suspended in the air. In the center of the room was a workspace constructed out of plywood and sawhorses. A few hard hats and vests littered the corners, and tattered blueprints were curled on the floor. The only item of interest was an opened laptop in the middle of the table.

While the three police teams swept the bottom level, pushing aside hanging sheets of plastic and ensuring no other threats were present, I went to the table. After circling around, I holstered my weapon and removed a pen from my pocket. The screen was dark, but the light indicators in the corner suggested the computer was in standby mode.

"Alex," Heathcliff hissed, but it was too late.

I tapped the spacebar with my pen, watching the screen blink to life. A live video feed filled the main window. The image was of the interior of the building we were occupying.

My eyes darted around, hoping to locate the camera. "We're being watched."

"It could be a trap." Heathcliff called to his fellow officers to proceed with caution, but he didn't stray from my side. He pointed to the wi-fi indicator. "This is being broadcast."

Before I could say or do anything, a computerized voice boomed from the speakers. "Agent Parker, you are wasting time. You should be on your way to collect our blackhat."

"Who are you?" I asked.

"We are Anarkhos."

"Alex," Heathcliff mumbled, "I don't like this." The ESU commander stepped behind us, checking the image on the screen to get a better idea of where the camera might be positioned. "Kill that camera," Heathcliff whispered.

"We have every intention of meeting your demands," I said. I hated negotiation. I wasn't particularly good at it, but I didn't have much of a choice.

"You do not. If you did, you would not be here. You would not be trying to stop us." The creepy computer voice referring to itself as a collective had me flashing back to childhood nightmares of *Star Trek*'s the Borg. If they said resistance was futile, I'd lose my shit.

"The FBI is prepared to do whatever it takes to stop you from carrying out your threat. I'm hoping we can reach a peaceful compromise, and violence will not be necessary." I strived for diplomatic while avoiding speaking my mind.

Two gunshots went off, and I immediately ducked, grabbing my weapon and aiming at the source of the sound. The ESU commander had shot down the camera. It sizzled and crackled before crashing to the ground. When I turned back to the screen, my breath shallow, the feed was blacked out.

"That was not peaceful," the computer admonished. "Goodbye." The black screen was replaced with a second image of an explosive device. From the angle, it appeared to be mounted to one of the beams above us. The display showed a large red clock counting down from five seconds.

"Bomb. Everyone out," I screamed.

I dashed to the exit on Heathcliff's heels. I wasn't even

sure I cleared the doorway before the blast decimated the building. While I remained on the sidewalk, flashbacks of another explosion that took the life of two FBI agents played through my mind. I hadn't been on the scene, but I could only imagine it must have felt something like this. Overcome, I rolled to the side, choking and gagging.

"Parker," Heathcliff patted his jacket over the hem of my pants, "stay down."

After my airway was clear, I put a hand against his arm. "I'm okay."

"The hell you are." He searched the scene around us. "You might have a concussion. Take it easy."

"I didn't hit my head." I pushed him away, watching as he pulled his jacket off my legs to reveal charring at the bottom of my pants. "Did everyone make it out?" The fear of casualties turned my stomach again, but I swallowed the bile.

His gaze swept the perimeter. "I think so. Are you sure you're okay?"

My ears were ringing from the blast, and my bruised ribs were on fire. But aside from that, I was fine. "I'm good. You?"

He nodded, and I hugged him hard. It wasn't professional, but after the number of times I'd put his life in jeopardy, I needed to hear that. He hauled me to my feet and let his hand linger on my elbow for several seconds.

"Let's not do that again." He offered a slight smile.

"Agreed." Inhaling, I added, "With our track record, there are a lot of things we shouldn't do again." Turning, I stared through the open door to what would have been a nice department store. Everything had been flash burned. The beams, the floor, every surface was covered in soot. The few items that had been inside were now nothing more than ash. "They wanted to make sure we wouldn't find any evidence to use against them. Whatever details we might have found concerning the location of another bomb just went straight to hell." Carefully, I stepped back inside, hoping I was wrong, but the computer was nothing but a melted plastic and metal blob. "They changed their M.O."

"Detective," one of the officers called, and Heathcliff

turned, "you need to see this."

After giving the interior a final glance, I took the two steps out of the building and went to see what the commotion was. An electronics store across the street had a display of televisions against the side wall which was visible from the exterior. Playing on a loop was our narrow escape from the latest bombing. The footage had been taken from nearby security cameras. Anarkhos really could hack anything.

"What should we do?" the officer asked.

"Find out where that feed is coming from," Heathcliff barked. Grabbing his cell phone, he entered the store and recorded the footage. Next, he dialed Moretti to update the lieutenant on the situation.

Before I could even think to dial Jablonsky, my phone rang. Fearful of whom it might be, I checked the display. My boss had a sixth sense when it came to things, and I hit answer.

"Are you okay? What the hell just happened?" Mark asked.

"I'm fine. There was another bomb. It didn't interfere with the electronics. It was meant to..." Inflict casualties? Scare us off? Demonstrate how serious the threat was?

"I know." He exhaled, and I knew whatever else he was about to say would only make matters worse. "The footage was sent to every agent at our field office."

"Shit. What about Vega?"

Mark grumbled something under his breath. "We had to let him go."

The words were like a punch to the gut. "Why?"

"He had a detonator. He said if we didn't let him leave peacefully, he'd take down an entire building full of people. We couldn't risk it. Director Kendall ordered us to stand down. After what could have been several law enforcement fatalities, we had to believe he was serious."

"I thought we didn't negotiate with terrorists."

"We don't have much of a choice." He spoke to someone in the background. "Our best bet at stopping this is to locate Kiter. So go find the bastard, and once you have him, bring him to HQ. Reece and his pals will take it from there."

"Dammit, Mark."

"That's an order." He disconnected, and it took all of my willpower not to throw my phone to the ground and stomp on it.

Within moments, dozens of vehicles arrived. The police had radioed for backup. Fire was called in to assist. The FBI and OIO sent several teams and techs to assess the area. The bomb squad rolled up, a bit too late in my opinion, and several ambulances responded, assessing the police for breathing difficulty and minor burns due to the blast.

After providing a quick briefing to those taking charge of the scene, I ducked back into my car. Heathcliff was bogged down with coordinating efforts, and I didn't want to waste precious time. Unfortunately, I wasn't any closer to finding Kiter or stopping Anarkhos. Aside from the hem of my pants being an inch shorter, I had nothing to show for the last twenty minutes, but that hadn't stopped the anarchist group from declaring war.

Kiter should be in a holding cell at the local jail. That's what was indicated in the police records. That was the intel Anarkhos had hacked. And that was where Detective Jacobs and two officers had gone. So that's where I needed to be.

I had barely made it a mile before Jacobs phoned. "Parker, where are you?"

"On my way to you."

"Don't bother. Kiter's not here. He was remanded into the custody of an Agent Reece due to matters of national security. Is Reece one of your guys?"

"No, he's the asshole who got us into this mess. When did he take Kiter?"

"Two hours ago. I have copies of the paperwork and sign out sheet, but the writing's illegible. To top it off, their computer systems have been experiencing extreme glitches. Everything is down, including their security cams. We have no way of verifying if Kiter was ever here or if this Agent Reece actually took him."

A million thoughts swarmed through my brain. "Get a

thorough description of Reece and double and triple check the prisoner he took into custody matches the photo we have of Kiter. I'll see what I can figure out on my end. In fact, get a sketch artist down there just to be sure. I'll call as soon as I know something."

I cursed several times, dialed Jablonsky, and altered course for the federal building. The call went to voicemail, and I pushed the worry away. He was busy. He'd call back as soon as he got the chance.

I stormed into the federal building prepared for war. "Where's Reece?" I received a few shrugs. "As soon as he arrives, I want to know about it." Slamming the door to the conference room, I shoved the chair to the side in a fit of rage. I could have died. Heathcliff and the other cops could have died because of this messed up op. Even now, Reece continued to screw us over every chance he got.

My blood was boiling. The images plastered to the walls of the destruction that previous IEDs had caused added fuel to the fire. At least those detonations didn't come with casualties. We were lucky. Anarkhos could have barbequed us, but they didn't. Instead, they wanted us to know they would use violence if necessary. That's why they sent the footage to the FBI and OIO and broadcast it from the nearby TVs.

A gentle rapping at the door drew my attention. I turned to find Agent Reece. "I was told you wanted to see me," he said.

"Where. Is. He?"

"I'm sure I have no idea what you're talking about." Reece's facial expression never changed. He was a company man through and through.

"Stavos Kiter. You located him. You removed him from police custody. Where is he?"

"I don't know."

Grabbing him by the lapels, I threw him against the wall. "Answer me," I screamed.

The bastard didn't flinch. He didn't move. He didn't even blink. He just stared with that superior look on his face.

"Parker," Mark bellowed, but I didn't release my grip,

"what's going on?"

"He has Kiter. Detective Jacobs went to the prison and found out Reece authorized a transfer." I yanked Reece forward and slammed him back against the wall. "Tell us where you stashed the blackhat."

"Agent Jablonsky, control your subordinate," Reece said in a bored tone.

Mark put a hand on my shoulder. "Walk away, Alex."

"Fuck." I slammed Reece into the wall again and stepped back.

Reece moved to straighten his tie, and Mark decked him. The CIA agent didn't see it coming. He stumbled sideways along the wall, dazed. When he recovered, he spat on Mark's shoe and let out a smug snort. "You'll regret that."

"I regret not doing it sooner. Now answer the question. Where's Kiter?"

"I don't know."

"Agent Reece, you're under arrest for obstruction of justice," Mark roughly spun the agent around and held him against the wall while removing his side arm and cuffing him. "Unless you change your tune, you aren't leaving this building." He dragged Reece to the conference room door. "Davis, make sure our guest is comfortable in one of the interrogation rooms and assign a few agents to guard the door. He's not going anywhere, and no one is to make contact with him. Is that clear?"

"Yes, sir," Davis said, giving the CIA agent an uncertain look before leading him down the corridor.

I sighed and dropped into a chair. Mark shook out his hand and took a seat across from me. "You better be damn sure you're right about this," he warned.

"I am."

"You're positive Jacobs got the facts straight?"

"The only other possibility is Anarkhos freed Kiter and blamed Reece, but why would they call in threats and demand we release Kiter if they have him?"

"They wouldn't." Jablonsky glanced out the conference room door. "Now we just have to break someone trained to withstand our interrogation techniques." He took a deep breath and stood. "Get out of here. I want you as far away from this building as possible. There will be fallout, and we have more important things to deal with. I'll speak to Kendall. We should assume Anarkhos has every intention of carrying out their threat. See if the PD can help determine the target, and tell Moretti to plan for an evacuation."

"You don't think Reece will talk?"

"He will if his superiors order it." He jerked his head toward the elevator. "Now go."

TWENTY-SEVEN

On my way to the precinct, I phoned Jacobs and Heathcliff. Jacobs was on his way back from the jail, and Heathcliff was still at the scene of the explosion. Since I had a few spare moments and the reality of the situation weighed heavily on my mind, I detoured to the Martin Technologies building.

Unlike most of my visits, I didn't waste time exchanging pleasantries with Jeffrey Myers, the head of security. Instead, I was escorted to Martin's office. Martin took one look at me and got up from behind his desk.

"Is everything okay?" he asked. "What happened?"

"History is not going to repeat itself. I'm not telling you to go. I'm not sending you away. You can do whatever you want. But I need to tell you something, and you can't repeat it to anyone. The city receives threats all the time. We don't report them or spread word because it would cause a panic. There'd be chaos. Most of the time, the danger isn't real. On the rare occasion it is, well, things could go to hell real fast."

He put his hands on my shoulders. "I won't say a word. What's going on?"

"There's a bomb. Somewhere. I don't know where. I...we

don't know what the target is. Or who the target is. I just want you safe. I don't want you to be here. You're in the business district. It's densely populated. There are plenty of high-rises. It's enticing. It'd be best if you got out of town until I give the all-clear."

He rubbed some soot off my cheek and examined his fingertips. "Why do you smell like smoke?"

"Because I was close, just not close enough."

"Could I convince you to take the next few days off and we'll go somewhere together?"

"I can't leave."

"Then neither can I." He pulled me into a hug. "But I'll be okay. You have to believe that, and I have to believe you'll stop this from happening. That we're both going to be just fine."

"What if I can't prevent it from happening?" I looked up at him. "I want to know you're safe, even if I fail."

"Sweetheart, I could get into an accident while leaving the city, and you'd feel responsible for that. Or I could stay, and shit could go wrong. It's not up to you. If you're staying, I am too. We're in this together." He kissed me. "I have faith." He released his grip. "Is there anything I can do to help?"

"Not really. It's up to Jablonsky and the police department." I gave him another kiss. "Will you at least leave early tonight, just to be on the safe side?"

"Okay," he promised. I moved toward the door, but he grabbed my wrist and searched my eyes. "Be careful."

I smiled. "You know me."

"That's why I told you to be careful. I'll see you Friday?"

"You can count on it."

My drive to the precinct didn't take long, but I allowed myself a few moments of self-indulgent doubt and fear. It wasn't surprising Martin refused to leave. I gave him the choice. It was his decision to make, but I didn't like it. My boss wouldn't be happy I disclosed the nature of the current threat to my paramour either, but I was already in enough hot water. How much worse could it get? Marching up the precinct steps prepared to grovel for any assistance they could provide, I entered the major crimes unit ready to work.

"Jacobs, tell me you have good news," I implored.

He tossed a sketchpad across the desk. "Does he look familiar?"

"Reece." I ground my teeth. "Son of a bitch."

"I guess that means we can call off the search. We know where Kiter is, or at least, someone in the federal government does." The words came out full of hatred and disdain, and I couldn't help but agree fully with those sentiments. "Why doesn't this pencil-pushing prick help us out?"

"I don't know."

Jacobs wrung his hands together. "Great. Just fucking great." He looked around the room. "Okay. What are your people planning to do now?"

"Jablonsky's working Reece, but we shouldn't assume that will pan out. We need to go back to your original play."

"You want us to find the bomber and the bomb."

"It's the best we can do, and we might need to prepare for an evacuation." I looked around the room. "Did Heathcliff get back yet?"

"I haven't seen him." He opened the drawer, removed something from his desk, and slammed it shut. "For the record, whatever happens from this point forward is on you."

"Noted." Pressing my lips together in a grimace, I shuddered when he slammed a second drawer.

"Start writing. I know you must have a profile on the bomber. I want to know everything. We need to figure out the target, and the only way to do that is to figure out what they hate the most."

"They hate the government. They hate structure. They're classic anarchists, but they hide behind computer screens. They want the complete sharing of information. Everything is passed along technologically. As far as I know, that's the only method they've ever used to interfere with our security, and it's the mode they use for disseminating classified information. Until now, their leader, Guillermo Vega, was personally responsible for two overseas bombings of military installations. It's believed those bombings were a direct attempt to rescue or kill Kiter. Neither incident resulted in any casualties."

"And there were no casualties today," Heathcliff said, stepping over to the desk to join us. "They had the cameras rigged. The bomb was triggered by a remote detonator, not the timer. Whoever set it off wanted to make sure we were out of the building before things went boom."

"Tell that to the cuffs of my pants," I retorted. "That blaze was quick. Are you certain he didn't want to flash fry us?"

"I don't think so." Heathcliff placed a copy of the bomb squad's report on the desk. "They used magnesium dust to make everything burn hot, fast, and bright. That's why nothing was left inside. Other than that, we don't have much to go on."

Jacobs picked up the report and keyed something into the computer. "We might be able to track suppliers. This might be the lead we need. It's better than the shit Parker's given us."

The truth of his words cut deep, and I pushed away from the desk, surrendering the chair to Derek. "I need to call the OIO."

I went into the small area outside the double doors and dialed my boss. Before I could update him on the situation, he informed me Anarkhos had phoned again. They were aware of Kiter's removal from police custody and believed it was in fulfillment of their demands. A tiny voice in my head hoped the same thing, even though we were dealing with yet another hitch in our plans. Due to our perceived compliance, Anarkhos was willing to renegotiate the timeframe for which their demands should be met.

"We have a twelve hour reprieve," I announced, returning to the bullpen. "Anarkhos knows we're cooperating, so they're willing to grant us more time to turn over Kiter."

"Why would they do that?" Heathcliff asked.

"We told Vega that Kiter escaped after we removed him from police custody. They're under the impression we're conducting a citywide manhunt to recapture the blackhat in order to turn him over to his brethren. We also made it abundantly clear that we are their best chance of getting Kiter back alive. I don't know if they bought it, but we have twelve more hours."

"That gives them another twelve hours to plant additional bombs," Jacobs said.

"And it gives us more time to disable them." Heathcliff looked at me. "I have an idea, but I need your help."

I glanced at Jacobs, but he was busy running down the supplies used in the earlier detonation. Perhaps that would be enough to put us on Vega's trail and apprehend him and the rest of Anarkhos before more damage could be done. I really didn't want to risk getting blown up again if I could avoid it.

Heathcliff led me down the stairs and back to the techs we had visited earlier. Bex and the crew were knee deep in recalibrating the hardware and restoring vital systems on the precinct computers. Before I could voice the obvious question on my mind, one of the techs handed him a slip of paper.

"Thanks, man," Heathcliff turned on his heel and headed out the door.

I jogged to catch up. At this rate, I'd end up with whiplash. "Do you intend to share the plan with me sometime soon?"

He snorted. "Only if I have to."

"Will you at least explain to me how Jacobs is upstairs running evidence through his computer while the tech department is struggling to get the system operational?"

Heathcliff held the door, waiting for me to exit. Once we were outside, he glanced around and headed for an unmarked cruiser. "Anarkhos destroyed our arrest records. Everything else remains operational." He slid behind the wheel, falling silent until I joined him. "They know we tracked their location to the construction site, but they wanted us to find that. They wanted us to go there. From the greeting you received, I wonder if they didn't want you to go there, but based on what I've been told, they were using an advanced version of facial recognition software to determine our identities. Yours. Mine. The ESU commander's. Hell, probably every officer and emergency responder who came within a hundred feet of that building."

"And while that's fascinating, I hope you have a point."

He twisted the key in the ignition. "What they didn't count on was us figuring out the computer at the construction site and the images streamed to the television screens in the electronics store had a different IP address than the one we followed."

"The suspense might kill me," I deadpanned. "Where are we going?"

"To an internet café disguised as a hipster coffee shop. It's the real world location for the IP address. One of our anarchists must have been set up there while we went to the construction site. You said Vega had a team with him."

"I said he might. Do you think this unsub's still there?" Vega had been surrounded by OIO agents at the time of the explosion, meaning he wasn't personally responsible for triggering the bomb, which meant another member of Anarkhos was here. Until now, we knew there was a high probability, but we had no proof. Now, we did. "Did you call for backup?"

He looked at me from the corner of his eye. "The last time we rolled up with backup, things went boom. This is a crowded location. We can't afford that. Moretti knows the situation. Since you're one of the few people in a position to positively identify these bastards, we need your eyes on this. If you can make an identification, we'll take him down quietly. In the meantime, we'll stake out the place, see what's what, and take it from there, unless you have a better idea."

"Not really."

He parked several blocks away, reconsidered my appearance and his, and approached one of the street vendors. He purchased several touristy items and handed me a pair of yoga pants, sweatshirt, and a baseball cap. "Find a bathroom and get changed. It wouldn't hurt to wash your face either."

"Thanks."

He rolled his eyes, removed his jacket, rolled up his sleeves, and pulled a jersey on over his dress shirt, making sure it was long enough and baggy enough to conceal his gun and cuffs. Then he put on a beanie and checked his reflection in the car window. "How do I look?"

"Very gangsta," I replied. "I'll be back in a second. Don't get hassled by the po-po while I'm gone."

TWENTY-EIGHT

"Talk about feeling old," Heathcliff whispered in my ear. We were seated on the same side of the table, like those nauseatingly lovey-dovey couples. Thankfully, Martin was too refined to try a move like that, or I would have been forced to knock some sense into him. But sitting beside the detective in this instance allowed us to have an equal vantage point in surveying the entirety of the restaurant. He slung his arm around my shoulders and took a slow sip from his cup. "These people cannot be that much younger than I am, but they have an entirely different existence. I feel like a grandpa watching preschoolers play."

I adjusted the lightly tinted sunglasses on my nose. "I don't think I was ever that naïve, and I doubt you were ever that relaxed or carefree."

"I can be relaxed."

I laughed, brushing my cheek against his shoulder. "Having to down a six pack to get there doesn't count."

The one thing Heathcliff was exceptionally good at was blending in. He'd done extensive undercover work before he transferred to the major crimes division. As far as I knew, the only time he'd burned a cover was for me. Even now, dressed like a couple of gullible tourists, he made sure the oddity of our presence wasn't actually that odd. In fact, in the last forty-five minutes, I'd seen at least three different groups of people enter in similar garb to order coffees. Although, most only stayed a few minutes before returning to their sightseeing.

"Can I get you another one?" the waitress asked. Most coffee shops didn't have a wait staff, but with the way these computer freaks were buried behind their screens, they'd stay for days at a time and never think to order a second coffee or muffin.

"Go ahead, honey," Heathcliff nudged me. "It's our vacation. You get to splurge."

"Don't tempt me, or I'm totally going to get one of those hot chocolate frappes."

Heathcliff smiled at the woman. "We'll take one of those and an extra large cookie." He reached into his pocket and pulled out a twenty. "Keep the change."

"You just bought me a hot chocolate," I cooed, leaning closer so I could get a better look at the man seated at our ten o'clock. He was across the room from us. I'd made him the moment we entered the coffee shop, but he hadn't looked up from his computer. He wore a dark red jacket and kept the hood up. He wore jeans and classic Adidas sneakers that I hadn't seen lately but were all the rage in Eastern Europe. "How did I get so lucky?"

"I'll make sure to get reimbursed," Heathcliff replied in a teasing, flirty tone. I'd never actually heard him flirt. Even when we'd been undercover as a couple, he had exuded dominance and possession. This was different and rather disconcerting. "Is that carefree enough for you?" His eyes scanned the room. "Red Hood looks like our best bet, but what about *Watchmen* t-shirt at two o'clock?"

I shifted against him, fumbling to pull my phone from my pocket. Stretching my arm out as far as possible, I held the phone up and snuggled closer to the detective as if taking a selfie. Instead, I clicked a few zoomed in shots of the man in the comic book t-shirt. While we waited for the waitress to return with our order before continuing our conversation, I examined the photographs.

She returned with a smile. "The two of you are

absolutely adorbs. Where are you from?" She placed the frappe and cookie on the table.

"A small town no one's ever heard of," Heathcliff replied easily. "It's insane how many things there are to see and do here." He squeezed my shoulder playfully. "And this one just wanted to spend the afternoon relaxing and indulging in sugar and caffeine."

"It's not my fault the only good coffee place in town closed down," I retorted.

She laughed. "Well, since you're splurging, I added some extra marshmallow whip to your drink."

"Awesome." I gave her a bright smile, and she disappeared behind the counter to assist the other baristas in serving the sudden influx of customers.

"What do you think?" Heathcliff asked, glancing down at the photos on my phone.

"I don't recognize him, but that doesn't mean much. We need to get a better look at the computer, but my bet's on Red Hood. It's also possible anyone of interest left when things got hot."

"I know." Frowning, Heathcliff took a bite of his cookie. His eyes narrowed and twitched, analyzing everyone in the room. "I don't think anyone's carrying. No one's spoken, so we can't pick up on accents. We'll give it another five minutes, and then I'll make a pass."

I chuckled, lifting the cup to my mouth to shield my lips while I whispered, "I thought we were just staking out the place."

"Stakeouts are boring, and we don't have time for this."

"Agreed." Taking a sip of the sugar-laden, cocoa-infused beverage, I was equally delighted and repulsed at the same time. It wasn't that dissimilar of an experience from the hot fudge sundaes and champagne. I really needed to start watching what I ate and drank.

When another two groups of people filed into the crowded café, Heathcliff stood and stretched. The main entrance was blocked by the lengthy line, making getting out in a hurry nearly impossible. Since that increased our chances of making an arrest should one of the men prove our suspicions right, he brushed past the *Watchmen* guy.

My gaze flicked between the man he just bumped into and the mark across the room. Red Hood didn't bother looking up, which meant he wasn't nervous. It might also mean he wasn't our guy.

Maneuvering through the waiting line, Heathcliff crossed to the other side of the room. The bathrooms were in the back corner, but aside from a couple of women darting in and out after placing an order, none of the computer addicts had used the facilities. Heathcliff stepped out of the way of a woman reaching for sweetener packets and jostled Red Hood. From where I was, I couldn't hear the exchange, but Heathcliff wasn't apologizing or backing off.

Sensing the detective might be a second away from announcing, I got up from the table and pushed through the line, uttering excuse me until I was within hearing distance. Glancing back, I made sure *Watchmen* t-shirt didn't make a break for it. Until Heathcliff made his move, I couldn't be certain anyone else inside the café wasn't part of the anarchist hit squad.

"Are you sure I don't know you?" Heathcliff blotted spilled coffee with a handful of napkins. "You look so familiar."

"No." Red Hood shook his head emphatically. "I'm just visiting." He had an accent, but I couldn't determine what it was. It sounded a bit British mixed with something else.

"Hey, me too," Heathcliff exclaimed. "Where are you from?" The man didn't answer. Instead, he folded up his laptop and shoved it inside a reinforced bag. Derek's eyes glanced back at our table. When he didn't find me, he did a quick scan of the room. He made eye contact and nodded. "Dude, you know Stavos, right?"

For a split second, Red Hood went completely motionless. The blood drained from his face. Then he bolted for the door. He made it eight feet before I grabbed the strap of his bag. He jerked sideways, grabbing the other strap with both hands and tugging hard.

"Fine." I let go, and the momentum flung him backward against the door. The door unexpectedly opened, and he landed on the sidewalk. I was on top of him before he had time to process what just happened. I shoved him over, clinking on the cuffs before the detective made it outside. "Stand up," I ordered, grabbing the crook of his elbow and hauling him to his feet.

Heathcliff stepped outside, giving the coffeehouse another uncertain look. "Are there any other anarchists inside?" He moved around to face the cuffed man. "Answer me. Are more of your people inside that café?" The man didn't speak. "We might as well take him to the car. If someone else is working with Anarkhos, they've already sent word of what's happened."

"What's your name?" I asked, dragging the man down the sidewalk. "We have an entire file on your group. We have photos and bios. I'm pretty sure I've seen your ugly mug glorified in black and white. So save us some time, and we'll work on making things a bit more pleasant for you."

The man abruptly stopped, refusing to move. I shoved him forward. He pushed back, dropping to his knees, determined to make everything as difficult as possible. Hell, he should work for the CIA.

"On your feet," Heathcliff ordered, noticing the looks we were getting from passersby. He held up his badge. "Police business. Move along." He knelt down, hauling the man to his feet. "We need to get him in the car before one of these chuckleheads records this and posts it on the internet."

"Agreed."

Taking one elbow while Heathcliff took the other, we dragged the man down the street to the car. I kept a hand on the man's arm while Heathcliff opened the rear door. When I moved to push Red Hood inside, he bent his knees and reared up, knocking his shoulder into my bruised ribs. The force knocked me to the ground, and I howled. Luckily, I tripped the anarchist, who fell face first onto the asphalt. Heathcliff pounced on top of him in a split second.

Furious, Heathcliff literally threw the man into the back of the car and slammed the door. "You okay?" he asked, offering me a hand up.

"Yeah." I winced, holding my arm against my ribs while I went around and got inside the car. Turning in the seat, I glowered at the man. The frigid cold of my death stare practically caused the windows to frost over. "Since you don't want to play nice, neither will we. We'll make sure we broadcast on every law enforcement channel and throughout every database that you are cooperating with the U.S. government and the CIA in providing technological skills and know-how to thwart all future intrusions into our systems and you are a valuable asset we will use in our fight to dismantle Anarkhos. Your buddies will never trust you again, and whatever they have planned for Kiter will pale in comparison to what they'll do to you."

The man swallowed. "If I answer your questions, you will make no record of my involvement."

"I'll consider it, but you have to tell us what Anarkhos is planning," I said.

"We need to know everything there is on the bombs and their locations," Heathcliff added, glancing at the man from the rearview mirror.

"I can't," Red Hood insisted.

"You have ten minutes to change your mind." Heathcliff pulled into traffic. "Once we take you through booking, it'll be too late."

I looked back at Red Hood. "Think fast."

While he was mulling over the possibilities, I put on gloves and checked the compartments of his computer bag for weapons. He didn't have any on his person when I frisked him while he was on the ground, but that didn't mean he didn't have something in his bag. He might even have a tracker.

"Loop around," I whispered. "We need to make sure Anarkhos doesn't have its dog on a leash." I searched every compartment, groove, and crevice of the bag. I didn't find anything obvious. Besides the computer, I found a blank notepad and pen, a few passports in various names, some stolen credit cards, and a wad of cash. He also had a receipt from a diner and a few brochures. Based on the date and timestamp on the receipt, I imagined that was where he ate last night.

"Anything?" The detective tore his eyes off the road to see what I had found.

"Maybe, but there's no smoking gun." I continued searching, but I didn't find anything else. "His computer might prove useful, but I'm not touching it. We'll let the professionals do that."

Heathcliff checked the rearview mirror again. "I don't think we're being followed." His eyes went to our prisoner. "What's it going to be, buddy? We'll send you home with a one-way ticket, or we'll make sure your friends want you dead. It's your choice."

"What do you want to know?" Red Hood asked.

"For starters, where's Guillermo Vega?" I asked.

He swallowed. "Busy."

"Planting explosives?" Heathcliff asked.

"No." He blinked a few times. "That's a bluff."

"Right." Heathcliff snorted. "The reason I was nearly burnt to a crisp was just a bluff."

"You weren't. We could have done it if we wanted, but we didn't. We do not hurt people. We do not kill people. You do."

"Do you want to make sure you learn that lesson firsthand?" I snapped. "We are trying to save lives. You're the ones threatening to destroy them."

"You kidnapped Stavos. You filled his head with lies. You used him. You forced him to betray us. We had to resort to these measures to liberate him."

"We've agreed to surrender Stavos. We just need more time." I stuck with the OIO negotiator's lie.

"That's doubtful," Red Hood replied. "You don't even know where he is."

"Do you?" I asked. From the look on his face, he didn't have a clue. "Call off the attack, and we'll locate Stavos together. Once you have him back, we'll send you home."

"I don't believe you," Red Hood insisted. Honestly, I didn't believe me either.

TWENTY-NINE

"How many bombs have you built? Where are they planted?"

Adrian Bashar, the man we arrested at the coffee shop, stared blankly up at me. I might as well be speaking another language. "Bring me my computer."

"Answer the fucking question. Where's the bomb?" I'd been asking the same questions or some version of them repeatedly for the last forty minutes, but Bashar wouldn't talk. We hadn't even officially arrested him yet. We had done what we could to conceal his identity from the security cameras on the off chance Anarkhos was watching, so we were protected for now. I just didn't know how much longer it would last.

"There is no bomb."

I leaned across the table, inches from his face. "It's within my right to treat you as an enemy of the state. Your actions reek of terrorism. You can be detained indefinitely, but if you prevent another strike, we'll let you go."

He rolled his eyes, illustrating his contempt for my words and empty promises. I was out of my depth, and he knew it. This was why those shmucks at the CIA had their black sites and enhanced interrogation techniques. Maybe they were illegal. Maybe they violated every moral and ethical standard of a civilized world, but perhaps it was the only way to get uncooperative assholes like this to talk.

"We believe in a free society, not one oppressed by government secrecy and rules. You are nothing but a mechanism of that oppression."

No matter what I did, he wouldn't stay on topic. He wouldn't answer the question. All he did was spout out ideological rhetoric. I slapped him hard enough to make his eye tear. "Just answer the question. Where are the bombs?"

"Parker," Heathcliff called from the doorway, "I need to speak to you. Jacobs will take over."

I leaned back. "In a minute."

"Now." Heathcliff stepped away from the door so Jacobs could enter.

I grabbed the Anarkhos file off the table and left the interrogation room, following Heathcliff into the adjoining observation room. The cameras had been disconnected inside interrogation to make sure they couldn't be remotely accessed. Lt. Moretti wasn't taking any risks, and the rest of the police department seemed to be equally onboard. I could probably get away with murdering the anarchist, but I didn't think hosting a séance to communicate with his spirit would yield better results. The man just wouldn't talk.

"Do we have an ID yet?" Heathcliff asked. "I'm getting tired of calling him Red Hood. He's not a supervillain."

"Adrian Bashar." I handed the dossier to Heathcliff and pointed at the photo. "Aside from a list of suspected hacker activity, there isn't much to go on."

"Where'd you get this?" He flipped through the other photos, analyzing Anarkhos' rank and file.

"Reece gave it to us. Jablonsky had Agent Lawson drop it off when he heard about the arrest."

"Why isn't your boss here? Isn't this a major breakthrough?"

"Mark trusts my judgment. He also needs plausible deniability in order to force CIA Agent Reece to turn over Kiter. So he doesn't want to know anything about who we have or what we're doing."

"Speaking of which, what are you doing?"

"Trying to stop another tragedy. Aren't we on the same page?"

"I'm not sure. I've been watching you inside that room. Bashar's close to breaking you."

"Funny. I'm the one asking the questions."

Heathcliff dropped the file back on the table. "He's not responding the way you'd like, and I don't think he's going to. He knows he's done. There is no out. There is no safe passage home. This is it. The promises we've made are nothing but lies. He realized it the second we arrested him. He's not going to talk."

"Then we make him."

The detective straightened his posture. "I will be damned if I let these shitheads detonate another explosive in my city, but there's a line, Alex. Don't tell me you weren't about to cross it."

"I wasn't."

"Bullshit." He blew out a slow breath. "We have Bashar's computer. Jacobs found half a dozen vendors that supplied the materials used in the construction site bombing. We have officers canvassing the shops and the area. The merchants are cooperating. We are exploring other avenues. More roads are opening as we speak. We are going to stop this. But first, I need to stop you from doing something you'll regret."

"I wasn't."

"Don't lie to me or yourself, not after the things we've seen and done." He shook his head, fighting to keep away the emotions. "I've gone down this road with you before. It was a different situation, but it royally fucked us over. So don't stand there and tell me you weren't half a second away from slamming his head into the table or worse."

"We have to stop this. Whatever it takes." Jacobs' words reverberated in my mind. If anything should happen, it was my fault. I wouldn't let innocent people pay for my mistakes. Bashar wasn't innocent, and neither was Anarkhos. That meant they could pay. They should pay for what they'd done and what they planned to do.

"Not like this." He took a step closer and lowered his voice. "I won't follow you over the line again. If you cross it, you're on your own. I won't cover for you, and I won't help you."

"I didn't ask you to."

"Good." Heathcliff stepped back. "From here on out, stay away from Bashar, unless you plan to make this official and take him into federal custody."

"You know I can't do that. Jablonsky doesn't want this to get back to the CIA. We're having enough trouble getting Reece's boss to force him to cooperate. If they find out we have a second asset, that'll botch our negotiation, and we'll never get Anarkhos to disarm the bombs. That's why Agent Lawson and the police techs are working on decoding Bashar's computer at the precinct. It's why we're keeping his arrest quiet. If he doesn't tell us how to disarm the bombs or what the targets are, then there's no point."

"Parker." Heathcliff tried to derail my rant, but I continued to sputter out all the reasons why I needed him to go along with my carte blanche interrogation tactics. "Stop." He grabbed my arm roughly and spun me around to face the glass.

"Mr. Bashar," Jacobs took the pen and a sheet of paper from Bashar's hand, "thank you for your cooperation. Sit tight. I'll have someone bring you something to eat."

"What the hell?" Before I could ask what I missed, Jacobs came into the room. "What'd he say?"

"They built three devices. Two have already been detonated. The third is with another member of Anarkhos, but Bashar doesn't know his location or the target," Jacobs said.

None of that made sense. "Why would he tell you any of that?"

"The man's hungry," Jacobs retorted. "I went inside, offered him a candy bar, and said I'd get him something to eat if he shared some information."

"And you believe him?" I stared through the two-way mirror, watching as one of the officers entered with a sandwich, bag of chips, and a bottle of water.

"Not necessarily, but it's a start. We need to build a

relationship. From what I've read, he's one of these cloistered, brainy types. He believes he's the smartest man in the room. It won't hurt to let him think that. He'll get cocky and slip up. They always do." Jacobs glanced between Heathcliff and me. "Did I interrupt something?"

"No." Heathcliff gave me another look. "I believe we're done here. That is, if Parker's done."

"I guess I am." I looked back into the interrogation room. "Make sure someone keeps a constant eye on him. I don't trust him not to do something asinine."

"We'll have two officers outside the door, one in the room, and one in here," Jacobs replied. "That's on Moretti's orders."

"Great." I went out the door, following Jacobs to the IT department. "Have we made any progress on cracking the computer?"

"Lawson's taken over, so I'll let you wrangle your people. I don't want to overstep." Jacobs gave me a friendly wink to let me know the jab was in good fun. Apparently, he and Heathcliff were in the midst of a role reversal based on our recent progress. While Jacobs was fine letting bygones be bygones now that we had a fighting chance of stopping another attack, Heathcliff had decided I was a liability and reckless. Perhaps it was because he knew me and realized I had turned into the thing I always despised.

Lawson and the police techs were having problems decrypting the password to access Bashar's computer. It was slow going on account of the fear of it being booby-trapped. As it stood, Lawson was certain that after a set number of failed attempts to access the computer, the hard drive would automatically initiate an internal wipe. After hooking it to various diagnostic tools and other equipment, Lawson gave me another look and shook his head.

"We need Bashar to bypass the biometric scanners. This laptop is rigged with more security protocols than the underground bunker at the White House."

"Don't say bunker." I glanced back at Jacobs. "The asshole kept insisting we bring him the computer. I'm not certain this is a good idea. What do you think, Detective? He's your new best friend. It's your call."

Jacobs sucked on his bottom lip. "What do you guys think?" he asked the police techs, who shrugged. "Is there any way to ensure he won't use the opportunity to contact other members of his team or erase the drive before you can access it?"

"We'll keep him cuffed," Lawson said. "We don't need his cooperation, just his fingerprint and perhaps his face."

"You decide, Parker," Jacobs said. I looked at Heathcliff, figuring he'd have some remark to add, but he stared silently at the laptop.

"Okay, let's give the man a chance to redeem himself. Shall we?" I gestured to the door, and Lawson unhooked the computer and placed it back inside the bag.

Heathcliff led the way up the steps and back to the interrogation room. Jacobs detoured to update Moretti on the situation and the potential progress we were making. The officer inside the room stepped out when the three of us entered.

At the sight of the computer, Bashar perked up. He wiped the crumbs off the table as best he could with cuffed hands and rubbed his palms together. He was like a junky about to get a fix.

"We need you to unlock your computer." Lawson knelt next to the table, checking the laptop again before hooking some other devices to it. "What's your password?"

"Fuck you," Bashar responded.

Ignoring the remark, Lawson put the computer barely within reach of Bashar's bound hands. He reached for the anarchist's fingers, but Bashar curled his hands into fists. "You're going to cooperate whether you want to or not." Lawson struggled with the prisoner, and I pinned one of Bashar's wrists to the table in an attempt to assist. He rocked side to side in the chair, attempting to buck us away.

Without a word, Heathcliff came around the table, locking Bashar in a one-armed chokehold against the chair. "Cooperate or I'll cut off your fucking finger."

At Heathcliff's deep, booming voice, Bashar stopped fighting, and Lawson used our captive's prints to unlock the outermost level of the computer's security system. We now had access to the main computer interface. Unfortunately, most of the data was protected by individual security measures and passwords.

"I'll get started cracking these." Lawson lifted the computer off the table. "It shouldn't be long now."

Bashar let out an angry, frustrated scream, and Heathcliff released him. The detective scooped the empty computer bag off the table to be cataloged as evidence.

When we left the room, I tossed a confused look at him. "Someone's being particularly mercurial today."

He tossed an annoyed glance in my direction. "I wasn't going to do it. We just needed him to believe it."

"Hell, I believed it." I nudged his shoulder with mine. "For the record, I would have covered for you."

Although he didn't look up from the bag, I could tell that comment aggravated him. We returned to the bullpen of the major crimes division, but Heathcliff was practically buried inside the bag. When we made it to his desk, he emptied the contents, placing each item in a separate evidence bag. The pen and paper caught his eye, and he flipped through the blank notepad. It was insignificant. The pen, on the other hand, made him pause. He rolled it between his gloved fingers and picked up the phone.

"Yes, maybe you can help me," Heathcliff said to whoever he called before identifying himself. "Do you have a guest by any of these names staying with you?" He reached for one of the evidence bags and flipped through the various credit cards, reading off the names as he went. "You do?" He paused. "Excellent. Please make sure no one enters the room. Call off housekeeping. I'm on my way." He hung up the phone, sealing several of the bags and grabbing a set of keys and his jacket. "We need to move on this. I know where Bashar's been staying. Maybe he left something useful behind."

THIRTY

"Housekeeping wasn't supposed to clean the room," Heathcliff insisted, "so where the hell is everything?"

"They must have packed light." The beds were unmade. The motel provided toiletries had been opened and partially used, but those were the only indicators anyone had been inside the room. "I'm guessing Vega was here." I nodded at the second bed. "We could have forensics check for prints and swab for DNA."

Derek gave me an incredulous look. "DNA in a motel room? We'd be running the samples for the next ten years, unless of course you have Vega's DNA on file."

"I'll let you call Agent Reece and ask."

"I'm sure Anarkhos hacked into the database and deleted it, just like they did the security footage and credit card records from the motel." Heathcliff continued to meticulously search the room. At the moment, he was on his hands and knees, checking beneath the bed and night table. "If the desk clerk I spoke to hadn't been the one who checked Bashar in with the stolen credit card, we never would have known he stayed here."

"How did you know he was here?" I moved into the bathroom and shook out the towels before removing the toilet tank lid.

"The pen had the motel logo."

"But it's a chain. How did you know it'd be this one?"

"It was closest to the coffee shop. Jealous you didn't come to that conclusion yourself? Damn, Parker, you're slipping."

Returning to the main room with a wet Ziploc bag hanging from the end of my pen, I cleared my throat. "Since you're the savant, would you call this a clue?"

He got to his feet. "What do we have here?"

I unzipped the bag and emptied the contents onto the bed. A metal tie clip, some cash, more brochures like the ones we'd found in Bashar's computer bag, and a rough drawing on a napkin spilled out. Heathcliff picked up the tie clip and turned it over in his hands. He crossed the room to the wardrobe, checked inside, and gave the closet and drawers another look. We'd already searched the furniture once, but he was looking for a suit or tie to go with the clip.

"Ah-ha." He held out his opened palm.

"That's the sound a real detective makes when he finds a clue," I teased, looking at the broken tie clip. "Shit. It's a memory card. I'll be damned."

Heathcliff grinned, the first sign I had been forgiven, and placed it and the rest of the items inside an evidence bag. Then he placed the wet Ziploc into a separate bag. "I'll have CSU check the rest of the room. We have copies of the security cam footage for the last two weeks to analyze, but like I said, these anarchist hackers wiped it. I don't think it's a priority given the givens, but it can't hurt to take it with us." He surveyed the room again. "Actually, there's one other place I want to check."

He opened the door to the balcony. Outside were a set of plastic chairs and a tiny plastic table. On the table was an ashtray, but it had been emptied. After examining every possible hidey hole for additional clues, Heathcliff returned to the main room. As we exited, two men in jumpsuits came in to give the room the full workup.

"What do you think is on the drive?" I asked. "Government secrets? The President's sex tape? A billion dollars in bitcoin?"

"I'd settle for a method to deactivate the bomb and the

time and place where they plan to detonate it."

While he drove, I studied the items we collected. Cash, credit cards, and a hidden computer drive made sense. These were tech-savvy terrorists. "Which of these items is not like the rest?" Mumbling to myself, I manipulated the materials inside the bag to get a better look at the brochures. From the outside, they looked like nothing special. They were for various shops, local outdoor events, and tourist sites, but they had to be significant if Bashar or Vega thought they were important enough to stow in the hotel's toilet tank. That also meant they didn't want us to find them.

"Do you think those are targets?" Derek asked, eyeing the bag on my lap.

"I don't see how taking the nature trails at the park would constitute much of a target." I recalled the locations the CIA asked us to protect. Digging my phone out of my pocket, I dialed Agent Davis. "E-mail me a list of the locations we've been monitoring. I'm working on a hunch." He tried to protest, arguing the units had been pulled off those buildings after Anarkhos made contact, but I didn't care. "Look, unless you know for a fact this is a waste of time, forward me the intel."

When we returned to the precinct, Heathcliff took the security cam footage and the drive to the IT department while I donned a pair of gloves and removed the brochures we'd recovered from Bashar's computer bag and the toilet tank. Quickly, I jotted down the ten locations depicted and brought up a map of the city. After a quick comparison to the locations the CIA asked us to monitor and protect when they were still determined to keep us out of the loop, I didn't see much of an overlap or any obvious pattern.

"Here," Detective Jacobs cleared off the desk and unrolled a map of the city, "this might make it easier."

"How are things going on your end?" I circled the possible CIA sites in blue and the brochure locations in red. Some were close, just not close enough.

"I made a copy of the photos in your anarchist file and showed them to the vendors. Get this, every transaction had been erased."

I stopped what I was doing and stared at him. "So we're nowhere."

"Not necessarily. These are vendors dealing in construction materials. Most of them had hard copies or carbon copies. They recognized our boy Adrian and your buddy Vega. I even tossed around Kiter's photo, but they hadn't seen him or anyone else in that dossier. I'm hoping that means we just need to capture Vega to put this thing to bed."

"From your lips to god's ears. So we know the quantities and items purchased. Any idea how many IEDs these shitheads made or how large of an impact we should expect?"

Jacobs picked up the brochure I put down and flipped through it. "The bomb squad is working on a mock-up based on what we already know of the previous devices. I forwarded the list to the FBI techs to conduct their own analysis. I figured two heads are better than one."

"Thanks." I opened another brochure and held it up to the light. "That's weird." Inside the brochure was a small map with directions to the location. Nothing was written on the map, but there were some pinprick holes through it. "Let me see that one." I took the brochure from Jacobs and held it to the light. Sure enough, that map had a few pinpricks too. Grabbing a green pen, I marked the pinpricks from each of the ten brochures on the city map. "Is your crime lab capable of imaging? I want these run through the full gamut. They need to be checked for holes, invisible ink, indentions and impression, and anything else that might be of use."

"No prob." Jacobs scooped up the brochures and led the way to the crime lab.

While we waited for the scans to complete, Heathcliff barged into the room. "The drive wasn't encoded. We have the schematics for the IED. We also have copies of the blueprints from the Branded Telecom building and several city maps."

"Was anything marked?" I asked.

"Nothing you don't already know about. They had extensive notes on accessing the BT building. From what we can tell, they never mapped out any other targets."

"That's not what the brochures indicate," Jacobs added, catching Heathcliff up to speed. "We know they have enough raw materials for at least another device, possibly more. I'm waiting for the bomb squad to get back to me."

Leaning against the wall, I closed my eyes, listening to the hum of the scanner and the detectives' chatter. We were missing something. Anarkhos wanted Kiter. They never planned to ransom the city in order to get him. They thought they'd come in, spring him from the CIA's secret facility, and what?

"Jacobs," I said, halting the conversation, "we need to know what Anarkhos planned to do with Kiter before their plan went to shit. Did Bashar tell you?"

"No."

"They want him on a plane out of the country," Heathcliff said. "We already know this. That's what they demanded from the FBI."

"What if it's bullshit? It could be another misdirection. We never knew if they planned to kill Kiter or take him back with open arms. We aren't even certain if he was abducted by the CIA or if he turned on Anarkhos."

"Alex," Heathcliff gave me that worried look of his, like I was close to having a break from reality, "why does this matter? How is that going to get us closer to locating their next target?"

My eyes flashed to the computer screen where the first of the brochures had just completed a final scan. The monitor was divided into six segments, each with a different scanned version of the paper. The pinpricks were illuminated, as were some indentions. Stray marks on the front were inconsequential, but the series of numbers that had been written above the map was not.

"Is that an address?" I asked the tech, ignoring Derek's question and pointing at the screen.

"It looks like longitude and latitude. It was probably written on a sheet of paper that was on top of the brochure and the pressure from the writing implement remained undetectable to the naked eye," the woman replied.

"Parker?" Jacobs queried, hoping I'd get back to

answering Derek's question.

"Don't waste time," I ordered, "just check the rest for pinpricks and indentions."

"Yes, ma'am." The woman clicked a few keys and changed the setting on the instruments. My foot tapped impatiently while the rest of the brochures were scanned. Each had a different set of coordinates. Whoever wrote them down did so while examining the maps on the brochures to make sure they corresponded. "That's all of them," the tech declared, and I scribbled down the ten sets of coordinates.

"We'll send units to check these out," Jacobs offered, reaching for the paper.

"This needs to be done carefully. No uniforms, no police cars, no nothing." Reluctantly, I handed over the paper. "I can have my people follow this lead."

"And a bunch of men in cheap suits isn't suspicious?" Jacobs challenged. "We're closer. We can get this done now. We won't fuck up."

"Okay."

"Parker," Heathcliff hissed while Jacobs raced up the steps to pass the coordinates on to Moretti so undercovers could scour the locations for additional devices, "tell me what's going through your head right now."

"From the dicta Bashar's been spouting and the rhetoric I've read in the Anarkhos file, they don't believe in violence. They don't believe in killing. The government kills, and their entire mission is to disseminate the evils the government commits in the hopes of causing an uprising. I think they plan to use Kiter as an example or a martyr. I'm not entirely sure, but since they threatened to detonate another device, they must know we'll come out in force." I focused on the wall, not seeing anything but the rampant thoughts that were fueling what might be nothing more than paranoia. "We need to question Bashar again. We have more evidence. We won't be able to bribe him or barter, but we have a better chance of pulling off a convincing bluff now that we possess these additional details."

"What if you're reading this wrong? Waiting might be

better."

"Let me go in alone. It'll give you a second shot if I screw this up." I gave him a grim smile. "Please."

"Okay, but I better not regret it."

"That makes two of us." I moved past interrogation in the hopes of tracking down Lawson. Hopefully, the FBI's resident tech had made progress on cracking the laptop. "I'm about to go in for round two," I announced to the IT department, most of whom ignored me. "Any idea what Bashar's weaknesses might be?"

"Whatever they are doesn't involve the use of computers." Lawson didn't even glance up. "His coding is ridiculous. It's beyond my capabilities. Unless he decides to unlock the entire CPU, we'll need to source this out. Sorry I can't be of more help."

"Update Jablonsky, and get back to the OIO as soon as you can."

"Roger that."

"Well, that didn't work out the way I hoped." I stepped back into the hallway. Cracking my knuckles, I smirked. "Guess this won't be an easy K.O."

"Make sure there isn't a K.O." Heathcliff moved past me into the observation room so he could watch the show.

THIRTY-ONE

I sat down, crossing my legs and smiling at Adrian Bashar. The first time I tried this I was rigid and desperate. This time, I wanted him to believe that was no longer the case. Playing with the tip of my ponytail, I twirled it around my finger a few times before letting it swing back into place.

"How was your stay at the motel?" I asked. "You didn't bother to fill out the comment card, but I'm guessing you must have enjoyed it. Continental breakfast, in-room coffeemaker, cable TV, it's the American dream, my friend." He didn't respond, so I continued. "You probably should have spent more time watching TV. Then you would have realized hiding contraband inside the toilet tank is a rookie move. That's where every drug dealer on every crime show always hides his stash. And I mean always."

He swallowed involuntarily, remaining stock still in the hopes I wouldn't notice a change in his posture. Too bad he was trying too hard. That had been my problem the first time around.

"Yeah, we found it. The brochures with the hidden maps. The bomb schematics. The blueprints for the Branded Telecom building. The stolen credit cards." I gave my ponytail another twirl. "Are you certain you don't want to offer a blanket denial or some sort of explanation? I'd even settle for an ominous warning." I waited. "No? Nothing? That's disappointing. I take it Vega's in charge of the ominous warnings. From what I've seen, he's also in charge of making things go boom, at least on military bases. What are you? His tech support in case he can't figure out how to trigger the bomb?"

"The devices we build aren't bombs," Bashar declared.

"I'll bite. What do you call them?"

He glared at me from across the table. "Delivery systems."

"For the EMPs?"

He nodded. "I've already told you we do not kill people. If we did, you would be dead. I made certain you and the police didn't turn to ash, even though you are the tools the government uses to enforce their structure and exert control. The world would be better off without agents like you."

"Yeah, but at least we get medical and dental."

He sneered. "Agent Alexis Parker," his eyes never wavered as he rattled off my home address and phone number, "we know you. Honestly, we thought you might be different. That you might have proven yourself to be an ally, but we were mistaken."

"I don't side with terrorists."

"But you have acted against your government, against their orders and rules, in order to rectify injustices. You have fulfilled a greater purpose to protect society and not just the few elitists in power. Wouldn't they imprison you for your crimes if they knew about them?"

My blood ran cold. "You're full of shit."

"Maybe, but we can create anything. We can make information disappear just as easily as we can create our own truths, plant them within, and make it appear as if they always existed." He leaned closer. "That's what your government does. That's why they wanted Stavos."

"What are you planning to do with him when you get him back?" I asked, glad that we were talking about something pertinent besides my alleged indiscretions that weren't quite so hypothetical.

"We don't have to do anything to him. Your government will show its true nature before they ever release him. They'll abuse their power and knowledge to keep their secrets in the dark. All we're going to do is shine a light on the truth."

"How?"

"You'll see."

I wanted to scream. But it was no use, he wouldn't say anything more. "Thanks for your time. It was illuminating." I went out the door, holding it open so an officer could enter to keep watch over the prisoner.

"Well?" Heathcliff appeared in the doorway with his arms folded across his chest.

"That was absolutely pointless." The conversation bothered me, but there were too many things to pinpoint exactly which one was causing the buzzing behind my eyes. "Actually, he just admitted to blowing up the construction site and nearly barbequing us."

"I heard." Heathcliff gave the closed door a concerned look. "That worries me. It's like he's given up."

"Or he knows something we don't." Before I could say anything else, my phone rang. "It's Jablonsky." Answering the call, I held it to my ear. "Do we have Kiter yet?"

"No. You need to get back to the office. I had to cut my conversation with Lawson short on account of Moretti calling. It sounds like you've done as much as you can over there. We're going to let the police scout those ten locations. In the meantime, Reece and the CIA are back on our side. I'll fill you in on the rest when you get here."

"Okay."

From his tone, he didn't sound particularly encouraged by our latest findings or the fact that we were back to being one big happy family with the intelligence operatives. Something was wrong. I just didn't know what. I gave the interrogation room another glance.

"I'm going back to the federal building, but if something shakes loose, you know the drill."

"Yep." Heathcliff gave me the quick once-over. "You might want to change your clothes so those CIA assholes will take you seriously."

I looked down at the yoga pants and sweatshirt. "Good call."

*   *   *

The drive back to the federal building didn't take any time. In fact, I was searching the trunk of my personal vehicle for a spare outfit when Lawson pulled into the garage. His brow crinkled, and he gave me a confused look.

"How'd you get here so fast?"

"Lights. Sirens. A general disregard for my own safety and that of other motorists."

"Huh." We got into the elevator together, and he turned his back while I stripped out of the yoga pants and slipped into a pair of dress slacks. "You should know," he said, glancing briefly over his shoulder, "that the tracker in your hip wasn't one of ours. It's possible the CIA buys their toys off the books for their clandestine ventures, but they're denying it."

I snorted, shedding the sweatshirt and slipping into a button-up blouse. "Of course they are. They've denied everything. Do you know if the Director confronted them about it?"

"I have no idea." Lawson faced the elevator doors while I hurriedly fastened the buttons. "I barely had time to run any diagnostics on it before Vega called again and pandemonium rained down on us." He chuckled. "I must say, these men are exceptional anarchists. A single call throws us into utter chaos."

"Don't let Jablonsky hear you fanboying out about it."

"I'm no fan. I just wish I had half the coding ability they do. We're out of our depth. Cybercrimes might be able to handle this better than we can." He patted the computer bag.

"Get clearance and pass it on to them." The elevator opened, and I picked up the clothing I just shed and went straight to Mark's office. "I'm not sure being exiled for most of the day was particularly productive, but I like being recalled even less. What happened?"

"A lot." Mark rubbed his eyes. "Vega just called.

Somehow, he discovered Kiter is still in U.S. custody. He knows we lied, so he changed his demands. No more airport. No plane. He wants Kiter released in the next two hours, or he'll detonate another device. Reece and the CIA are now assisting us in stopping another attack on U.S. soil. After what happened to you and the police officers, we have no choice but to assume Vega plans on inflicting as many civilian casualties as possible."

"Dammit."

Mark grabbed some things off his desk. "Vega says he'll meet us at the designated location and hand over the deactivation code and location of the device." He gestured to the door, waiting for me to lead the way out. "But he has something up his sleeve. Walking into that situation, bomb or no bomb, he has to know he won't be walking away. He must realize we won't willingly turn over Kiter. That's why he used such extreme measures on the bases." He shook his head, biting back whatever curses he might have wanted to utter. "This is a ploy. I don't imagine it will end well."

"What did Reece say?"

"That prick has his head so far up his own ass he can't see the light of day."

"But he's cooperating?"

"If you want to call it that. Kendall had to call in every chit he had. The CIA thinks they have the market on stopping imminent attacks and their actions are wholly justified. The last thing they want is for any of this to become public. It's bad enough they are operating several black sites right under our noses, but now that one of their assets is the cause of the current threat, I don't know what's going to happen. Those Anarkhos assholes know exactly how to strike. They've demonstrated the rift between our own agencies, the line between what the government does and what the people know about, and to top it off, they'll probably blow us all to kingdom come before everything is said and done." He let out a lengthy exhale as we continued down the corridor. "That's why you're staying here."

I stopped dead in my tracks. "What? You need every

available agent in the field."

"No, I need every available agent to do her damn job. We have tac teams on standby. The exchange will be covered. The CIA is sending a team to deliver Kiter to us twenty minutes before the deadline. From there, we'll take a convoy to the drop site. This way, the spooks get to keep their site secure and secret. While I'm gone, you are expected to stay on top of everything. You'll be coordinating. Lawson is decrypting Bashar's computer. The PD is checking every location you uncovered. I sent teams to scout the locations the CIA originally asked us to protect. We have enough help in the field. I need someone to work as overwatch, and you're the best agent I have and the only person I trust not to crumble under agency pressure or disclose details to these chuckleheads that will jeopardize our op further."

"Mark," I protested, "I'm more useful out there. I can't do this."

"You've been doing nothing but this for the last two weeks. You know how to coordinate intel." He opened the conference room door. "We'll be on comms. After the briefing, come back here and set up shop. Moretti knows to call you personally should something develop. He trusts you. I trust you."

"That's ridiculous. You're the supervisory agent. You should stay here and coordinate. I'll go to the exchange."

He smiled sadly. "I swore I'd never lose another agent on my watch, least of all you. You're not going on this suicide mission."

I grabbed his arm. "Thinking like that means you shouldn't be anywhere near this."

"Stand down, Agent Parker. It's my show." He patted my hand. "And no matter what goes down tonight, it's not your fault. Remember that."

THIRTY-TWO

Jablonsky's pep talk sucked. His pep talks always sucked. He wasn't good at sugarcoating things. He never had been. It's probably why he'd been divorced three times. I didn't want him to lie and tell me everything would be okay, but based on his words, I was positive nothing would be okay.

"How'd you enjoy visiting our interrogation room? We use drab, boring colors here instead of painting everything a blinding white, so your retinas should thank us," I said.

"You don't like me much," Reece replied.

He'd been hovering in the doorway for the last five minutes. After the briefing, the tactical units had started to prep, and Jablonsky had been summoned to the Director's office for a few final words. That meant the CIA agent was free to wander, and he'd chosen to wander into my path. Too bad I wasn't a speeding train.

"Brilliant observation."

"I'm curious. Is it because we abducted you off the street? I've been told I make a lousy first impression."

"First, second, third. It's not the impression. It's just you."

He laughed, a phony, mechanical sound. "You don't approve of what we do."

"No, I don't."

"Do you have any idea how much of the information you receive comes from the tips and intel we gather? You wouldn't be able to do your job without us."

"Right. I really needed you to toss me into a van and try out your enhanced interrogation techniques, and I couldn't have survived another day without you and your people breaking into my apartment and implanting a tracking chip under my skin. I'm not your bitch, so don't treat me like a dog."

"What the hell are you talking about?"

I let out a derivative snort and shook my head. "My mistake. The CIA would never do something like that, just like they wouldn't authorize a black ops mission on U.S. soil."

"We messed up, but we're fixing it. You're helping us fix it." Reece stepped closer, extending his hand. "What I said earlier was out of line. I'd like to call a truce."

"Why?"

"Jablonsky left you in charge of coordinating the teams. You're going to be the voice in my head." He tapped the earpiece. "I'd like to know that voice isn't hostile."

"Fine," reluctantly, I grasped his hand, "but if anything happens to any of my colleagues, I will hold you personally responsible."

"Okay."

"What is this?" Mark entered, pulling a windbreaker over his vest.

"I wanted to make sure everyone's on the same page," Reece replied.

"Yeah," I gave Mark a pointed look, "and I wanted to make sure Agent Reece understands everyone is coming home alive."

"So we're set?" Mark asked, and I nodded.

Reece checked his phone. "My team will leave the facility twenty minutes before the deadline. We don't want Kiter to escape again, and we don't want Vega or any other member of Anarkhos intervening beforehand. They will meet us at the agreed upon spot. Your team will conduct the exchange. As soon as we have a location and deactivation code, you'll redirect to deal with the IED, and my people will pursue Anarkhos and recapture the asset."

"Easy as pie." Mark took a breath. "Parker, you'll stay on top of things here. Our surveillance teams will head out first to scout the location and make sure it isn't a trap. Each team is using a different radio frequency to make it more difficult for Anarkhos to intercept our communications. You'll have to pass word along. Go with your gut. If anything unforeseen occurs, handle it."

"Are you sure you don't want me in the field?"

"You've already been blown-up once today. Let's not tempt fate." Mark checked his watch. "We'll be waiting at the staging area. Keep the chatter to a minimum, and only report what is absolutely necessary."

"Yes, sir."

Jablonsky gave me a tight smile, and he and Agent Reece left the room. If that was the last time I ever spoke to Mark, I'd resurrect the son of a bitch just so I could kill him for putting me through this. As soon as they were gone, I went to collect the necessary equipment and turn the conference room into my command center. Since we were going to war, I wanted to be ready.

In an hour and thirty minutes, we were handing Stavos Kiter over to a group of anarchists. What could possibly go wrong? I snorted. Everything.

The table was covered in maps, several laptops with live footage from city cameras, and half a dozen different handheld radios, each properly labeled. The boards against the wall were littered with the profiles we'd created on Guillermo Vega, Stavos Kiter, and Adrian Bashar. To a lesser extent, the rest of the CIA dossier was taped to the wall. Until now, we hadn't encountered any other member of Anarkhos, but prior to this afternoon, we didn't know Bashar was stateside. For all we knew, the upper echelon of the anarchist hacker group might all be involved in the attempt to retrieve Kiter. Reece said they were stateside, but he said a lot of things I didn't believe.

My phone rang, and I grabbed it off the table. "Did you find something?"

"We're not sure," Detective Jacobs said. "Units have

cleared six of the ten locations. No devices. No one has seen any of our suspects. We didn't pick up any traces of explosive materials either."

"That's reassuring."

"Is it? It means we aren't any closer to finding the device, unless one of the remaining four locations turns up something."

"What's the delay?"

"They're high-rises. We have to work the area, and then we have to do it again vertically. It'll take time. Time we might not have."

"Give me the remaining locations." I circled them on the large map. Any four points could make a circle, but they were grouped too close together for my liking. The only positive I could determine was the four remaining points were nowhere near the exchange. "We have something in play, so we're spread too thin to help on this."

"We might have one other problem."

"What's that?"

"I just spoke to the bomb techs. Based on the schematics we found in the motel room and the volume of materials purchased, they estimate Anarkhos could have created another three devices."

"Right, and two have been detonated." This was old news.

"No, Parker. That's where the miscommunication occurred. They have enough to make three more devices, not counting the two we've already seen." He coughed a few times. "Heathcliff's taking another run at Bashar to see if we can coax some additional details out of the man. It'd be best to know if we're dealing with one big bomb or three smaller ones."

I rubbed my eyes and stared at the map. "You find something, call me. I'll do what I can."

"I thought you were spread too thin."

"That doesn't matter."

After disconnecting, I pulled the preliminary report from our bomb experts. They weren't committed to the same hard and fast numbers as the PD, but they speculated several smaller impact devices could have been created from the raw materials purchased. Glancing at the map again, I grabbed a ruler and calculated the square miles involved.

"Hey, Davis," I shouted into the bullpen, "grab the list of CIA locations and get in here."

"Who died and left you in charge?" he teased, and I scowled at his words. He flinched, remembering my checkered past when it came to coordinating raids from the office. "I didn't mean that." He placed the file on the only empty corner of the table. "What do you need?"

"I've already checked to see if any of these locations coordinate with the areas we were assigned to monitor, and they don't. But," I pointed to the area I had circled, "what if it's not a direct attack?"

He flipped through the pages, marking each spot with a small black x. "They aren't that close. We already evaluated the possibility of a threat when you originally gave us the coordinates. I don't think we're wrong."

"How much are you willing to bet on that?"

He didn't respond. Instead, he went back to his desk and returned with a copy of the larger file we'd been using to determine potential targets Anarkhos might use to launch another strike and cripple the city. "I'll get started on the comparison and see if any of these are close to those four points. What happened to the rest of the coordinates?"

"They've been cleared. We're waiting for the PD to finish the job with these four."

"But with agents in the field, you wanted to be certain it was safe," Davis surmised. "I'm on it."

"Thanks."

He nodded and leaned over the table, scanning the maps while I studied the live video feeds and marked the most likely routes our teams would take. I wanted to make certain none of those overlapped with possible Anarkhos targets.

When my phone rang again, my stomach did an uncomfortable flip. "Did our suspect volunteer any new intel?" I asked.

The sound of Heathcliff's lengthy inhale meant I asked the wrong question. "I can't get anything from him."

"Try again."

He let out a huff. "That's not possible. He's dead. He went into anaphylactic shock. The medics believe it was an extreme allergic reaction to something. Maybe he had a food allergy. I don't know. My guess, it was self-inflicted and intentional."

"Are you positive it wasn't poison?" My mind raced through the possibilities. Did the CIA kill him and make it look like natural causes?

"We took a blood sample. We'll run a tox screen. No one came into contact with him except the officers guarding him. Moretti kept him locked up tight."

"Were you in the room when it happened?"

"No." A loud bang thundered through the receiver, which might have been the sound of Heathcliff's fist hitting the wall. "I was working him over when Jacobs called with an update. I stepped out of the room. My back was turned for maybe twenty seconds, and then I spotted him through the glass, foaming at the mouth."

"Was it a seizure?"

"I don't know. IA doesn't know about this yet, but they will. Moretti's already assessing the situation. Given the circumstances, they can't pull me off the case, but I don't know what happened. The cameras were off. There's no way to know anything."

"Listen to me, we'll figure out what happened. If someone got to him, we'll find out. Let Moretti do his thing, and don't say a fucking word to anyone. The OIO can handle the pressure. It's our op. You're assisting. The extreme stipulations were our call. I'll take the heat if need be."

"I'm not worried about me right now." He slammed his fist into the wall again. "How are we going to find these IEDs without Bashar's help?"

"We're on it. Be prepared to mobilize."

Disconnecting, I squeezed the bridge of my nose. I needed to phone Mark. Davis glanced at me. He heard my half of the conversation and knew the shit had hit the fan.

"Are we okay?" he asked.

"I don't think so." I closed the conference room door.

"Was Agent Reece aware a member of Anarkhos was taken into police custody?"

"I don't think so. Jablonsky said it was hush-hush. I'm not even sure how many of our people know about it. It's possible he overheard a conversation, but he spent most of the day locked up. It doesn't seem likely. What happened?"

"Bashar's dead."

"Dammit. He was our second best shot at locating the devices, assuming Vega double-crosses us."

"I know." My mind went to Lawson and the laptop and USB drive. "Maybe Bashar can't help us, but his computer might. Monitor the channels for a few minutes. I'll be right back."

Racing up the steps, I went straight to the cybercrimes division. Lawson was working on the USB while several members of the unit worked on decrypting the computer. After giving them a quick update on the situation, they decided to throw caution to the wind and try a more aggressive method of breaking into the password protected files. We might lose the entire hard drive, but we didn't have time to waste. The clock was ticking, and with Bashar dead, I knew the anarchists were willing to sacrifice themselves for their cause. The nonviolent hackers became suicide bombers, and Jablonsky and several tac units were on their way to meet the ringleader face-to-face.

"Do whatever you have to. We need answers." I shifted my weight from leg to leg, waiting impatiently for access to Bashar's laptop. The voice in the back of my head scolded my decision. If this didn't work and we fried the computer in the process, we'd lose the only advantage we had against Anarkhos.

"Bingo," one of them said.

Lawson stopped what he was doing and assessed the screen. "That was sheer brilliance. Is everything viewable?"

"Yep. We redid the user interface, reset the default, and removed all password protection."

"And without wiping the drive." Lawson pressed his palms together and bowed. "You are the masters."

"Enough," my impatience wouldn't allow this to continue further, "I need everything Bashar had on the bomb and their plans for it. Let's get moving people."

THIRTY-THREE

"Parker," Lawson bumped his forearm against my thigh to make sure he had my attention, "Bashar just received an encoded message."

"From whom?" Davis asked before I could utter a word. We had moved the computer to the conference room, along with Lawson and a few cybercrimes agents who were working on the computer and drive while Davis and I continued to monitor our teams and determine likely targets.

"Give me a sec," Lawson replied.

Crossing my arms over my chest, I tapped my fingers against my elbow and paced back and forth, my eyes never wavering from the screen. This had to work. It had to be something. My phone buzzed, and I jumped, my hand involuntarily traveling to the handle of my nine millimeter which remained secure in my shoulder holster. It was Jacobs.

"We found a device," the detective said. "We've evacuated the area. We're waiting for the bomb squad to determine the safest way to disarm it. If it can be moved, we'll relocate it before attempting to disarm."

"Where are you?" I snapped my fingers at Davis and

pointed at the location on the map as soon as I had the coordinates. "How large is the IED?"

"It's hard to say for certain. They've encased it in some pretty thick housing. We haven't seen this before."

"Pull up everything you can on bomb schematics with a thick housing," I said to the agents analyzing the drive. "Has the bomb squad consulted the intel we recovered?" I asked, switching the call to speakerphone.

"They didn't find anything useful." The detective sounded anxious. "The explosion this afternoon was remotely detonated, but this is different. With no visible timer, we don't know if it's inside the housing. We're assuming there's an external trigger. We won't know until we open it up, but we're waiting on the robot to run some scans. Given what we do know, it might be booby-trapped. That's why we're clearing out as many civilians as possible."

"I can take a team to assist," Davis offered. "Our bomb experts have been analyzing explosives made by this group since the attack on our military base. We might be able to lend a hand."

Jacobs sighed. "Yeah, okay."

I nodded to Davis, and he and one of the cybercrimes agents left the room. The only problem was our best people were already moving into position to assist Jablonsky. Even though the police located one device, that didn't mean Vega didn't have another one up his sleeve.

"Agent Davis and a team of agents are on their way to you. Have you gotten word yet on the other three sites?" I asked.

"Negative. We have search teams checking the remaining areas, but this might be it. From what I've been told, this is a lot more complicated than what we normally encounter. There appears to be some programming involved. A few of our IT guys have been called in to assist. I'll let you know how things turn out." The detective hung up, and I forced myself to take a breath.

"All right, people," I said to the motley crew of FBI agents who remained in the conference room, "you heard the man. We found one device, but there might be more.

Jablonsky and our tactical teams might be facing something similar. Stay on your toes." I turned to Lawson. "Did you decode the message yet?"

"I need another minute."

"Hurry."

Picking up the radio, I updated Mark on the situation. He had no choice but to share the intel with our CIA counterparts. It was imperative we prepare for worst case scenarios. Jablonsky wanted us to tread lightly. Depending on how the exchange went, Vega might be persuaded to hand over the detonator. That was assuming the device we discovered was the only device. Should we deactivate it prior to the exchange, I was to radio back. If Vega's leverage was removed, the risks associated with the exchange would be minimized. It wouldn't be necessary to take the anarchist alive.

Lawson pressed his hand over mine, stopping the rat-a-tat-tat of my fingernails on the table. "The message is decrypted." He angled the computer toward me. "Anarkhos knows where Kiter is. They plan to liberate him."

"Who sent the message?" I stared at the jumble of letters and numbers.

"It originated from an online box. The e-mail address has already been closed." He looked at one of the cybercrimes agents. "I sent the info to you. See what you can run down. I don't want to use Bashar's computer to do it."

"I'm on it," the agent responded.

"They don't know he's dead. We might be able to use this." I studied the message, but it was curt and straight to the point. Whoever sent it didn't waste words. There was no need when the entire thing had been written in code. "Is it possible to send back a response?"

Lawson stared at the screen. "I can try. Like I said, the box is closed, but they might have other means of monitoring it. More than likely, the message would be rejected and returned with an error message. They might be monitoring this box and receive the rejected message. It's all guesswork at this point."

"But you could write something using the same code?"

"Theoretically."

Nodding, I strode across the room and stared out the window.

After a few moments, he cleared his throat. "Do you want to send a reply?"

"I don't know." For once, I wasn't being indecisive. I just had no idea how to respond to the message. "Are there any other messages on the computer? Any indication of what's about to happen?"

"I'll continue to look."

The cybercrimes agent glanced up. "I'm sorry, Parker. It's a dead end."

"Yeah." I rubbed my neck and went to the radios. The tac team was checking in to notify me they were in position. For the next fifteen minutes, I coordinated their positions, passed along the information to the other teams in the field, and relayed everything back. I wouldn't have minded if I knew these extra precautions would make a difference, but I doubted anything we did was beyond Anarkhos' capabilities.

I placed the final radio back on the table. We were a go. We had another thirty-five minutes until the designated meet. In fifteen minutes, CIA agents would spring Kiter from their undisclosed location and rendezvous with Jablonsky. I looked at my cell phone, willing it to ring. The police department needed to deliver.

"I'm going downstairs to check on some things. There might be a way to trace the sender's location even if we can't identify him," the cybercrimes agent said.

"Go." Turning my focus to the live feeds on the monitors, I scanned the streets for signs of something amiss. As I clicked the images, I glowered at the train depot. "I should have fucking caught him."

Lawson looked up. "You got dinged by a bike."

"Then why didn't Reece run him down? Kiter got hit by a taxi. He was in the hospital for a while. You can't tell me Reece didn't see it happen. He must have been right there. How incompetent is this guy that he can't give chase?"

"I thought you were the only one who spotted Kiter."

"Yeah, but a guy in a suit ran past me after I was down.

It must have been Reece or some other CIA goon. They were tracking me."

"Are you positive? Did Reece confirm that?"

"Of course not." At that moment, everything became clear. "If the CIA didn't break into my apartment and tag me, it must have been Anarkhos. That's why Bashar knew my home address. The man in the suit could have been Bashar or Vega. That means they know where Kiter's been this entire time, but breaking him out of jail would be too difficult. So they had us do it for them. Bring up the message again." I leaned over his shoulder and read the words. "They know where Kiter is, not where he'll be. They're not waiting for the exchange. They're going to intercept him at the CIA site." Grabbing the radio off the table, I relayed the information to Jablonsky.

"That's ludicrous," Reece interrupted. "What proof do you have?"

"Did you stick a subdermal tracker in my hip?"

"No."

"Then Anarkhos did. They were at the train station Saturday night. They must have been keeping tabs on Kiter. When you took him from the jail, they followed you, waited, and now they're planning to attack. We need the location."

"There's no way I was followed," Reece said. "Keep this channel open. We're sticking to the original plan."

"Jablonsky?"

"Hold position," Mark responded in an unfamiliar, clipped tone.

I slammed the radio to the table. "This is ridiculous." Picking up my phone, I dialed Jacobs and told him my suspicions. "Is there anything nearby that could be a black ops site? If so, some serious shit is about to happen."

"We'll do what we can," Jacobs said.

One of the radios crackled and chirped. "Switching to a private channel," Mark said.

I spun the dial and clicked the button. "Jablonsky?"

"I think you're right. Reece is on the phone with his team. Tell our tac units to abort and remain at the staging area. They need to be ready to move. The showdown isn't happening here."

"Do we have a location?"

"Negative." Mark's voice became quiet and muffled. "Run the locations we were told to guard. I'm betting it's one of them."

"Roger."

Leaning over the table, I studied the files. The map was marked and covered in notations. Davis hadn't been able to pinpoint much of anything. Dividing my attention among the live feeds, the maps, and the files, I considered everything we knew about Anarkhos.

"You want to make the whole city stop and take notice, so where do you strike?" I asked.

"Power grid," Lawson replied.

Turning off the lights was the best way to get attention. It would prevent people from being glued to their screens. "Assuming they've created an even more powerful method of delivering an EMP, it would fry all nearby electronics, right?"

"Potentially."

"They'd want to knock out the equipment inside the CIA facility. If they take a good chunk of the city with them, that'd be a plus." Quickly, I cross-referenced the locations we'd been asked to monitor with the list of possible targets. Several corresponded. My eyes zeroed in on the circles on the map. "There." I scrawled a large red x and grabbed the phone.

"Heathcliff," I said, knowing Jacobs was busy with the current device, "can you send units to—"

My cell phone let out an angry, shrill crackle. I looked down, seeing the connection had been lost and I had no bars. Something outside caught my eye. I looked out the window. Night had fallen, making it apparent that a large portion of the city was blacked out. The lights overhead flickered, went out, and then the hum of the backup system kicked in, bringing the power back on.

Grabbing the radio, I clicked the button. "Jablonsky, it's happening." As quickly as possible, I gave him the suspected location.

"Mobilize units, and get down there and stop this,"

Mark ordered.

Grabbing another radio, I gave the tactical teams the general vicinity of Anarkhos' attack. "Lawson, you're in charge. Make sure everyone knows what's going on. Notify the police and emergency services that we might be looking at casualties."

Racing out of the room, I pushed the button for the elevator but reconsidered when the lights flickered again. Taking the stairs two at a time, I reached the garage and burst into a run. Clicking the unlock on one of the SUVs, I slid behind the wheel and headed for the epicenter of the blackout. I didn't know how large the blast radius was or how many people were hurt. We failed.

THIRTY-FOUR

I heard the boom before I felt the rumble. Gripping the wheel tighter, I couldn't help but think a second device had detonated. Traffic was at a standstill. The lights were out, and practically every intersection was the scene of an accident. Despite the siren and flashing lights, I laid into the horn and did my best to maneuver around the pileups. Eventually, I ended up using the alleyways to cut through the mess. When it became necessary, I drove through a gate.

Every few seconds, I clicked the radio, requesting ETAs and asking for updates on the situation. No one knew what the situation was. I tried flipping to police bandwidths, but my efforts were met with nothing but static. Cell service was out. It was chaos—the beginning of anarchy.

Where was I going? Back on the main drag, I leaned over the steering wheel, searching for something. Everything was dark. No lights. No power. This had to be the right place. Traffic drastically lessened the closer I got to the water. Then I realized why. The traffic from both sides of the bridge was completely halted. Not a single car in the area had functioning headlights. They had been fried.

Clicking the radio again, I offered my location to the tactical units en route. They were close, coming from the other side. We fanned out to search for signs of Anarkhos, Kiter, or the CIA. Toggling to another channel while moving at a crawl, I reached Jablonsky and Reece over the radio.

"Anarkhos is at your black site. I need the address. Based on what I'm seeing, it's already been compromised."

"And if it isn't, telling you over an unsecured channel will lead them right to it. Don't you think that might have been their plan all along?" Reece's words made sense, but he wasn't staring through a windshield at a scene from a post-apocalyptic movie. "I have received no such communication from my people. This is a ploy, Agent Parker."

"What about the fact they've detonated a device in the area?"

"Casualties?" Jablonsky asked.

"Not that I've seen, but it's impossible to see much of anything." I glanced toward the rows of automobiles. Several people were standing outside, yelling, congregating, cursing, and asking questions. At least none of them appeared hurt, just annoyed. Maybe scared.

"Patrol the area. We'll continue as planned," Reece spat.

"Mark?" I waited for confirmation, but all I received was an acquiescent grunt.

Headlights from one of the tactical vans bounced off the asphalt in front of me. We got out of the vehicles. The HRT commander placed a map on the hood of my car, and we worked out a search grid. Switching to a different frequency, we spread out. A second tactical van joined the mix, and we drove up and down each block, moving outward toward the water.

"Nothing to report. We'll continue on foot," one of the teams said. The crowd was getting boisterous at the sight of our flashing lights. "Bravo team, we need some crowd control."

"Roger that," the reply chirped through the radio speaker.

Anarkhos had to be here. Kiter had to be here. I

checked the time. Maybe Reece was right. His team was set to deliver Kiter to the exchange point in five minutes. If they couldn't comply, they would have made contact by now, unless they weren't able. Still, the blast had to have happened somewhere in the vicinity. Recalling the locations we'd derived from the brochures in Bashar's belongings, I knew one of them was close. The police had ruled it out earlier and left, but that didn't mean Vega hadn't returned after it was cleared. Maybe the device Jacobs found was meant to be a distraction.

Every building in the area looked the same. Any one of them could be a CIA facility or safe house. Gunfire caught my attention, and I whipped the car around and headed toward the sound.

"Shots fired," I gave an approximate location as I prepared to intercept.

I turned the corner, and bullets impacted against my windshield. Instinctively, I ducked down, despite the bullet resistant glass. Slamming the SUV into park, I flung open the door, using it as cover while I aimed in the direction of the incoming gunfire.

"FBI," I shouted.

My headlights illuminated the area in front of me, but I didn't see anyone. We were close enough to the river that I could smell dead fish. The water was probably a hundred yards away. This area was primarily an old industrial park with several large warehouses. A Branded Telecom utility van was parked at my two o'clock. Several wooden pallets and a few crates were between my position and theirs. Bullets zoomed toward me, impacting against the SUV's grill. I ducked behind the door and blindly returned fire. It was a good thing I had extra ammunition.

"Hold your fire," someone yelled from the vicinity of the van. "He has a bomb."

"Identify yourself," I commanded. Before the speaker could respond, another barrage of bullets took out my headlights. "Dammit." I was blind. I didn't know how prepared the shooter was or even how many shooters there might be. Grabbing the radio off the seat, I spoke quickly. "Be advised, we have an active shooter." When I released the button, the response I received was static. I clicked it again. The son of a bitch had a jammer.

"Guillermo Vega?" I asked, hoping to get a response. "I'm here to negotiate." The gunfire ceased, and I edged to the end of the door, glancing around for another cover position.

"You lie," a voice responded from somewhere at my eleven o'clock. "Your government has done nothing but lie throughout our negotiations. You aren't here to negotiate."

"Are you?"

A dark silhouette moved around in the shadows. "I'm here to free Stavos and expose the truth. No more lies. No more cover-ups. The people of this country and the world need to see how the United States operates. Your government has lied to you. You should know the truth. Throw down your weapon, and you will not be harmed."

"It's hard to see the truth from the lies in the pitch black." I considered making a move while he was distracted. "It would have been easier if you didn't shoot out the lights."

"Everything will be illuminated soon."

"Do you have a bomb?" I asked. He didn't say he did, and I hoped whatever device he used to short out the power was the extent of it. "You deal in truths. You told the negotiator you would detonate another device in the city if we didn't give you Kiter. We'll give you Kiter. Tell me about the device."

The sound of van doors sliding closed echoed loudly in the quiet. Surprisingly, no more gunfire ensued. With catlike stealth, I slipped away from the SUV and moved to the nearest cover position. The wooden crates were practically rotted. They wouldn't stop a bullet, but I forced my mind not to think about that. More sounds emanated from the direction of the van, distracting the dark silhouette.

"Don't move," the silhouette said, and I halted. "Your vehicle is disabled. You can't escape. Release Stavos."

Realizing he wasn't speaking to me, I continued to the next cover position. This one wasn't any better than the last. I dashed to the closest building and pressed against the brick wall. For a second, I thought I saw lights.

The two tactical teams were close. Even if they hadn't received my radio calls, it was just a matter of time until they happened upon us. In the meantime, my priority was determining how real the threat of a bomb was.

The silhouette moved out of cover, marching toward the van. He held something in his left hand. In the dark, I couldn't tell what it was. It could have been a detonator, cell phone, or a brick. I didn't see a gun, but someone had fired several shots. The realization that there could be two men didn't dawn on me until I was halfway across the expanse. As soon as I reached an alcove at the next building, I took a deep breath. So far, so good.

Gunfire erupted fifty yards in front of me. The silhouette went down, clutching his shoulder. The sound of an engine filled the sudden quiet as it roared to life. Whoever was driving must have gunned it because the van took off like a bat out of hell.

The silhouette managed to sit up, and then the back end of the van lit up bright, going airborne before crashing to the earth. The screeching of tires and the pungent smell of burnt rubber filled the air. The van careened sideways, skidding and sliding until it crashed into the guardrail overlooking the water. The speed and force at which it traveled was enough to break through the metal with a loud shriek before disappearing from sight with a splash.

Gun aimed, I dashed toward the downed silhouette. "Don't move." I came around to face him. He held up his hands. The gun was on the ground, and I kicked it away. But in his left palm, he held a black box. "Drop it."

"This will be too big to hide. Everyone will know." He looked up to the sky at the sound of chopper blades. A bright spotlight bounced off the ground, stopping on us. "They now know." In the blinding white light, I recognized the man as Guillermo Vega. "Run."

A loud rumbling shook the earth, and the building directly behind us started to collapse. The windows shattered, exploding outward. Vega ran for the water, diving over the edge. I sprinted after him. Luckily, I was in perfect alignment with the destroyed portion of the guardrail when the rest of the building blew.

The shockwave propelled me forward, but I managed to get into a dive position during the twenty foot drop. The water was frigid and deep. I wasn't sure how far down I went, but I spotted the white van slowly sinking and swam toward it. The helicopter must be close since streams of light cut through the inky blackness. Glancing around, I didn't spot Vega.

At the van door, I heard muffled banging. The blast that had taken out the back tires also damaged the back windows. I swam through the opening. A few inches of air remained in the back of the van, close to the ceiling. I treaded water and gulped down the much needed oxygen. The driver was unconscious, slumped against the wheel. Kiter was in the seat next to him, panicking and handcuffed to the handrail above the window.

The front cab was entirely submerged. This wasn't good. Something moved past me. I jumped, prepared to fight if necessary. The man held up his palms. I had encountered him during my abduction. He gestured toward the top of the van, and we popped up in the quickly decreasing air.

"Agent Parker," he inhaled several ragged breaths, "I need your help to get them free." He tilted his head back, hoping to grab another breath before the entire van was underwater. "Handcuff key."

I reached into my pocket, removing mine while he swam toward the front of the van. While he worked on freeing the unconscious CIA agent from the front seat, I went to work on Kiter's handcuffs. The anarchist was now unconscious. Both men were drowning. If we didn't get out of here soon, we'd all drown. I wasn't sure how deep the river was or how quickly we were sinking, but we needed to hurry.

The agent grabbed his partner and hauled him toward the back. Everything turned dark. I cursed, fearing the helicopter had been rerouted. They probably didn't think there were any survivors, or maybe they had gotten a visual on Vega. The thought that the anarchist might be close was a very real possibility.

After several blind attempts to get the cuffs free, I unlocked one side. Removing Kiter's wrist from the bracelet, I made sure to fasten the bracelet before maneuvering it around the handrail to prevent it from snagging. Then I wrapped my arms around him and kicked off against the dashboard. The force propelled us toward the back of the van, as my lungs started to burn.

Trying to force Kiter through the rear window ahead of me wasn't an easy feat. His mass was greater than mine, and with the water making us practically weightless, I felt myself shifting backward instead of moving him forward. Kicking with all my might, I pushed him free from the rear window, just as the agent returned. He grabbed Kiter around the middle and kicked off against the roof of the van, heading for the surface.

I hurried to follow. My need for air growing by the second. I pushed off, and the van lurched suddenly. The rear door swung open and latched shut, catching some part of my clothing in the lock. I fumbled around in the dark, hoping to get unstuck. Finally, I broke free, kicking with ferocity toward the surface. But my need for air was too strong to overcome. Before I breached the surface, everything went fuzzy. Involuntarily, my body inhaled the freezing cold water, and I blacked out.

THIRTY-FIVE

Coughing up the putrid water, I blinked through the tears. The tactical teams were assessing the situation. Several police cruisers had just pulled up, and the man who dragged me out of the river was taking a few deep breaths next to me.

"I'm glad they taught you how to swim," I said between choking gasps.

"We learn a lot of things at The Farm." He looked over at his teammate and Kiter, both of whom were being treated by members of HRT until ambulances arrived. "Where's Vega?"

I jerked my chin toward the water. "Didn't you see him? Oh wait, that's right, you tried to run away, and he blew up your van and your building."

"We were protecting our asset."

"You were protecting your asses."

From our position on the shore, I could see the headlights of several disabled vehicles powering back on. The crowd gawked at the emergency vehicles. Several choppers were in the air. They didn't all belong to the police. The news outlets had been advised there was a situation. Vega was right. Everyone would know what happened.

Another patrol car pulled up, and Jacobs got out of the passenger's side. "Parker," he called, finding me soaking wet and seated on the ground. Returning to the trunk, he grabbed a blanket and wrapped it around my shaking shoulders. "Lawson phoned. What the hell happened?" The detective's eyes traveled to the man beside me.

"Have you located Vega?" the CIA agent asked.

"The bomber got away?" Jacobs wasn't pleased.

"He took down that building, and during the blast, he dove into the water. I followed, but I didn't see him. Instead, we mounted a rescue." I glared at the CIA agent, wanting him to disappear like the rest of the spooks.

"We'll comb the river." Jacobs gave me an uncertain look. "You good?"

"Yeah."

Nodding, he went to speak to HRT about establishing a perimeter and search grid. Radio communication had returned, but it was spotty. The only long-term damage seemed to be to the city's power grid. Smaller battery-operated electronics were starting to function again, like the cars and radios. Even cell service was returning.

"He hit a power relay," the CIA agent said as if reading my mind. "That's what blacked out the city. He detonated a second EMP that took out communications arrays and disabled the vehicles. He wanted a captive audience."

"How'd you get the van to start?"

"We anticipated his move and shielded the electric system."

I coughed a few more times and pulled the blanket tighter. My chest burned with enough intensity to dull the aching in my ribs. "You didn't realize he planted a small charge on the back of the van?" I looked back at where a large building once stood. "Or that he used a much larger charge to take out your entire facility? How'd he gain access?" The CIA agent didn't say anything. He looked away, and I struggled to my feet. "Do you even know?"

"We attempted to trap him inside. We allowed him to enter through the bottom. The building was empty, aside from my team and Kiter. It was a safe house."

"Some safe house. It wiped out half a city block. This shouldn't have happened."

"Aren't you tired of pointing fingers yet?" Reece asked.

Jablonsky and our primary response units rerouted as soon as word got out and had just arrived. I didn't bother to answer. My body couldn't withstand a screaming match, and that's precisely what would happen if I confronted him. Jablonsky rubbed his palms up and down my arms, produced a small smile, and pulled me in for a quick hug.

"I'm glad you're okay," he whispered.

"Vega's in the wind. Or the water. He's still out there."

Mark released me and took charge, speaking to the agents and police assembled. Boats were already searching for survivors, and we were in the midst of establishing a perimeter. We would find him. Another dozen vehicles pulled up in rapid succession. I noted the government plates. Homeland wanted a piece of this mess too.

They carted Kiter and the CIA agents off for what I hoped would be a lengthy and excruciating debrief. In the meantime, we were left to clean up the mess. The police department was out in force. Patrols were beefed up throughout the blacked out areas to deter the crime wave that was likely to ensue. Vega's photograph had been passed around. Every cop was hunting him, as was every federal agent.

"Keep a lid on what happened. No one is using the words terrorism or bomb," Jablonsky said. "We don't want to cause a panic. We still aren't sure what his plan was or what's going on. Stay vigilant." He grabbed a hold of Detective Jacobs, and the three of us sat inside one of the SUVs. "What happened with the device you located?"

Jacobs leaned forward, glancing out the windshield. "It was a dud. The housing contained all the necessary bomb materials to set off our sniffers, but there was no detonator. The other three locations were clean."

"How many casualties have we seen since the blackout?" Jablonsky asked.

"The only reported injuries were related to auto accidents," Jacobs said.

"Vega had the devices with him," I said. "He set them as

he went. He wanted to expose the CIA. He wanted the attention. Setting off a random explosion wouldn't further his agenda." I blinked a few times. "He told me to run. I don't think he meant to hurt anyone, except the people who took Kiter."

"Let's hope he sticks with that mindset." Jablonsky opened the car door. Taking the hint, Jacobs went to assist the growing number of police officers in conducting the search and dispersing the assembled crowd that remained above us on the bridge. "I'll have someone drive you back to the office. Write up your report, help Lawson get things squared away, and grab a couple hours of sleep. I don't need you coming down with pneumonia."

"Okay." Glancing around, I recognized some of the agents. "Where's Davis?"

"He's taken over your job of coordinating with the PD. I spoke to him while I was on my way here. He can handle it." Mark looked at me. "Do you have any idea where Vega might have gone?"

"He disappeared into the drink. He could pop up anywhere."

"We'll find him."

* * *

"Are you sure you don't want to get changed?" Lawson asked. I probably smelled like dead fish and toxic chemicals. I'd seen a few of the support staff crinkling their noses when I went by.

"I'm out of clothing." I looked at the time. It was nearly midnight. "And I really want to go home. If I shower and change, I'll stay here all night. And all day."

He looked just as harried as I felt.

"We could both use a break," I said.

We'd spent the last few hours making certain we hadn't dropped the ball on anything. There had been so many radio calls back and forth, I was convinced we'd have to change the batteries before the end of the night. We'd spent the early part of the evening coordinating the teams. Now someone else was playing phone operator while we went over the computer intel, the police files, and everything the CIA had given us for the millionth time.

"I think we're pretty much done," Lawson said. "Cybercrimes is with the laptop. We've picked apart the police files, everything from their encounter with the phony IED to their last encounter with Adrian Bashar. Nothing suggests any other Anarkhos members are in play."

"We need to find Vega. He's the last missing piece."

Lawson rubbed his eyes. "Do you think he made it? A building exploded. He was tossed into freezing cold, pitch black water. We don't even know if he can swim."

"It was probably part of his plan."

"Like how he had messages delivered to the major news stations that a breaking story was going down right around the time he blew up the building?"

"Yeah, like that, except I showed up too early, and he blew his load prematurely."

"It happens to the best of us." Lawson pushed me out of the conference room. "Go type up your report and get out of here. You're making the place stink like week old sushi."

"Is this the thanks I get?"

Returning to my desk, I hunkered down behind the keyboard, the soggy blanket still wrapped around my damp clothing. My hands hadn't stopped shaking. I didn't know if it was cold or nerves. Probably both. After another hour and a half of recalling everything in a painstaking amount of detail, I concluded my report. It encompassed everything from the incident at the construction site to my encounters with Bashar and his arrest to the details regarding our plan of action and the lengths we had to go in order to rectify the CIA's oversight on the matter. However, I was professional enough not to throw Reece or any of his cohorts under the bus. After saving, printing, and filing the papers in the proper places, I turned off the computer.

"All right, I'm out of here. If Kendall or Jablonsky need me, tell them I'll be back by seven," I said to the room.

"Yes, ma'am," one of the support staff responded. "Before you go, you have a message." The secretary dropped a note on my desk.

It was late. Beyond a reasonable time to make a phone call, but I had a feeling Martin had seen the news and wouldn't go to sleep until he heard from me. Lifting my desk phone, I dialed his number.

"Hey, I was just about to leave work. I'm in desperate need of a hot shower and some sleep. Is everything okay?"

"Have you seen the news? Your apartment's in a blackout zone. They estimate it'll be another forty-eight to seventy-two hours before power is restored."

"Great," I exhaled, stifling a cough. Maybe I would stay at the office after all.

"You could come here." It was the first time he'd offered to let me back into his house since our break-up, but I didn't want to go under these circumstances.

"I would, but you're too far away. I'll just shower here and curl up on Mark's couch. Thanks for the update."

"What about a hotel?"

"I imagine, in the chaos, they're probably over capacity."

"You could go to the apartment. We don't have furniture, but the building has a generator. Plus, it's close to your office."

"Maybe I'll do that." I grabbed my purse and keys. "It's late. We'll talk tomorrow. I love you." Normally, I wasn't so curt with him, but I was dead on my feet. Thoughts of a hot shower filled my mind.

Leaving the office, I drove to our new apartment. When I pulled up, grabbing a hodgepodge of items from the car, like the tourist getup I'd worn earlier in the afternoon and a clean pair of underwear I found in my go-bag, I was surprised to find the doorman waiting to greet me. He held out the key to the apartment and provided instructions on how to use the elevator.

After letting myself inside, I locked the door, put my gun on the kitchen counter, dropped everything else on the floor, and went into the bathroom. Martin's staff must have been busy. The bathroom and kitchen were stocked. Dozens of clean towels were in the cabinet. Stripping out of my disgusting clothing, I tossed everything into the trash can and stepped under the steaming hot water.

It took twenty minutes of intense scrubbing before I felt reasonably clean. Wrapping a towel around my hair and another around my body, I realized my teeth were still chattering. I moved into the living room, located the thermostat, and cranked up the heat. Then I slipped on my underwear but couldn't bring myself to put on the clothing I'd worn at the police station. Instead, I dried off, grabbed a few extra towels, and curled up on the living room floor next to the vent. It was nice to be dry and safe.

The faint sound of a key scraping brought me out of my daze. I glanced at my soppy gun still on the counter. I should have cleaned that. The door opened, and Martin stepped inside.

"Alex?" he called, dragging a large rolling suitcase behind him.

"What are you doing here?" I pulled myself off the floor, wrapping a towel around me. "You shouldn't have come. The dark brings out the psychos."

"I wasn't going to let you spend your first night in our apartment alone." He assessed my appearance and the pile of towels I'd been using as blankets. "It's a good thing I brought supplies."

"Do you have a hairdryer?"

"Of course." He unzipped the bag, and I held out my hand. He noticed the shaking and frowned. "Let me get you something more practical to wear first." He pulled out one of his t-shirts and handed it to me. "I thought Marcal said he filled the linen closet with extra bedding."

"I don't know." I took the shirt and headed for the bathroom. "Where do we dispose of toxic waste?" After slipping into his t-shirt and hanging the towel on the rack, I returned with the trash can.

He regarded the contents, removed the bag, and placed it in the hallway. Grabbing his phone, he sent a text and stopped me from rummaging through the suitcase for the hairdryer.

"Are you okay?" he asked.

"It's been a hard day. I just need to sleep."

"Check the closets. Some of your things might be here. I don't know how much moving in we've done. I'm sorry the bed hasn't arrived. I'll call some hotels."

"Martin, it's the middle of the night. I just want to curl up near that vent and sleep for three or four hours before I have to go back to work. That's it."

He nodded. "Stay right here." Moving to the closet, he grabbed a few spare pillows, five or six blankets, and some sheets. Layering the bedding on the floor near the vent, he made a comfy nest. "Lie down." He patted the pile, and I complied, not needing to be told twice.

He plugged in the hairdryer and sat beside me, the length of his thigh pressed against my side. His free hand alternated between stroking my back and combing the knots out of my hair. The droning of the hairdryer and the warmth of his body pushed me into oblivion.

When I woke, the room was dark, and Martin was wrapped around me. I slept for a couple more hours until the first glimpse of sunlight came through the large windows. We needed curtains.

My chest burned, and my body ached from everything it had been put through the day before. I needed to get up. I had to get back to my apartment in order to get dressed, and I needed to clean and oil my service piece before it rusted. As it was, it wouldn't fire after being waterlogged, and with Vega on the loose, I might need it. Staying here last night was a bad idea. But then I felt the gentle touch of Martin's fingertips against my cheek, and I realized this was exactly where I needed to be.

"I hope you don't mind that I sent Marcal to pick up your things. You seemed out of sorts."

"Thank you." I turned away, holding my ribs and coughing until my lungs didn't feel quite so heavy.

"According to the news, there was a gas leak. It destroyed several empty buildings and damaged the power relay. The electric company is working to fix the problem."

"A gas leak, huh. Sure, that makes sense."

He pressed his lips together. "You were there." It wasn't a question, and he didn't wait for a response before holding me close. "Is it over?"

"I don't know." I couldn't talk about it, and he knew it. "Most of the team worked through the night. I need to get back."

"I'll make breakfast." Martin looked at me. "I sent your clothing to the cleaners. It'll be ready Friday."

I stared at him. "How do you have time to run a company and take care of me?"

He smiled. "I'm just that amazing."

"Yes, you are."

THIRTY-SIX

"We just got word," someone said, holding the phone to his ear, "Guillermo Vega's been found dead. His body washed up on the shore a few miles from the incident." A collective breath was released inside the federal building. Barring the possibility Anarkhos had other operatives in play, it was over. The city wasn't being held hostage. The danger had passed.

Mark stepped out of his office, giving a few words of encouragement and gratitude for our hard work. Despite the sudden dissipation of tension in the air, there was still a lot of work left. Anarkhos existed. Their recent behavior made them a potential future threat. More thorough assessments needed to be conducted.

"Alex," Mark called, "can I see you for a minute?" I followed him back to his office and waited. "The tox report was inconclusive concerning Bashar's death."

"Is Detective Heathcliff going to take the heat for it?" I asked. "I cannot be responsible for ruining that man's life or career more than I already have."

"Heathcliff will be fine. You didn't do this." He glanced out the blinds of his window. "This doesn't bear repeating, but I've heard rumors Reece and his buddies wanted to make certain their mess was cleaned up."

"They might have had something to do with Vega's death."

"I wouldn't bet against that possibility." He rubbed his palm over his mouth. "We made some enemies working this case."

"Are they going to snuff us out too?" I wouldn't be surprised if the answer was yes.

"I'm hoping that would raise one too many red flags. Killing a bomber or two won't garner any bad PR, but doing in a federal agent is a whole horse of another color."

"What bombers? It was a gas leak. Total accident. The city was never in any peril. Everything was a gas leak. The reported explosion inside the Branded Telecom building, the fire at the construction site, the explosion that took out half a block, all freak gas related accidents."

"That's the official story. That's what the media's running, and that required cashing in a lot of favors."

"This is precisely why Vega wanted the audience, why he did everything he did. He wanted people to know the truth, to witness the propagation of deception."

"And he was fucking insane. He wanted governments to crumble. His manifesto would lead to mass murders, death, destruction, and utter mayhem."

"I'm not siding with him. I'm just saying." I blinked. "Actually, I don't know what I'm saying. I can barely see straight, let alone think straight."

"I get it. I read your report. Yesterday was a hell of a day. Get started on the threat assessment. We want to make sure Vega didn't have any other tricks up his sleeve."

"Yes, sir." I moved to the door, but another thought stopped me in my tracks. "What will happen to Kiter?"

"From what I've been told, he was a willing CIA asset. He's agreed to work for them in exchange for a new identity and protection. He also wants his family brought to this country to join him. The logistics are up to the CIA and state department."

"Do you believe that? He escaped from their facility. He snuck into that sex toy company and called 9-1-1. He intentionally eluded us every chance he got. He committed several felonies while on the run. That doesn't sound like someone who's willingly cooperating."

"As long as they get him the hell away from here and out of our jurisdiction, I'm happy not to think about it."

"What isn't our jurisdiction? We flew to Turkey for fuck's sake."

"Get back to work." This was the CIA's mess.

*   *   *

For the rest of the week, our job was damage control and risk assessment. Based on the intel we collected, we were fairly certain no other members of Anarkhos were in the United States. Furthermore, the cybercrimes division was monitoring their dark web and internet activity to make sure they weren't planning another attack. With a change in their leadership and a decrease in their ranks, they were focusing their efforts in Europe. After we passed the intel over to the proper authorities and governments abroad, the only remaining task was putting the rest of the case to bed.

My desk phone rang, and I picked it up. "Parker here."

"Director Kendall would like to see you in his office."

"I'm on my way." Unsure why I was being summoned, I ran through a few possibilities. It was unlikely I was getting another commendation since officially none of the events over the last three weeks happened.

When I made it to his office, I was surprised to find the outer office empty. Normally, he had support staff manning the phones and making his appointments. Something about the situation didn't sit right.

"Sir?" I asked, knocking gently on the door.

"Come in, Alexis." He offered a congenial smile. "Why don't you take a seat?" Decidedly, whatever was about to happen wasn't good.

Taking a breath, I sat on the edge of the chair and returned the uncomfortable smile. He moved around the desk and shut the door before coming back and sitting on the edge in front of me.

"As far as I'm concerned, you and Jablonsky handled this situation professionally. You did what you were trained to do. You followed the investigation where it led.

Be that as it may, I'm sure you're aware several red flags were raised in regards to your behavior. Since these concerns came from outside this office, they have to be addressed."

"Of course." My mind ran through the possibilities. The commander on the base wasn't happy with my snooping, and Agent Reece was the biggest douche I ever met. I was oh for two. "What can I do?"

"Nothing yet." Kendall looked truly pained when he said, "OPR is conducting an investigation. They will want to speak with you and SSA Jablonsky at some point. At the present, they are evaluating your performance based on the reports you filed. Jablonsky's vehemently insisted you only acted upon his orders, which does not help him any."

I could read between the lines. I knew where this was going and what it might mean for Mark's career. He'd already put in his twenty years. I didn't want to see him lose his pension over something this ridiculous. He punched Reece and placed him in custody, but if he hadn't, I would have.

"If I crossed any lines, I did so without his knowledge or approval," I said.

Kendall snorted, clearly amused. "Yeah, Jablonsky said the exact opposite."

"It looks like OPR's going to have a hell of a time."

"Looks that way," Kendall said. "I just wanted to give you the heads up. The terms of your reinstatement make you the easy target, but I will back you and fight for you as much as I can."

"I know." I was more afraid OPR would want to open a criminal investigation, and given what I knew of the CIA and Kiter's computer aptitude, I was afraid of what they might uncover or falsify. Just being investigated would stall a career if it didn't end it altogether. With the way Kendall remained at the edge of his desk, I knew there was something else. He wanted to say something, but he didn't know how. So I asked, "How do we make this go away?"

"Off the record, the investigation will cease if either you or Jablonsky take full responsibility and resign."

"Okay." Standing up, I knew what I had to do. It was

time.

"Parker," he touched my arm, "there's no reason to think you won't be cleared."

"I know."

He searched my eyes. "If you do what I think you're planning, you need to know there is no coming back. No consulting work. No temporary reassignments. This really will be it. I don't want to lose you or Jablonsky over some pinheads making unsubstantiated allegations." But his eyes showed the truth. One of us had to go, or we both would.

"I don't see how five MPs, the word of another OIO agent, and the commander of a military base can be considered unsubstantiated, but I appreciate the blind faith and loyalty." I nodded goodbye and went to the door.

Back at my desk, I brought up the resignation letter I kept on file and made some quick changes to it. There wasn't a chance in hell I was turning this over until I was certain Mark's career would continue unimpeded. Then I cleared out my desk. The bottom drawer contained several thick files concerning the murder of Julian Mercer's wife. I'd used every connection I had to get these files, and even if they might be considered work product and government property, I was taking them with me. I promised I'd find a lead, and I hadn't done it yet. But I would. Maybe my character wasn't up to the standards of the oath I'd taken, but my word still meant something.

After a quick trip to my car, I returned and knocked on Mark's open door. "How long have you known?" I asked.

"What are you talking about?"

"Don't bullshit me." I pulled the door closed. "This has been going on since we got back from Turkey, hasn't it? It's why you kept trying to keep me away from key parts of the investigation. You wanted to make it look like you were in control."

"Alex, we'll weather the storm. It's not a big deal."

"It is. This won't go away, and we both know it's a long time coming too." I flinched, thinking of some of the darker turns I'd taken recently. "I won't let you jeopardize your career for me."

"My career?" he balked. "You have a long, bright future

ahead of you. You have another fifteen years easy. I'm a couple away from retirement. Hell, I probably should have given the OIO the finger a long time ago and found a nice spot to fish."

"Kendall said we could make this go away."

Mark shook his head. "No."

"I can't afford to have them digging around."

"No," he repeated much more forcefully.

"I'll be okay."

"What are you going to do? Chase around cheating husbands?"

"Maybe."

"No, you won't." He went through his desk, pulling out a handful of business cards. "Let me make some calls. I'll see what else we can do."

By the end of the day, I was ready to call it quits for good. Leaving this time was different. I wasn't running away because I was scared or broken. I wasn't doing it because I lost someone. I was doing it to save someone. Mark meant the world to me, whether his stubborn ass realized it, and I wouldn't let him sacrifice his life's work over my actions. I didn't consider them mistakes. Everything I'd done during the course of this case was necessary, just like it was necessary for the CIA agents who screwed up to try to cover their asses and culpability by passing the blame. It was a dirty game to play, and I didn't want to have any part in it.

"Director," I said from the doorway, "I'm hoping we can reach an agreement." A member of OPR was waiting in the office. Jablonsky was also there, and after a lengthy argument in which we both attempted to take the blame, I placed my resignation letter on the desk. It was my ace in the hole, and Mark didn't come nearly as prepared. After a few handshakes and turning over my credentials, I left the federal building for the final time.

Jablonsky followed me back to my apartment. It was Friday night, which meant I had plans with Martin, but he didn't seem to care. Instead, he made himself at home, pouring a drink while I packed a few bags.

"I shouldn't have let you do it," Mark said.

"You didn't have a choice."

"I should have resigned before you got the chance. Shit, I should go back and resign now."

"And that will make falling on my sword completely pointless, so don't you dare."

He reached into his pocket and fished out several cards. "I spent the afternoon making calls. When I realized there was no way to derail OPR's investigation, I did some checking. You're a hot commodity, Agent Parker."

"It's just Alex now."

He waved his hand in the air, hoping to brush off my words as if they were nothing more than a pesky fly. "So far, two other federal agencies are vying to have you on their payroll, as is the police counterterrorism unit. That's three job offers already. I'm waiting to hear back from two others, but you have options."

"Shit." I laughed, picking up the cards and checking the insignias. "How many favors did you call in?"

"You're qualified, and they want the best." He stared at me over the rim of his glass. "You can have your pick."

I stared at the cards before placing them on the coffee table. "I need time to think." As if on cue, Martin knocked on my door, and I stuffed the cards in my pocket. "Don't tell him. Let me do it."

Opening the door, I smiled and let him inside while Mark finished his drink. After making small talk, Mark left for the night, reminding me that I needed to make a decision.

"What was that about?" Martin asked.

"Nothing." I hefted a bag over my shoulder and reached for a box of things to bring to our weekend home. "Let's go see our new furniture."

THIRTY-SEVEN

The place was magnificent. It had been cleaned since the night we slept on the floor, and the best part was it didn't smell like the river. The furniture arrived, and I perched on the couch. Martin went to the bar, making sure it was fully stocked. The kitchen was ready to go. The bedroom furniture was in place. He had his weekend clothing and a few spare suits already tucked inside the closet and dresser. Of course, it helped to have staff who could do these things for you. The bed was made, and I dragged myself away from the couch to unload some of my things. It would be odd living here part-time, but it would make our weekend getaways much easier.

"Dammit."

"What's wrong?" Martin asked, coming up from behind and wrapping his arms around me.

"We forgot the most important thing."

He nuzzled my ear. "No, we didn't. You're right here." I made a gagging sound at the sentimentally. "Protection's in the bathroom," he offered, trying again.

I let out a displeased growl. "We don't have a TV."

He laughed. "Why do we need one?"

"Movies. TV shows. Your compulsive obsession with

- 273 -

keeping up-to-date with business news."

"I'm trying to reform. You should work on some of those annoying work habits of yours too. Then maybe we'll get to spend an entire weekend together. Is it too smothering to want to actually spend the time we're together being together?" He released his grip and opened the closet door. On the top shelf, he had piled several board games. "These are in case we get bored." He grinned. "Get it."

"After that pathetic pun, I'm reconsidering our part-time cohabitation."

"You know you love me." He grabbed me around the waist and tossed me onto the bed. "And we have much more important things to do right now rather than unpack." Slowly, he crawled across the bed and kissed me. The shrill sound of the phone broke the spell, and he dropped his head in defeat. "We should make this a phone-free zone." Thankfully, the call wasn't mine. It was his.

"Hello?" Martin asked. I slid out from beneath him and flopped against the pillow. At least I could pretend to have no interest in his conversation. "That's right. I want to sell the place in Aspen." He paused. "I don't care. I'm not unloading the beach house." He grunted a few uh-huhs. "Let's get a few offers on the villa, and I'll think about it."

When he hung up, I quirked an eyebrow. "Who was that?"

"My accountant."

"You have a place in Aspen?"

He smiled. "Do you want to go skiing?"

"I don't ski. Do you?"

"Snowboarding, actually, but I haven't in a while. I don't think I've been there in years, at least not since I met you."

"So it was your snow bunny bachelor pad." I narrowed my eyes. "Is there any particular reason you're selling it now?"

"Alex, don't overthink this." He rolled onto his side and stretched his arm beneath my pillow. "I don't need to have seven properties, especially when I have no use for a ski chalet. As it is, I'm fairly certain the caretaker's been listing it on AirBnB."

"Seven properties?" My eyes went wide. I knew of three.

"Okay, Mr. Rockefeller, why don't you list them on AirBnB and quit your day job?"

He smirked. "I'll quit mine if you quit yours."

I swallowed, sobering at the tease. "Actually, that's going to be a lot easier than you'd imagine." I sat up straight, chewing on my bottom lip while I figured out the best way to give him the news. "I lost my job."

"Ha ha. Very funny." When I didn't respond, he studied me for a long moment. "You can't be serious. Jablonsky wouldn't do that to you."

"It wasn't up to him. It came from Director Kendall."

"Shit." Martin stood, running a hand through his hair and spiking the dark brown locks in all directions. "Okay." He took a deep breath, grabbed his phone, and scanned the contact list. "I have the number for an excellent attorney. He specializes in wrongful termination suits. I understand it's a government job, but that shouldn't have any real effect on the process. We'll find some way to fix this. They can't do this, not after everything you've sacrificed for that job. It'll be okay. Everything's going to be fine, sweetheart."

"Hey," I grabbed his arm as he made another pass in front of me, "why in the world do you want to fight this? Shouldn't you be popping champagne bottles and shouting from rooftops?"

His eyes were intense, and he cupped my face in his hands. "Of course not. Your life is that job. I won't celebrate someone taking that from you. We're going to fight this. I'll help you fight this."

"No, you're not." I took his hands in mine. "I'm not fighting this. I had the opportunity, and I let it go. I want to be done. This is the only way that will ever be true. Jablonsky can't ask or guilt me into going back. I won't be reinstated again. It's over. I made my decision. I chose you."

"Alex, I didn't ask you to choose. We're figuring it out."

"I already did. I don't want to have to cut our weekends short because I have to chase an international criminal through a train station. I don't want to feel guilty for breaking my oath to warn you about a possible bomb or lie to you about a case because I can't tell you where I am or what I'm doing." I took a breath. "Right now, I'm planning to take the weekend to lick my wounds and recover from being axed, but after that, I might need your help."

"Anything."

"Do you know any good headhunters who might be able to find me a position at some security consulting or P.I. firms? I met one at that conference we went to, but I don't remember his name. And I threw out his card a long time ago."

"I can make some calls and ask around." A grin tugged at the edges of his lips. "You're going back to your old gig?"

"You didn't really expect me to change my spots, did you? At least this way, I have some control over my caseload, and barring a crazy eccentric millionaire who forces me to sign an NDA, I don't see any reason why I can't talk about my work with you. No more secrets."

"I'm placing a moratorium on your interactions with eccentric millionaires, and for the record, I never asked you to sign an NDA. In fact, I wanted you to disclose everything to the authorities and the courts and anyone else who might have been able to help."

I smiled. "Wow, that's some ego. I forgot how much you value your own self-worth, as if every example I come up with has to be about you."

"It should."

"Even when I'm talking about criminals?"

"Only if they are devastatingly handsome."

"Good to know."

Slumping back against the pillow, I exhaled a long slow breath. I just spent the last few minutes explaining why this was a great idea, but in truth, I was scared. After the way things had gone at the OIO, I was glad to finally nail that door permanently shut. Mark had even gone to the trouble of making some calls on my behalf, but I knew, in the end, a government job would destroy what I had with Martin. We needed some freedom without the oversights and stipulations the U.S. government placed on its federal agents. Perhaps, in some ways, I wasn't that different from the anarchists.

Martin skimmed the calendar on his phone and nestled

beside me. "I have a crazy idea."

"No."

"You haven't heard it yet." He sat up, excited and eager like a kid who just got his first car. "Let's go away. We'll leave in the morning. Your passport must be up-to-date since you just went to Turkey. You don't need to fill out paperwork or get approval before leaving the country anymore, so let's go."

"Where?" His giddiness was infectious.

"Didn't you say you trusted me to be your travel agent?"

"I need to know what to pack."

"Lingerie can be worn in any climate." But sensing my inevitable protest, he clarified by adding, "I was thinking it's about time I make use of some of these properties before I sell them off. Let's visit my villa in Spain. We'll stay a week. I might have to do a bit of work, but we can sightsee and recharge our batteries. Then we'll take it from there. I'd like to visit the place at least one more time before I unload it. What do you say?"

"Okay."

"Okay?" he asked skeptically.

I smiled brightly. "Yes. After these last few weeks, it'd be nice to be away from everything except you."

He kissed me. "Ditto." Then he made the arrangements to take the company jet and have the property ready for our arrival. Sometimes, it paid to have a good travel agent.

ON TILT, THE NEXT INSTALLMENT IN THE
ALEXIS PARKER SERIES IS NOW
AVAILABLE IN PRINT AND AS AN E-BOOK.

DON'T MISS IT.